The Clockwork Dragon

— SECTION 13 · BOOK 3 ·—

The Clockwork Dragon

JAMES R. HANNIBAL

Simon & Schuster Books for Young Readers
New York   London   Toronto   Sydney   New Delhi

SIMON & SCHUSTER BOOKS FOR YOUNG READERS
An imprint of Simon & Schuster Children's Publishing Division
1230 Avenue of the Americas, New York, New York 10020

SIMON & SCHUSTER BOOKS FOR YOUNG READERS
is a trademark of Simon & Schuster, Inc.
For information about special discounts for bulk purchases,
please contact Simon & Schuster Special Sales at 1-866-506-1949 or
business@simonandschuster.com.
The Simon & Schuster Speakers Bureau can bring authors to your live event.
For more information or to book an event, contact the
Simon & Schuster Speakers Bureau at 1-866-248-3049 or
visit our website at www.simonspeakers.com.
Book design by Lizzy Bromely
The text for this book was set in Weiss.
Manufactured in the United States of America
0119 FFG
First Edition
2 4 6 8 10 9 7 5 3 1
Library of Congress Cataloging-in-Publication Data
Names: Hannibal, James R., author.
Title: The clockwork dragon / James R. Hannibal.
Description: First edition. | New York : Simon & Schuster Books for Young Readers,
[2019] | Series: Section 13 ; book 3 | Summary: From London, through the Austrian Alps,
and to central China, Jack, Gwen, and new friend Liu Fai face a clockwork dragon as they
try to prevent Gall from finding ancient artifacts said to grant immortality.
Identifiers: LCCN 2018009717| ISBN 9781481467155 (hardcover)
| ISBN 9781481467179 (eBook)
Subjects: | CYAC: Antiquities—Fiction. | Dragons—Fiction. | Immortality—Fiction.
| Voyages and travels—Fiction. |
Friendship—Fiction. | Secret societies—Fiction. | Adventure and adventurers—Fiction.
Classification: LCC PZ7.1.H3638 Clo 2019 | DDC [Fic]—dc23
LC record available at https://lccn.loc.gov/2018009717

For all those who believe there is still room in the world for
a few kindhearted fire-breathing dragons

The Clockwork Dragon

—— · Chapter One · ——

A BRONZE NANO-DRONE ROSE from the cemetery behind Saint Paul's Cathedral and tilted northward, four spherical engines glowing blue. It ducked beneath a cab on Cheapside, weaved through hurrying knees and boots, and paused in the shadow of a white stone building. When the pedestrian traffic thinned, it popped up over the rooftop, dropping into a hidden courtyard and pushing in through the mail slot of a weathered black door.

Several minutes later, a light *ding* echoed through an ancient chamber of wood and slate, announcing the arrival of a lift. A man and woman in scarlet robes stepped off and turned toward a judges' platform at the curve of the horseshoe-shaped room, oblivious to the tiny drone slipping out behind. With a flare of its engines, the drone shot up into the safety of the rafters and set a drifting course among oaken beams, widening its iris to take in the scene below.

A crowd was gathering.

Four separate groups assembled in four separate sections of polished wood bleachers. The first, to the left of the judges' platform, looked serious, even dangerous, in gray overcoats that sat heavy on their shoulders like steel armor. Every man and woman among them wore a red scarf, bunched up beneath battle-scarred faces as fierce as the fire-breathing dragons sculpted into their high-backed chairs.

Those across the chamber bore more placid expressions and yet appeared no less dangerous, wearing a mix of high-collared suits and black robes. They kept their eyes fixed straight ahead, matching the marble unblinking eye set into the wall behind them. And they remained eerily silent, fingers flicking and tapping at their thighs in a sort of code.

The occupants of the next section down were not silent. They whispered and chattered, guarded by a pair of giant golden statues at the rear corners of their bleachers. They were stuffy sorts in tops and tails, casting dour looks across the chamber at the fourth and final group.

The looks of these *toppers*, as they were called, were not

lost on that last group, known to the rest as the *crumbs*. A few of the crumbs scowled back through thick spectacles. Others nervously tugged at tweed waistcoats. They were the smallest group by far, huddled in a bunch at the center of chipped and abused bleachers carved with falcons, wolves, owls, and bears.

But unlike the toppers, there were real giants among them.

The nano-drone settled above the judges' platform and zoomed in on the second judge from the left, an olive-skinned woman in a scarlet robe. She had just pulled a bronze cylinder from a pneumatic tube and cracked it open. She drew out a parchment. The drone snapped a picture.

PLAINTIFFS:

SIR IGNATIUS GALL, MINISTRY OF SECRETS

SIR BARRINGTON ROTHSCHILD, MINISTRY OF

GUILDS

DEFENDANT:

JACK BUCKLES, MINISTRY OF TRACKERS

As soon as the judge opened the pneumatic tube to return the cylinder, the drone idled its engines and dropped, barely scraping the wood backing of her chair.

The woman turned to the judge beside her, cylinder dangling above the open portal. "Did you say something?"

"Only that I hope this doesn't take all night. The Royal Arbiter and I have a nine o'clock table at the Wig and Pen."

"I can't imagine it should. Then again, you know how vicious these ministry squabbles can get." She dropped the cylinder into the tube, closed the portal, and pressed a brass button. Off it went through twists and turns with the nano-drone clinging to the front, flaring its blue engines in delight.

Jack Buckles sat on a plain wooden bench in a small waiting room, head resting in his hands, trying to clear his mind.

It didn't work.

Three blue-green pings lit up the corner of his brain, like sonar in a submarine. *Ping. Ping. Ping.* Jack waited for them to stop. *Ping. Ping. Ping.* They didn't. He left the bench and walked over to a brass grating set high on a wall papered with burgundy and gold silk. Blue light glowed behind.

The moment Jack pulled the grating free, a nano-drone shot out. It coasted around the room in a slow descent and came to rest on the bench beside Jack's nine-year-old sister. The two exchanged a glance. Sadie—that was her name—shrugged and smiled.

Their mother, meanwhile, looked befuddled, but not by the drone. She patted her coat pockets, holding a single red glove by the fingers. On the way back to his seat, Jack knelt beside her and lifted a matching glove from under her chair.

"Ah. There it is." She spoke with a British accent, even though she had spent the first thirteen years of Jack's life in Colorado, pretending to be American. "Just like old times."

Jack glanced over at a black slate door, looming in the corner. "No, Mom. It isn't."

"Everything is going to be all right, Jack."

Nothing had been *all right* for more than a year, ever since a mad Clockmaker had kidnapped his dad, luring Jack out of an exile no one had bothered to tell him about. Jack's discovery of his birthright as a member of a cloak-and-dagger British detective agency had caused him nothing but trouble. Since then, he'd been cut off from everything he'd known and locked in an underground tower—his mother and sister prisoners with him, his father in a coma. Returning from exile had made Jack lonelier than he could have ever imagined.

Jack shoved his hands into the pockets of an old leather jacket, one he knew Mrs. Hudson would frown upon. The matron of the Ministry of Trackers had strongly advised him to wear a suit for the trial. Jack had chosen a T-shirt and jeans.

"You're strong, you know," said his mother. "Your father

and I grew up together on Tracker Lane, embedded in the rigors and traditions of the ministry from birth. You were denied that, and yet you're stronger than he was at fourteen, both mentally and physically." She poked the knot of muscle at his shoulder and combed his dark brown hair with her fingernails before sitting back again. "You can handle whatever they throw at you tonight, Jack. I know you can."

He hoped so. London's oldest secret agencies—the Ministry of Dragons, the Ministry of Secrets, the Ministry of Guilds, and the Ministry of Trackers—all played by a different set of rules. Simply by learning his true identity, Jack had violated Section Thirteen of the tracker regulations, the rule mandating the exile of the thirteenth generation.

And he had broken many more rules since.

A girl with honey-blond hair pushed in through the opposite door, along with the scent of strawberries, staring down at her smartphone. Gwen Kincaid snapped her feet together directly behind Jack's mom and looked up. "There you are."

Jack frowned. "Where did you think I was?"

"Not you, you wally." She unraveled a purple-and-black striped scarf with one hand and pointed her phone at the nano-drone with the other. "Him."

"You mean, *it*," said Jack.

"No. I mean, *him*." Gwen drew a walnut pillbox from the pocket of her gray wool coat and flipped it open, exposing the blue velvet padding inside. "Fun's over, Spec. In you go."

Spec approached the box as if intending to obey, but then zipped away at the last moment and flew around the room. He settled in a high hover, out of Gwen's reach, and did a little flip.

"Get in the box or spend the next week as a paperweight on Mrs. Hudson's desk."

Gwen's threat did the trick. The nano-drone cut its engines and dropped into the pillbox, snapping it closed with the weight of the fall, and Gwen squished herself down between Jack and Sadie to show them the smartphone. "He took a picture of tonight's lineup."

"Risky." Like he needed another mark on his record. "What if the judges had seen him?"

"They didn't, did they?" Gwen bumped Jack's shoulder with hers. "You see, before it became a courtroom, the Black Chamber was the Elder Ministry station of the Royal Mail, so there's all these pneumatic tubes, and some of them connect to the air ducts, and—"

"Gwen." Jack placed a finger under her arm, lifting the phone. "The lineup?"

"Right." She tapped the screen, bringing up the photo of the judge's parchment. "Gall is scheduled to speak."

Ignatius Gall—the Undersecretary for Things Unknown at the Ministry of Secrets—was the creepiest of all their agents, with a clockwork monocle in place of one eye and a skeletal clockwork prosthetic in place of his right arm. Jack had it on good authority that Gall had enlisted the mad Clockmaker to kidnap his dad so he could experiment on a tracker brain, causing his dad's coma. Jack also had it on good authority that Gall wanted his family dead. "He . . . uh . . . wouldn't try anything in front of all those people, would he?"

Gwen gave him an indefinite shrug. "Probably not. Right? Too many witnesses."

It was not quite as confident an answer as Jack was hoping for.

She switched to the video. All those people, four secret societies, had come together for one purpose—to determine Jack's fate. The camera zeroed in on Gall, at the center of the Ministry of Secrets section. Jack bent closer to the screen. The spook, as agents of the Ministry of Secrets were called, appeared to be talking to the empty space beside him. "Who's he talking to?"

"An imaginary henchman?" offered Gwen. "Who knows?

Madmen talk to all sorts of things—rabbits, pigeons, shopping trolleys. In any case, it looks like—"

"They're ready for you." Sadie finished the statement for her. But Jack's little sister wasn't looking at the video with the others. She had turned to face the big black door.

It opened slowly, ghostly silent, and a boy in a three-piece suit with glossy black hair poked his head in. His eyes settled on Jack. "Master Buckles, I presume?" His manner was posh, as Gwen would say, but not his accent.

"Yeah. That's me." Jack stood, straightening his jacket.

The boy pointed at him, turned his finger over, and curled it twice. "You're with me, yeah? The rest of ya can watch from the cheap seats."

———·· Chapter Two ··———

POSH-SLICK-HAIR BOY LED JACK down a long arching bridge to a circular podium elevated above the chamber floor. The whole place smelled of old wood with a hint of lemony polish, a spotty orange scent in Jack's intersecting senses. He took care not to touch the podium's slate railing as he took his seat. Those mixed-up senses allowed him to *spark*—to see the memories trapped in stone and steel by feeling molecular vibrations, drawing out the light and sound trapped within.

Metal had a vibrant memory, but short. Stony materials like slate had long, deep memories, but contorted and shadowed, often terrifying. A high heart rate or a rush of adrenaline could cause any tracker to accidentally spark, and Jack's heart was pounding.

Murmurs and whispers from the bleachers reached out in gray tendrils to grasp at him.

Section Thirteen.

He's gone too far.

They disintegrated in smoky wisps as his escort dropped into the chair next to him. "Name's Will. Welcome to the Black Chamber."

Jack shook the boy's offered hand, furrowing his brow. "Are you . . . my lawyer?"

"We call 'em barristers, Jack. And no. I'm not one. I'm an adjudicator's clerk, your guide for tonight's proceedings." Will pronounced *clerk* as *clark*, the way Gwen and Mrs. Hudson always had. "I work for that lot." He thrust a thumb toward the panel of judges. "The Royal Council of Adjudicators for Disputes Wiffin the Elder Ministries, the infamous RCADWEM."

In a year and two months of navigating the strange world of the four Elder Ministries, Jack had never heard of the RCADWEM, *infamous* or not.

Don't look so grumpy, silly.

The thought entered Jack's mind unbidden, and he looked to the crumb bleachers in time to see Sadie and his mother entering from the hall, with Gwen right behind them.

Sadie waved, wiggling her fingers. In the last year, she had gone from being way too good at hide-and-seek to reading Jack's emotions and pushing thoughts into his mind.

Jack gave her a subtle shake of his head, hoping she'd read his answer. *Not here. It's not safe.*

Among the *spooks* of the Ministry of Secrets and the *dragos* of the Ministry of Dragons were two ancient bloodlines—Arthurian fire-wielders and Merlinian telepaths. Jack's troubles were partly a result of his tracker abilities manifesting far too early in life, along with some Arthurian-slash-drago tendencies. He dared not imagine what the spooks might do if word got out that Sadie was showing signs of Merlinian blood.

A gargoyle-esque sneer drew Jack's gaze a few seats over to a blond and bulbous teen on the verge of gianthood. Shaw—journeyman warden, protector of artifacts, enforcer of rules, and all-around glory hound—had made Jack's comeuppance his primary ambition in life. He gave Jack a disturbing wink, clearly enjoying the night's spectacle.

"Noggins up, Jack. We're startin'." Will shoved a hand

under Jack's armpit and hauled him to his feet. He had some muscle under that suit.

The woman Jack had seen in the nano-drone's video cleared her throat. "All rise for the Right Honorable Sir Alistair Drake."

The assembly rose with a great thumping and shuffling of feet, and an elderly black judge with a tight gray beard walked to the center seat at the judges' desk. He paused to survey the room, then seemed to remember something and drew a white wig from the pocket of his robe.

"That'd be the Royal Arbiter," whispered Will, "the head of the council."

Sir Drake flopped the wig onto his head, where it sat slightly askew. "Be seated, please. Master Recorder, read the complaint."

The woman untied a green ribbon from a bundle of parchments and raised the top page to her eyes. "We the undersigned, his lordship the Minister of Secrets, the Unblinking Eye of the Realm, Master of Mysteries, Sultan of Spies—"

"Just the salient points, if you please, Asha."

The Master Recorder glanced at the Royal Arbiter sideways, then set the first page aside and picked up the next. "The Ministry of Secrets and the Ministry of Guilds do hereby raise the following complaints. Number one: that the apprentice tracker John Buckles the Thirteenth, sometimes called Jack, did willfully infiltrate the Ministry of Guilds by use of a submarine, which subsequently sank and now rusts at the bottom of the ministry's granite lake."

Jack couldn't help but glance at Gwen. The submarine had been her idea. She blushed, making her freckles glow.

The Master Recorder continued. "Number two: that this same Jack Buckles did willfully remove a potentially world-ending artifact from the Ministry of Trackers and hand it over to a madman—namely, the Clockmaker."

Jack squirmed in his chair. The complaint failed to mention that he had needed that dangerous artifact, known as the Ember, to rescue his father.

"Number three: that this Jack Buckles did alter the DNA security files of the Ministry of Secrets and use said access to aid in the theft of the Crown Jewels."

Jack leaped out of his chair, grabbing the slate railing. "That's a lie. I was set up by—"

The chamber went dark. Jack's podium dropped into a black ether, slamming down into a ghostly version of the same room. He had done exactly what he had told himself to avoid. He had grabbed the rail and sparked into the past, right in the middle of his own trial.

Stone, without fail, had always taken Jack far into the past, usually to some traumatic event in the object's history. But this spark felt different, more familiar. People—of a sort—milled about in the bleachers, black-and-gray silhouettes polished to a dull gleam like the slate rail itself. Similar creatures assembled on the platform, taking the places belonging to the arbiters' council. This was a rocky version of the scene Jack had watched on Spec's video. The slate had brought him only a few moments back in time. Why?

One silhouette from the spook section looked Jack's way, and not by chance. It *saw* him. One eye—the eye that should have been covered by a clockwork monocle—glowed orange. "Hello, Jack," said Gall in a voice made grating and raspy by the slate. "Surprised?"

Once before, in the headquarters of the Ministry of Secrets, Jack had suspected Gall of seeing him in a spark. He had let it go as fear and fancy, but this time there was no doubt. The imaginary friend Jack had seen Gall addressing in the video had been Jack himself.

How? Jack wanted to ask, but he couldn't. A tracker couldn't speak during a vision without first pushing his consciousness fully into the spark, and that came with big risks.

"Must you really ask?" said Slate Gall as if he'd sensed Jack's question. "You've heard the rumors about me by now, I'm sure. Miss Kincaid is always keen to share what she knows."

Merlinian, thought Jack. *A telepath, maybe even a seer—able to look into the future.*

"And now you are asking yourself, 'Is he *really* all those things? Or was he simply smart enough to know that I would spark back to this moment?'" Gall chuckled, a gravelly laugh emanating from stone lungs. "We haven't time to delve that deep. For now you need to know that you and I are about to embark on a journey. And you would do well not to resist."

Fat chance, thought Jack.

The orange eye shined a little brighter. "I suspected you would feel that way. Not that it matters. At this moment, I *am* your reality, Jack. I am your past, I am your present, and most importantly, I am your future—both the long and the unbelievable short of it."

Slate Gall thrust out a rocky hand, and Jack stumbled back from the rail, instantly coming back to the warm lights and the orange, woody scent of the present. No more than a fraction of a second had passed. Before Jack could gain his bearings, Will grabbed him by the arm and sat him down. "You will *not* do that again. Ya get me?"

"No," breathed Jack, catching a disturbing grin from Gall. "No, I won't."

Section Thirteen.

Out of control.

For the first time, Jack agreed with the whispers in the crowd.

Out of control. They had no idea.

─────── · Chapter Three · ───────

"I APOLOGIZE, MY LORD," said Will. "The accused will not speak again." He caught Jack in the shoulder with a backhanded thump. "Will ya?"

Jack shook his head, but when Will sat down, he risked an earnest whisper. "Don't I get to speak?"

"Where do ya fink you are?" Will whispered back. "America?"

"But what happens if they find me guilty?"

"The judge'll lock ya in the Mobius Tower 'til ya go mad. Maybe feed ya to a dragon." The clerk settled back into his chair, utterly relaxed. "The usual punitary constigations."

"Neither of those is a word."

"Really? So now you speak legalese?"

Jack crossed his arms and faced forward. "That's not a real word either."

The Royal Arbiter rolled a finger in the air, signaling for the Master Recorder to continue.

A few of the complaints were not Jack's fault, like blowing up a hyperloop transport system belonging to the Tinkers' Guild. Several were, like starting a flaming rave among a dozen live specimens in the Ministry of Dragons Collection.

Through all of it, Jack had only been trying to do the right thing—to rescue his dad, to stop the Clockmaker from burning London to the ground, and to stop Edward Tanner from unleashing a power upon the world that had once wiped out a tenth of its population. It was Gall who had set it all in motion, and now he would hang all the consequences around Jack's neck.

Once the Master Recorder had finished, the Royal Arbiter turned to the section of dark-robed spooks, still flicking their fingers in silent conversation. "Who speaks for the Ministry of Secrets?"

Gall stepped up to a podium at the center of the spook section, his clockwork eye twitching and clicking as he focused on the Royal Arbiter. "Lord Ignatius Gall. Undersecretary for Things Unknown."

"These are serious complaints, Lord Gall."

"True." Gall gripped the podium with one good hand and one mechanical prosthetic. "But these are not mere complaints, are they? These are symptoms, festering sores that give testimony to an underlying disease within the Ministry of Trackers."

Jack winced. Was he a *festering sore*, an *underlying disease*? He felt like he needed a shower, maybe some antibiotics.

"Oh, he's good," said Will. "A regular oraficorial genius. You're done for."

Gall gestured with his good hand toward the crumb bleachers. "The Ministry of Trackers is rotting from the inside. For more than a year they have harbored this dangerous boy. And as we all know, *another* tracker, Professor Edward Tanner, went rogue two months ago and sought to resurrect the power of Genghis Khan, putting the whole globe at risk."

"And I stopped him." Jack jumped up again before Will could restrain him, careful not to touch the railing this time. He couldn't believe Gall would bring up Tanner. After all, it was Gall himself who had sent Tanner to recover Genghis Khan's ruby.

Gall's clockwork monocle gleamed, as if he had

foreseen—even planned on—Jack's response. "Yes, you did. And how, Mr. Buckles? How did you stop him?"

Jack opened his mouth to answer, but he faltered, and dropped his eyes. He couldn't answer that, not in front of this crowd. Will pulled him down into his seat.

The spook addressed the rest of the chamber, raising his voice. "Don't let this boy's tender age fool you. There are rumors that he *burned* Tanner to death from the inside out."

Gasps rippled through the bleachers.

Jack shot a questioning glance at Gwen, who shook her head, eyes wide. They had spoken to no one about the fire that had started during Jack's subconscious battle with Tanner. How could Gall have known?

Mrs. Hudson jumped up from her seat. "That is *outrageous*, Lord Gall! Even for you!"

The arbiter looked from one to the other, his expression growing stern. "Do you have any proof to back up this accusation?"

"Not at this time, my lord." Gall grinned at Jack—a shameless, open leer. "Not at this time."

"Then what is your point, sir?"

"Only this: that the Ministry of Trackers, an agency guarding a cache of artifacts with the collective potential to bring about the apocalypse, has allowed this child—this Section Thirteen with unknown and uncontained powers—to hide within their midst. We, the Ministry of Secrets and the Ministry of Guilds, are asking, nay, *demanding* that this"—he shoved a finger toward Jack—"*creature* be destroyed, and that the crumbling Ministry of Trackers be dissolved."

Chapter Four

"SO THAT WENT WELL," said Gwen as she and the Buckles family reached the Lost Property Office. The little office served as the front for the Ministry of Trackers. It also served as the top level of the Keep—a huge Gothic tower that jutted down into the caverns beneath London's Baker Street like a crashed rocket ship.

Jack gave Gwen a hug goodbye, and then he, Sadie, and his mom followed a pair of giant wardens through the upper offices to the Great Stair that wound its way down around the tower's outer rim. He kept silent in the long descent, still trying to process what had happened.

The moment Gall had called for the dissolution of the Ministry of Trackers, all the crumbs had jumped to their feet, shaking their fists. The toppers, golden giants grinning behind them, began chanting, "End the trackers! End the trackers!" And no amount of shouting from the Royal Arbiter could shut them up.

To Jack's surprise, the dragos, led by a tall blond woman with piercing blue eyes, had taken the trackers' side. And so it went, dragos and crumbs versus spooks and toppers, for a half hour, until the Royal Arbiter finally made himself heard and declared an end to the night's proceedings. He had a dinner reservation that he did not intend to miss. The trial would reconvene in two weeks.

Two weeks. In that short time, Jack had to find a way to save his agency and head off a death sentence, all while outwitting a crazed spook who could read his mind and see into the future. Great. No problem.

At the bottom of the Great Stair, the wardens took their leave. Jack's mom turned a bronze key and pushed open an ancient wooden door, and the three stepped out onto a cobblestone lane lit by gas lamps. The bottom, or rather the top, of the Keep tower stuck out from the rocks above, with eight gargoyles looking up at the ceiling instead of down at the houses below.

Four seventeenth-century cottages surrounded a cul-de-sac

with a burbling fountain. House Fowler, House Tanner, and House Mason all stood empty, thanks to the exile of the unlucky thirteenth generation and their parents. Only House Buckles still had lights burning.

"We should eat," said Jack's mom, hanging her hat and blue peacoat on a hook beside the door. "We need to keep up our strength for the storms ahead."

Dinner was quick and cold—mutton and toast. When he finished, Jack excused himself and went upstairs. He sat down in the big red chair beside his father's bed and took up a frail hand beset with plastic tubes. "Gall is coming, Dad. And I don't know how to stop him."

John Buckles the Twelfth, Jack's dad, said nothing, leaving only the beeping of his life-support monitors to answer.

"He'll kill us. And then he'll have the trackers disbanded." Jack bobbled his head, trying to look on the bright side. "I guess that means the ministry won't be able to prosecute you and Mom for the Section Eight thing."

Jack's mom, Mary Buckles, had been born Mary Fowler, a daughter of another tracker family, and Section Eight of the ministry regulations strictly prohibited the mixing of tracker bloodlines. But Jack's parents had fallen in love. His mom had run away to America and the two married in secret, using the exile of the thirteenth generation as cover.

So Jack was a double whammy—a bad luck Section Thirteen and the cursed child of a Section Eight violation. His return had exposed his parents. The ministry planned to put them on trial as soon as his dad woke up. But Gall would probably kill all four of them before it came to that, and maybe Gwen as well.

Jack let go of his dad's hand and slumped back into the chair, yawning. "If we don't beat this, none of us will survive." It was his last thought as he drifted off to sleep.

The dream began as usual. Jack stood by himself in a crystalline cave, the type of world he experienced whenever he sparked on a jewel and stepped into the vision. The walls sparkled like diamonds.

Gwen appeared beside him, dressed in the gray coat and black leggings she favored. "Oh, very nice. Is this a spark?"

It wouldn't matter how he answered. Jack had seen it all play out before, night after night. "No, Gwen. This is a nightmare. Please go away."

She didn't hear him. "Cool. I've never been in a spark with you before."

Jack adored the way her freckles rose with her smile, the way they responded to her every expression. He had never told her that. There wasn't time to tell her now. "You have to leave."

"But I just arrived."

Too late. The creature had already come.

A faceted silhouette grew at the far end of the cave, taking the shape of a man in a bowler hat.

Gwen glanced back at him. "I think that's your dad."

"No." Jack's voice had grown weak, barely a whisper. "No, it isn't."

Something moved in the diamond shell, like the larva of a moth, twisting and seething until the jeweled cocoon shattered into dust. A man emerged, wearing the same blue-green body armor he had worn when Jack had last faced him. "Hello, Lucky Jack."

From that point on, Jack's words were scripted. He could not control them. "You're dead. I saw you fall from Big Ben."

"No, *mon ami.* I am alive. And I am coming for you." The Clockmaker pointed at Jack with a stump instead of a hand. "You stole my flame."

Jack hated that stump. He had never wanted to cut anyone's hand off, but the Clockmaker had turned it into a flamethrower. "You gave me no choice. You were going to burn London."

"Liar." The Clockmaker let out a wry chuckle. "You stole the Ember because you could not resist the beauty of the flames. And now you have a fire of your own burning inside." His eyes shifted down to Jack's closed fists.

Jack slowly opened them. A tongue of white fire rested in each palm.

The Clockmaker took a menacing step forward. "I *will* have that flame. It belongs to me."

"No. Leave me alone!" Jack thrust out his hands. The flames shot away, merging into a diamond fireball that slammed into the Clockmaker with a brilliant flash.

That should have been it. The nightmare should have been over.

It wasn't.

The fire consumed the Clockmaker, transforming him into a dragon of titanium, steel, and the same blue-green alloy that made up his body armor. Red eyes glowed. The creature came roaring forward, cracking the diamond floor with metal talons.

Gwen charged out to meet it. "You should have stayed dead!"

"Gwen! Don't!" Jack tried to pull her back, but his fingers swept through her shoulder.

The dragon opened its metal jaws and released a torrent of flame.

"Gwen!"

"Jack!" Someone was shaking him. "Jack, wake up!"

Jack's eyes popped open. He was still in the chair, listening to the eternal beeping of the monitors.

"Oh, thank goodness. You're conscious." Gwen—the real Gwen—had her coat off, frantically swatting the arm of his chair.

Jack blinked. "What . . . What are you doing?"

"Saving you. As usual." She shook out her coat, nodding down at the arm of the chair. Scorch marks marred the wood. Smoke drifted up from the burgundy quilting.

Jack opened his right fist, the way he had opened it in the nightmare. A little yellow flame rested in his palm.

Gwen puckered up her lips and blew it out. "We really *must* get control of that."

The grandfather clock standing in the corner read ten o'clock. Jack had been asleep less than an hour. "How did you get in here?"

She laughed. "As if I ever left after we said goodbye. I followed you in and waited for the wardens to close up shop. I have a lead, Jack, something I saw at the tribunal. It's solid."

"Did you pick the lock on our door again?" Jack was still trying to push away the fog of the dream. "You know how Mom feels about that."

Gwen slipped her coat on over a green sweater. "You're not listening, Jack. I have a lead."

"Yeah. No. I heard you." He rubbed at the scorch marks with the corner of his T-shirt, trying to wipe them away. "What kind of a lead?"

"The kind of lead that could put Gall away, save your life, and perhaps save your dad's in the process."

———·Chapter Five·———

GWEN SPOKE LITTLE AS she dragged Jack across the bridge beneath the roaring waterfall of the Keep's power station, making for the unguarded utility door at 221B Baker Street. Stealth was key. As a Section Thirteen, Jack could not leave the Keep without an order from Mrs. Hudson, which he did not have.

Soon they were safely aboard a cylindrical carriage on the Ministry Express, the underground transport system of the four Elder Ministries. The purple glow of the maglev ribs flashed by the windows, casting their light across the quilted blue upholstery.

Gwen handed Jack a grainy photo.

"*This* is your lead?" he asked, tilting the picture to take better advantage of the globe lanterns at either end of the carriage. He had seen it before. Two men were posing before a green marble fireplace, arms across each other's shoulders. One was Jack's grandfather, John Buckles the Eleventh. The other man remained a mystery. Jack dropped his hand to his lap. "I found this, remember? In Grandpa's journal where the page had been torn out. It was a dead end."

Jack and Gwen had started a quiet investigation into Gall after Tanner had let it slip that Jack's grandfather had died to keep a dangerous artifact out of the spook's hands—a small red sphere that Jack called the *zed*. According to Tanner, the zed could bring Jack's dad out of the coma. Only Gall knew how. But the investigation had drifted into a black hole of missing journal pages and meaningless pictures.

"We don't even know who that other guy is."

"Don't we?" Gwen took the photo back and pointed to the mystery man. "Picture him twenty years older, wearing a scarlet robe and a white wig—looking terribly, *terribly* bored."

Jack drew in a breath. "The Royal Arbiter."

"I recognized him during the hearing," said Gwen, tucking the photo away. "And I've taken measures to keep tabs on him." She held her phone between them, showing Jack what appeared to be a live image of Sir Drake—without the wig—leaving a restaurant.

"You have the *judge* under surveillance?" Jack put a hand to his neck. He could already feel the noose closing.

"Relax. It's Spec. He's quite discreet." The carriage hummed to a stop, and the clamshell doors hissed open. "Hurry. He's on the move."

They rushed across a multilevel platform of red granite. Cylindrical maglev trains flew through bronze rings above and below them. The Ministry Express side of Temple Station was drago territory, and Jack could feel their eyes boring into him as he ran. Dragos always stared at him. No one had ever told him why.

During the elevator ride to the surface, they checked Spec's video. Sir Drake strolled up Fleet Street. Gwen expanded the picture and tapped the screen, activating blue lines that identified his possible routes. She pointed to a large station three blocks on. "There. That's Ludgate Circus. Trains. Buses. If he reaches it before we catch up, we'll lose him."

She had not timed the statement well, since the elevator ride was not over. Muzak played from a speaker above them. And the two stood side by side in awkward silence. Gwen coughed. "Um . . . so, are you going to tell me why you lit your chair on fire and thrashed around in your sleep, all whilst calling my name?"

Jack's face went tingly. "I was"—he swallowed—"calling your name?"

Gwen nodded.

"Well . . . I was . . . I mean, you were . . ." The elevator bumped to a stop, saving him.

Gwen slid open the door and took off at a quick walk, eyes on the video. "We'll circle back to that one, shall we?"

Their quarry did not take the projected route to the train station. Instead, he took a sudden left into a rat's nest of alleyways, stairwells, and courtyards. Even with Spec's video to help, it took all of Jack's tracker skills to follow the judge's trail through the rapid turns—the gray *scuff* of a leather sole on cobblestone, the yellow *flap* of a wool overcoat lined with silk.

Jack slowed as they passed through a tiny courtyard. At the center stood the bronze memorial of a cat, seated on a dictionary. He wrinkled his nose. "Is that . . . ?"

"A predecessor," said Gwen, tugging him onward. "The Archivist of the eighteenth century lived on this lane. Brilliant man. Naturally, the cat gets the statue."

Moments later, the two caught up to Spec at the entrance to a tavern. Wooden barrels beneath the awning read YE OLDE MITRE.

Jack had assumed Sir Drake was heading home, not hopping from a pub to a tavern. "So our only lead is an old judge out for a bender?"

"I very much doubt that." Gwen coaxed Spec back into his box and pulled open the door. "After you."

Only a few patrons haunted the front room. Grizzled faces flickered in the dim orange light. "Look." Jack gave a subtle head tilt toward a green marble hearth where the last embers of the night's coal lay dying. "That's the fireplace from the picture."

The barkeep fixed them with a steady scowl, cleaning a glass with an old rag. "Whadda you two want?"

Jack lowered his chin, avoiding eye contact. "We were looking for someone."

"In the snug." The barkeep waved his rag at a tiny side room with YE OLDE CLOSET painted across the doorframe. "He's waitin' for you."

"Um . . . He is?"

The scowl intensified.

"Thank you. Thank you very much," said Gwen, pulling Jack toward the room. "*Snug* is a bit generous, if I'm honest," she whispered once the two had squeezed inside.

The dying firelight hardly breached the threshold, making

the little room uncomfortably dark. Jack could make out a single table, a couple of chairs, and a leather bench against the back wall. All were empty. "I think that barkeep is messing with us."

But as his eyes adjusted, a falcon and a dragon took shape in the wood moldings above the bench. Jack had seen them together before, on an heirloom from his father's armory. "Gwen, there's—"

"I see them." She pulled out her phone, letting the glow from its screen wash over the panel. The wings and tails of the two creatures touched to form a seal, with a Latin phrase etched beneath. *"Familia in Aeternum,"* read Gwen. "Forever family. What do you suppose it means?"

On a hunch, Jack pressed the seal inward, and heard a soft *clank*, followed by a scraping of wood. The bench, along with a section of the wall behind it, rotated outward. He laughed. "It means the barkeep wasn't messing with us after all."

Chapter Six

A FALCON, THE SYMBOL of the trackers.

A dragon, the symbol of the dragos.

Familia in Aeternum.

Forever family.

There was more to Sir Drake than Jack had first supposed.

A spiral staircase, lit by a hissing gas sconce, beckoned them onward. Three steps down, Jack pulled an iron lever, and the bench and panel swung back into place, closing them in.

At the bottom of the steps, they found a tavern built from an old crypt, with patrons wearing anything from chalk-striped suits to ragged street clothes. A kid with green spiky hair and a black leather jacket glanced up from a nearby table. He gave Jack an indifferent nod before returning to a plate of bread and cheese.

"This is . . . odd," said Jack, and he wasn't talking about the crypt layout or the mixed scent of bread and blackberries. A girl circled a finger in the air, gathering a disc of vapor into a globule of water. She flicked it away to splash against a boy's head at the next table over. Across the room, two little boys of Arab descent sat back to back, each with half of a chess set on a separate board. One slid his queen diagonally across the squares. The other dropped his forehead into his palm and knocked over his rook.

Gwen lifted Jack's chin to close his mouth, which had been hanging slightly open. "Why have we never heard of this place?" She pointed to several men and women brooding over a table strewn with maps. "There's the arbiter."

The moment she spoke, Sir Drake looked up, smiled, and gestured toward an empty table.

Jack answered with a nervous nod. "It's like he *sensed* we were here. That's not disconcerting at all."

The three took their seats, and a fourth chair slid over from the table next door of its own accord. A well-dressed teen with shiny black hair sat down opposite Gwen. "Hello, miss. Remember me?"

Jack did. "Will." He narrowed his eyes. "How'd you do that?"

Will touched two fingers to his temple, as if that was the answer. "Welcome to Fulcrum, Master Buckles. It'll be good to 'ave a tracker 'round 'ere again."

"Whoa," said Gwen. "Slow down. What *is* Fulcrum, some kind of tracker-drago speakeasy?"

The clerk laughed. "Not likely. There's no alcohol down 'ere, too much business goin' on. And *we* are Fulcrum." He used an elbow to point at the patrons around them. A few answered with solemn nods. "This *speakeasy*, as you call it, is the Cellar—a right and proper lair." He took a swig from the wooden mug he had brought with him, leaving a swath of pink foam on his upper lip. "Best brambleberry cider-milk in the Elder Ministries."

Jack tried to wrap his brain around that one. "Brambleberry what?"

"Want some?" Will wiped his lip and stood up again. The chair moved out of his way on its own. "'Course you do. Two cider-milks coming up."

As Will sauntered off, Jack turned to Sir Drake, raising a finger. He meant to ask what Fulcrum was all about, but the Royal Arbiter answered that very question before he got the chance to ask it.

"We are the secret society within the secret societies, Jack—a catalyst of equilibrium, using our modest skills to keep the balance of power among the Elder Ministries."

Gwen sat forward in her chair, lips parting with a question of her own.

"What sort of skills?" asked Sir Drake, doing to her what he had done to Jack. "For one, the sort of skill that allows me to finish your sentences. I can hear your most prominent thoughts, moments before you speak them."

The slightest smile lifted the corners of Gwen's mouth. "You're Merlinians."

Will sat down again, setting two mugs of frothy pink cider on the table. "And Arthurians, yeah?" The mugs slid over to Jack and Gwen on their own. "In my case, that means tele-kinesis. Pretty cool, eh?" He winked at Gwen. Her freckled cheeks flushed.

Jack glowered at him. "I thought the Arthurians were a subset of the dragos, and the Merlinians were a subset of the spooks, fire-wielders and mind-readers from—"

"The bloodlines of Arthur and Merlin," said Sir Drake. "True. But Fulcrum stands apart, Jack. Think of us as . . . outcasts." He bent forward. "Just. Like. You."

"Ahem." Gwen found her tongue, turning away from Will.

"Are you saying Jack is part drago? Or part spook?"

"Both, I should think. As all trackers are." Sir Drake sat back and snapped his fingers. Spiky-green-hair kid strolled by, sliding a plate of rolls, apple slices, and cheese onto the table. "The same sensitivity that allows me to see the thoughts on the tip of your tongue, allows a tracker to experience every piece of his environment in four additional dimensions."

Will rotated a finger, and Gwen's mug moved in a circle, pink foam curving to a swirly peak. "An' the same brand o' telekinesis that lets me to do that, lets Jack, 'ere, read the molecules of a door knocker. It also lets a drago ignite the air molecules in 'is palm." He raised his mug in toast. "But you know all about fire, don't you, Jackie Boy?"

Jack wasn't about to confirm his budding abilities with fire in front of the judge—not after Gall's accusations. He kept silent, but he raised the mug to appease the clerk.

Will took a great big swallow and smacked his lips. "Aah. Good, yeah?"

Jack tried to match him, but he wound up coughing into his sleeve, eyes watering. "It's . . . sharp," he wheezed.

"That'd be the brambleberry juice. If it weren't for the moose milk, you'd never get it down."

Sir Drake frowned at them both. "Jack's ancestor Johnny Buckles was the first to discover the connection. At the same time, he saw the dragos with their raw power, the spooks with their secrets and mind-reading, and the toppers with all their money, and realized that any one ministry might quickly overpower the rest."

"So he created Fulcrum to keep the balance." Gwen took a swig of her cider without so much as a flinch.

Will grinned. "That-a-way, miss. Very nice."

"Johnny Buckles," said Sir Drake, ignoring the exchange, "searched among orphans like himself for the unacknowledged children of the ministry aristocracy. He found many with . . . unique . . . variations of the Arthurian and Merlinian skills."

"Like a girl who can make water magically appear." Jack took a roll and a slice of cheese from the plate. Discovering a new secret society had made him hungry.

Sir Drake cast a glance at the girl in the corner. "Kaimana doesn't use magic, Jack. She draws moisture out of the air, making London a veritable playground for her."

"And the twins playing chess?"

"Ahmed and Rahim. They remotely sense each other's movements, but *only* each other's for the moment." Sir Drake picked up an apple slice and popped it into his mouth. "We shall see what time reveals."

Jack split his roll down the middle and slipped the cheese into the gap, making a perfect little sandwich. As he tried to take a bite, the roll flew out of his hand, straight into Will's.

"Thank you, Jackie Boy."

Sir Drake placed a cautioning hand on the clerk's arm, as if to say *be quiet for a bit*. "That brings us to Jack's grandfather, John Buckles the Eleventh. As I'm sure you've guessed by now, he was Fulcrum. During his last assignment, keeping Gall's power in check, we lost him. All we know is that he fell from a cliff in the Bavarian Alps, a few miles south of Salzburg."

Will polished off Jack's roll and called another from the platter. It flew right past Sir Drake's nose. "That's where you come in, Jackie Boy. We need ya to find out what 'appened, connect his death to Gall."

There must have been twenty people in that secret underground lair with untold telepathic and telekinetic skills. Jack sat back, crossing his arms. "Why me? Why not Will or Water Girl?"

"This mission needs a tracker." Sir Drake picked up another apple slice. "And you're motivated. You have the most to lose."

"But aren't you the Royal Arbiter?" Gwen laid her elbows on the table. "Can't you rule in Jack's favor? Besides, Jack is the accused. He not supposed to leave the Keep, let alone London."

"That is not quite correct, Miss Kincaid. Jack is the object of a complaint, nothing more. What the Ministry of Trackers chooses to do with him is still their own affair. And *I* am an *arbiter*, not a dictator. I am but one voice on the council."

Another roll flew off the platter. Sir Drake intercepted it and slapped it into Will's hand. "*Stop* that. I feel as if I'm caught in a reverse food fight." He let go of the roll and sighed. "Jack, I've left this mystery unsolved for far too long. Gall's actions tell me that battle lines are being drawn. We must have answers if we are to be ready for the fight."

Jack took an absentminded sip from his mug, forgetting the pink-burning-death-drink lurking within. He coughed. "What . . . will we . . . find in Salzburg?"

"Evidence, I hope." Sir Drake removed a yellowed paper from his inside pocket and laid it on the table, covering its faded script with his hand. One edge was ragged, as if the page were torn from a book. "Your grandfather gave his life racing against Gall in the hunt for a powerful artifact—the Mind of Paracelsus. That is why he went to Salzburg. Find that artifact's trail and you'll find his." He lifted his hand. "This may help—the last words of Paracelsus, translated from an entry in an innkeeper's ledger."

Gwen passed a magnifying glass over the script. "I know this handwriting. This is the missing journal page."

She handed the glass to Jack, and he read the words aloud. "'Once I held a treasure worth the fortunes of pope and king. It rests on high beneath the seasick saint, now far beyond my reach.'"

"Your grandfather found the ledger in a New York bookstore," said Sir Drake, folding the paper again. "After recording these lines, he had that ledger destroyed to keep Gall from finding it." He handed the paper across the table.

Jack tucked it away. "But what *is* this Mind of Paracelsus?"

Sir Drake's expression turned grave. "The Mind unlocks the one treasure that powerful men cannot take for themselves— the one treasure that would enable a man like Gall to hold on to power indefinitely." He stood, indicating that the interview was over. "The search for the Mind is the search for immortality."

·────· Chapter Seven ·────·

JACK AND GWEN WALKED north of Baker Street, avoiding the Keep for a while longer. They found a quiet bench in Queen Mary's Rose Garden. The lamps were doused for the night, but Spec hovered above, spreading a cone of yellow light around them.

"Do you have it?" asked Jack, holding out an open palm.

Gwen shoved a hand into her pocket, rummaged around for a few seconds, and produced a mother-of-pearl lighter with the initials *JB* in gold lettering. "You know, if my Uncle Percy catches me with this, he'll think I've started smoking."

Jack pressed his lips together. "Uncle Percy knows you better than that."

When Jack had first confessed his budding ability with

fire, Gwen had suggested a policy of dual control—given Jack's history with the zed. The little sphere had gradually sucked the life out of him for a year, all while he thought it was boosting his abilities. It had been a life-threatening addiction. Gwen worried that the fire thing might turn out the same, so she kept the lighter, and Jack practiced his fire-craft only under her supervision. Recent events, however, had made it clear that this new power was beyond either of their control.

It had started a week earlier, when Jack woke up to a charred pillow. Then, three nights later, he burned a hole through his blanket. Both had occurred after the clockwork dragon nightmare. The chair fire had been the worst yet. He shuddered to think what might have happened if the flames had reached his dad's oxygen tanks.

Jack could produce fire in his sleep, like an Arthurian drago. But he could not duplicate that skill while awake. He could only play with an existing flame.

Gwen drew the lighter back. "Are you sure you want to do this? Now?"

"It helps me think." Jack lowered his outstretched hand. "And you used to think my fire-play was cool. But I guess it's not as cool as making food fly across a table."

"What's that supposed to mean?"

"I could practically see your heart flutter when Will winked at you. If you're into guys with bad grammar and no manners, I'm sure I could get you his number."

"Now you're just being absurd."

"Am I?" Another zinger had made it halfway from Jack's brain to his lips when Spec dropped down and bonked him on the head. "Hey!"

The nano-drone zipped around Gwen, messing up her hair, and settled in front of them, camera twitching back and forth, looking from one to the other.

"Oh, relax," said Gwen, straightening her hair. "We're not fighting. We're just talking."

"Speak for yourself," grumbled Jack.

Spec pushed in closer.

"Fine." Gwen struck the lighter. "We're sorry. Look. I'm giving him the flame." She put on an exaggerated smile. "Everyone's happy. Right, Jack?"

"Uh . . . right." Jack matched her ridiculous smile and passed a hand across the lighter. He opened his palm, showing Spec the little tongue of fire.

The nano-drone stayed put for a moment, then slowly rose into the air, canting toward them as if to say, *I'm watching you.*

A long while passed before either spoke again. Jack played with his flame, holding it in his palm and twirling it with his finger. He tossed it from one hand to the other, which was his best trick. Not very impressive. Whenever he tried to throw a flame as he had done in the nightmares, it snuffed itself out within a few feet. He checked to see if Gwen was watching, and then tried something new, rolling the fire from his palm to his knuckles and back again. It worked.

"You *are* getting better," said Gwen, bumping his shoulder. "And I noticed your hands are getting farther apart when you toss it. Pretty soon you'll be throwing fireballs like a true drago."

Jack held the flame in both hands and lowered them to his lap. He sighed. "How are we supposed to get to Salzburg?"

She gave him a smile, a devious lift of her freckles that Jack knew all too well. "I've been working that out. Come on. Douse that light. It's time to get you home." Gwen explained her plan as they walked.

It could work.

Maybe.

Gwen followed him partway down the Great Stair, instead of going home to her mother's flat near King's Cross. The two had an early training session with Ashley Pendleton the following morning, so she would sleep in her uncle Percy's office on the quartermaster level. "Just so you know," she called, pausing in the doorway as Jack continued down the steps, "if I want Will's number, I can get it myself."

The door fell shut behind her.

——·Chapter Eight·——

THE NEXT MORNING, JACK met Gwen on the quartermaster level. He leaned against a walnut panel in a long, arched hallway lined with oil paintings. Men and women in bowlers and top hats posed with canes, bullwhips, and copper discs—the ministry's most famous quartermasters, trained in the many arts required to get trackers deep into trouble and out again.

Jack tugged at his sweats. The waistband itched, needling the back of his brain with orange and yellow spikes. He cupped his hands to his mouth. "Anytime now, Gwen." They didn't want to be late. They had to stay on Ash's good side if they wanted his help with the plan.

"Relax. I'm right here." Gwen emerged from her uncle's

office wearing black sweats with the word APPRENTICE down the right arm and QUARTERMASTER down the left. She had her favorite black-and-purple striped scarf wrapped around her shoulders.

"Nice scarf," said Jack, pushing off the wall and walking beside her.

She nudged him with an elbow. "Have you forgotten how cold it gets in the arena? Trust me. You'll wish you had one before the hour's over."

A leather-padded side-a-vator brought them along a jerking, lurching route to the arena—the Keep's indoor stadium. Jack had seen the ministry's workforce of Quantum Electrodynamic Drones, or QEDs, configure the place into everything from a castle setting to a garden village. Most mornings it was empty, nothing but a giant ironwood cylinder.

Jack swayed as the side-a-vator stopped. "Are you going to ask him, or should I?"

The doors slid open. Gwen just looked at him and walked out.

Jack nodded. "You're right. It's better if you ask him."

"Ask me what?" Ashley Pendleton waited on a simple ironwood walkway that ran around the upper level. White clouds collected above, near the lights. Thanks to its size, the arena had its own weather system. The dashing black quartermaster tipped up his newsboy cap with a wolf's-head cane. "I'm sensing an ambush," he said, then twirled the cane and pointed at his trainees. "I can see it on your faces."

Gwen took a half step forward. "We need a favor."

"A favor?" He gave her the winning smile that had made him Mrs. Hudson's favorite. "I'm intrigued. But let's chat once you've run a few laps. Make it four."

"But, Ash—" said Gwen.

"Four laps." He tucked the cane into the crook of his arm and clapped. "Off you pop."

Once they had finished, huffing and puffing, Ash put Gwen off again. "I don't want to lose our momentum," he said, and tossed each a pair of fingerless gloves. He pointed the wolf's-head at a platform jutting out from the walkway. "Over there. I have something special for you."

Out in the open space of the arena, the bronze quad-style QEDs were busy pushing oak and mahogany obstacles into a loose formation. Ropes, climbing walls, monkey bars, and stairwells all floated on glowing white thrusters. "Who designed your course?" asked Jack. "M.C. Escher?"

Ash helped them both onto a single floating disc, barely

large enough for one person, let alone two. They had to hug to keep from falling off. "This will be an exercise in dynamic problem-solving," he said, poking Jack's hip with the cane to send them drifting out into open space.

Jack peeked down over his arm. A dark fog churned at the bottom of the arena, nine stories below. "More like an exercise in certain death."

"Oh, don't be melodramatic." Gwen found her balance and pulled on her gloves one at a time, wiggling her fingers. "That sort of thing is far too American." She raised her voice in a humdrum tone. "We've done obstacle courses before, Ash."

"Not like this one." On cue, the obstacles eased into motion, moving left and right and up and down. A black rope hanging from a thruster disc wheeled around a central staircase. "Welcome to the moving maze. Only certain obstacles, passed in order, will get you to the other side." Ash dug his thumb and forefinger into the front pocket of his waistcoat and drew out a stopwatch.

The motion cracked Gwen's bravado. She chewed her lip. "I know you, Ash. You wouldn't send us off without a clue."

"Too right. Try this one, then. 'Chess master.'"

"Chess master?" asked Jack.

"You have fifteen minutes. Fail and you can forget that favor you wanted." Ash raised the stopwatch and pressed the button. "Go."

With a sudden leap that almost sent Jack careening off the disc, Gwen caught a rising set of wooden monkey bars. "Come on!"

After a quick glance at Ash, who held up the watch, swinging from its chain, Jack rolled his eyes and leaped after his partner.

The two dangled from the bars a foot apart, facing each other, while Gwen muttered to herself. "Chess master. Chess master."

"What does it mean?"

"Haven't the foggiest." Her pupils were shifting all about, scanning the obstacles.

"Shouldn't we have figured that out before we left the stand?"

"No," Ash called from the platform. "That's why we call it *dynamic* problem-solving. Think, Jack. How does a chess master win?"

Gwen answered for him. "By looking three and four steps ahead." Her eyes locked onto a target. "That's it."

Ash thumped the platform with his cane. "Keep moving!"

"That climbing wall," said Gwen, "moving right to left. Now!"

They both swung for it at the same time, and Jack grunted as his cheek squished against the wood. The polished grain left dark furrows across his tracker brain. "How . . . can you be . . . sure?"

Gwen was already climbing. "We find the good path by eliminating the bad—follow each potential path in our heads, looking for the obstacles to avoid." She reached the top and helped him up beside her. "Concentrate, Jack. *See* the vectors like the tracker you are."

"Right." He let the data fill his merging senses. The gray whoosh of the moving obstacles. The bronze hum of the thrusters. The play of light and shadow against the ironwood walls. All of it merged into one picture—one confusing picture.

"Two minutes down," Ash called from the platform. "You'll never make it at this rate."

"Yes we will," countered Jack. Vectors emerged amid the chaos in his head as ghostly white lines. "Those stairs," he said, pointing to his left, "and that trapeze. They're dead ends."

Gwen slapped his arm. "Well done! That leaves the rings. Keep on it!"

Jack identified the obstacles to avoid, and Gwen picked the proper path. Each new phase revealed a new piece of the moving puzzle. They chose the rings, a rope bridge, and an annoying leather bag that jiggled and rotated whenever Jack shifted his weight, and within three minutes they had reached the motionless stairway at the center of the maze.

They had the course licked.

Until it started to rain.

"Really?" asked Jack, looking up into the arena clouds. A slow drizzle wet his cheeks. "I think you people take the whole 'always rains in London' thing a little too far."

"Massive space. Poor ventilation. A common tale." Gwen dabbed her face with her scarf. "There's nothing for it. We have to finish if we want that favor from Ash."

Without further complaint, Jack climbed up onto the stairwell railing and grabbed the rope swinging past. A series of knots made the climb manageable at first. But the more the rope sailed through the drizzle, the wetter it became.

His feet slipped.

He couldn't get them back into place.

Down below, the yawning chasm of the arena opened up to claim him.

Jack tightened his grip. "Uh . . . Help?"

"Hang on!" Gwen reached the top of the stairs, waiting for the rope's next pass.

Jack's steadily growing panic gave way to a burning sensation—not in his stomach, in his right hand. Steam and flames shot out between his fingers. "What the—?"

The rope snapped.

Jack fell at the same speed as the rain, as if the drops had frozen in space, and the arena was rising around both them and him. He could read his own vector the way he had read the vectors of the obstacles. A ghostly white line traced down from his eyes to the mists below. A purple-and-black scarf whipped through it.

"Grab hold!"

Jack caught the scarf with his left hand, patting his right against his hip to put out the flame. He crashed into the side of the floating stairwell. Gwen hauled him up over the rail.

"Thanks," he said, panting as he dropped to the floor.

She laughed and eased herself down beside him. "Didn't I say you'd want my scarf before the end?"

A pair of QEDs pushed the stairwell to the platform, and Jack tucked the burned glove into his sweat suit. He did not want Ash to see.

The quartermaster scratched his head with his cane. "I've

never seen one of our ropes snap like that. Not a big deal, mind you. The QEDs would have caught you." The two drones hovering on either side rotated to face him, widening their camera lenses in what Jack could only take to be surprise.

"Right," said Jack, stepping down onto the platform. "Sure."

Gwen hopped down behind him. "Ash, about that favor. I know we didn't finish, but—"

"You solved the maze, and you saved your partner. That'll do." The young quartermaster folded his arms. "Shoot."

"We need you to use that smile of yours to convince Mrs. Hudson to do something."

"And what would that be?"

"We need her to send all three of us on Jack's first sanctioned tracker mission."

Chapter Nine

DESPITE ASH'S IRRESISTIBLE SMILE, Mrs. Hudson said no.

Sort of.

Jack squirmed in a coach-class seat, unable to get comfortable. The FASTEN SEAT BELT sign flicked off with a melodious *bong*, and the captain announced that they had reached a cruising altitude of thirty-five thousand feet, well on their way to Salzburg.

"Are you asleep?" he asked, poking Gwen's shoulder.

A rose tint at the edge of the window promised a magnificent sunset washing over the tops of the clouds, but Gwen had blocked the view with her squishy pillow. She nestled deeper in. "I'm trying to be."

"I'm kind of disappointed."

"Are you now?" She sounded kind of miffed that he was still talking.

Jack didn't care. "Since we've met, you've taken me on levitating trains, a submarine, a supersonic underground transport, and a rocket-powered zeppelin. All while going rogue. Now we're out on our first ministry-sanctioned hunt, and we're on a regular old airliner." Jack pressed the little button on his armrest and bounced against his seatback, trying to recline. It wouldn't budge. He sighed. "In coach."

"What can I say, Jack? Welcome to the glories of official ministry ops." She held up a tiny snack bag. "Have some improbably small pretzels."

After the obstacle course, Ash had kicked his charm into high gear and made his pitch to Mrs. Hudson. She could send Jack and Gwen to Salzburg after the mysterious Mind of Paracelsus, an artifact that had come to light thanks to a clue Jack had uncovered in his grandfather's notes—which was mostly true.

Ash would supervise, of course, and the three would return victorious, showing the council that the Ministry of Trackers could still do its job, and that the spooks and toppers were making noise over nothing.

"Yes to the first part," Mrs. Hudson had said, looking down on all three through her spectacles. "And no to the second. I am not opposed to your plan, but Section Thirteen is clear. If Mr. Buckles is to leave the country"—she focused her stern gaze on Jack—"to conduct an *official* tracker investigation, he must have a warden looking after him, not a quartermaster. I am sorry, Mr. Pendleton. You do not fit the requirement."

Ash was out.

Shaw—with whom neither Jack nor Gwen would dare share the real purpose of their mission—was in.

The oversize teen now snored in the aisle seat beside Jack. His big, weighty arm fell into Jack's lap. Jack tossed it back over the armrest. "And where is our gear?" he asked, taking the bag of pretzels and stuffing it into the seat pocket. "All we brought were overnight bags."

At this, Gwen opened her eyes and smiled. "You'll see soon enough."

Thirty minutes after landing in Salzburg, they were standing at the bus station.

Spec came zipping around the corner.

"Wot's that, then?" asked Shaw, swatting at the drone as it did a lap around his head.

Gwen opened the pillbox. "My nano-drone. I couldn't

very well send him through the scanners, could I? In you go, Spec."

Instead of returning to the case, though, Spec pushed closer to Shaw's bulbous nose, making him go cross-eyed. With uncanny speed for his size, Shaw snatched the drone out of the air and tightened his fist, squeezing hard. "Gotcha!"

"Stop it!" cried Gwen. "You'll hurt him!"

She needn't have worried. Spec's engines flared from blue to white, and in schoolyard-bully-why-are-you-hitting-yourself style, Shaw's own fist rammed into his forehead over and over until he let go.

Spec gave him an extra bonk and then did a backward triple-flip with a half gainer into the pillbox, snapping it closed.

Shaw growled and stormed off toward the bus kiosk. "We need tickets into town. Don't none of you move 'til I get back."

Waiting until the warden was out of earshot, Jack turned to Gwen. "What's the deal with Spec, anyway? Not even the QEDs are that . . . quirky."

"Uncle Percy made him. The smallest QED ever built. Gave him to me as a Christmas gift." She checked on Shaw, making sure he was still a good distance away. "He used a very special crystal as the foundation for the artificial intelligence chip."

"What sort of crystal?"

"Let's just say Uncle Percy never logged in all the artifacts he and your father found. There've been a few *other* Christmas gifts as well." Keeping her hand close to her body, she touched her scarf, then her coat.

"I knew it. That's why your pockets never run out of room." Gwen only smiled.

The bus dropped them off on a snow-dusted riverbank in view of a hilltop castle with train tracks running up through the lower ramparts. At the base of the castle hill, they found a market square dominated by a statue of Mozart. Gwen nodded toward a shop in the darkest corner. Gold stenciling on the windows read ARNULF UND SÖHNE. Vests and neckties hung behind the glass.

"A tailor?" asked Jack. "Seriously?"

Gwen frowned at him. "*Outfitter.*"

"Whatever. Are those lederhosen?"

A sign hanging between the ties read GESCHLOSSEN, which Jack knew from middle school German to mean CLOSED. Gwen and Shaw pushed through the doors anyway, tinkling a little bell. An older gentleman stepped out from behind the counter, waving his hands. *"Nein. Nein. Wir sind geschlossen."*

"Not for us, if you don't mind," said Gwen, dragging Jack forward. "You have a contract with our agency, Herr Arnulf. A very old contract." She snapped her fingers at Jack, which he had long ago learned meant, *Show him the card.*

Jack pulled a platinum business card from the inside pocket of his leather jacket, showing Herr Arnulf the family name printed on the front. JOHN BUCKLES.

A look combining wonderment and dollar signs filled the Austrian's eyes. "Ah, *wunderbar.* I have not seen a tracker for many years, many years indeed." He made a grandiose gesture toward the back. "Please, follow me."

Herr Arnulf led them past cherrywood shelves filled with a rainbow of shirts, socks, and handkerchiefs to a short platform with a three-sided tailor's mirror.

Jack knew what to do. His mom had taken him to get fitted for a suit when he was eleven. He stepped up on the platform and raised his arms, holding them straight out to the sides.

Shaw laughed.

Gwen did a face-palm.

Herr Arnulf coughed and pressed Jack's arms down again. "Perhaps . . . a little closer, yes?"

Confused, Jack stepped deeper into the arc of the three

mirrors. Something beeped. Red lasers ran up and down his body from both sides, and his ministry mug shot materialized over his own reflection. "What on earth?"

Red boxes sprang up all over the combined faces, turning green in rapid sequence. A female voice, exactly like the voice that constantly reminded Tube passengers to *Mind the gap*, said, "Identification confirmed. Tracker. Welcome, John Buckles."

It was an access system. Jack glanced over his shoulder, not knowing the protocol for the others. "Um . . . and . . . guests?"

"And guests," said the voice. The mirror slid up into the ceiling, revealing a long hall filled with clothes, fabrics, and gleaming gear.

———·Chapter Ten·———

JACK WALKED ALONG A wall of miniature crossbows and dart guns. Titanium spheres and tungsten discs
rested on satin cushions lit by pink lights. "This is a tailor's
shop?"

"*Out-fit-ter*," said Gwen, correcting him once again. "The
ministry has contracts with masters across the globe. Our
travel accommodations may be lacking." She chose a titanium ball from a cushion and twisted the bottom half. The
top sprang out into spinning blades, lifting it from her palm.
"But there *are* perks."

Gwen wandered off to look at hats while Jack inspected a
row of shiny gold and silver fountain pens. "Let me guess," he
said to the tailor. "Lasers?"

Herr Arnulf removed a pen's cap and pressed its clip inward. Blue-white flame shot from the tip. "Torches. These will make quick work of any alpine ice encasing an artifact."

Next came canes with heads in the shape of animals. Several had blue or purple sparks arcing within glass chambers on the shafts. Jack brought down a plain oak cane with a pewter bear on the end. "These are longer than I'm used to."

"A lengthy shaft is best for mountain work." Herr Arnulf delicately retrieved the cane and returned it to the rack, trading it for another—onyx, ornately carved and topped with a silver leaping lynx. "Might I suggest this one?" He waved Jack back a few steps and pressed an unseen button on the shaft. With a pronounced *shink*, a tungsten spike stuck out from the end. "For icy mountain passes, yes? But that is not all." He spun and fired. The spike shot out, dragging a microfilament line, and stuck into a dressing dummy at the far end of the room, missing Shaw's nose by a fraction of an inch.

"Oi! Watch it!"

"My apologies, Herr Warden," said the tailor as both the line and the spike came whistling back.

Jack caught a twinkle in the old man's eye.

Herr Arnulf handed Jack the lynx cane. "It is interesting,

mein Herr, that your eyes were drawn to the bear first. Your grandfather favored that same icon."

"My grandfather came to this shop?"

"Oh yes. I kitted him out for two weeks in the Alps." Herr Arnulf sized Jack up from his head to his sneakers, and selected a leather satchel. He strolled down the line of satin cushions, filling it up. "Sadly, I did not see him after that." He paused, touching his chin. "Although there was an incident with a package."

"What package?"

"A boy, a street urchin, brought me one of my own hollow copter scouts a week after your grandfather left. He would only say that John Buckles had asked that I give the contents to John Buckles."

"So . . . my grandfather sent a package to himself."

"Strange, yes?" Herr Arnulf glanced back at him. "I sent the item to London—a sphere, wrapped in packing paper—addressed as requested." He returned and lifted the strap over Jack's head, adjusting the satchel at his hip. "Now, will you be needing a suit?"

A sphere, wrapped in packing paper. That was exactly how the zed had come to Jack's father.

"Herr Buckles? A suit?"

"Hmm? Oh. I don't think so." Jack had always preferred jeans and his dad's leather jacket.

"Mein Herr, you are in Austria. In February. This"—he gestured up and down Jack's form, frowning—"will not suffice."

Jack knew Herr Arnulf was talking about his clothes, but he could not help noticing the tailor had gestured to his general person.

"Perhaps I should explain. We are not talking about the usual fabrics." Herr Arnulf took Jack's elbow and steered him along the racks. "Our shirts turn your kinetic energy into heat to keep you warm. Our suits are lined with Kevlar to protect you from falls and . . . other threats."

They came to a selection of boots and wingtips. "The soles of our shoes are covered in carbon nano-spikes to keep you upright on the most slippery ice."

Stepping close, Herr Arnulf gave a subtle tilt of his head toward Gwen, who was trying on a purple stocking cap a few feet away. "And in an *Arnulf und Söhne* suit, you *will* look sharper than any man she has ever seen."

"Any man?" Jack pictured Will in his three-piece suit, making mugs slide around the table—Gwen's cheeks flushing when he winked. "Okay. Do your worst."

Twenty minutes later, Jack came out of the dressing area. Herr Arnulf had put together a full ensemble—a rugged three-piece suit and overcoat, complete with a Homburg hat. Jack gave Gwen a nervous shrug. "Whaddaya think?"

Gwen's jaw went slack, if only for a moment. "I . . ." She recovered quickly. "It'll do." She rose on her tiptoes, pulled the Homburg from his head, and tossed it aside, giving him the slightest smile. "Yes. It'll do nicely."

The others got new threads as well. Shaw could not stop looking at himself in the three-way mirror.

"That suit is tweed," said Jack, standing behind him, "exactly like all your other suits."

"Yeah, but this'n's a full shade lighter, innit? Complements my complexion. That's wot 'err Arnulf says."

Gwen picked out a beige cable-knit sweater—Kevlar-impregnated—and the purple hat she'd been admiring, along with a willow walking stick with a bluish cobalt owl for a handle.

"Herr Arnulf," said Jack as the tailor walked them all to the door. "Did my grandfather say anything else about his mission, anything at all?"

"Let me see . . ." The tailor removed the measuring tape from around his neck and laid it on the counter. "He *did* ask me for directions to the White Horse Inn. I expect he had a room there."

The White Horse Inn. Why did Jack recognize that name? He patted his pockets, looking for the page from his grandfather's journal.

"Jack?" asked Gwen.

"Hang on." Jack unfolded the page, and there, in the margin, he saw it. "The White Horse Inn. That's the inn where the ledger came from—the inn where Paracelsus died."

The square outside had gone dark, lit only by a spotlight shining on the statue of Mozart. Gwen checked her watch. "It's getting late. We need to find rooms for the night, and now we know the perfect place."

Chapter Eleven

JACK, GWEN, AND SHAW took a bus from the city center to the White Horse Inn.

Gwen spent most of the ride nose down, buried in her phone. "The inn has existed in one form or another for a thousand years," she said, reading from a web page, "as a common stop on the Catholic pilgrimage trail through Bavaria."

Jack pulled himself up from his seat to look over her shoulder. "Is that Wikipedia?"

"Archivipedia." Gwen glanced up at him. "Maintained by the Archivist. Far more accurate, if you ask me."

A touristy hotel came into view, and Jack sat down again. "I'm not so sure."

The White Horse Inn did *not* look a thousand years old. Sure, it had an old-school German facade with dark timbers and white plaster, but it also had balconies with plastic lawn furniture and an asphalt parking lot.

"So yer sayin' Paracelsus might a' used that Jacuzzi over there?" asked Shaw, pointing a fat finger at the pool.

The trio checked into separate rooms and spent several fruitless hours exploring the grounds. There were no clues to the fate of the Mind, and Jack's sparks proved pointless. Every stone, brick, and timber had been replaced since Paracelsus's day, likely ten or twenty times over.

Shaw gave up and went to bed, while Jack and Gwen collapsed onto a couch near the great room fireplace to take a breather.

"We'll never find Grandpa's trail in time," said Jack, laying his head back and closing his eyes.

"That's the spirit, Jack. Well done." Gwen wasn't listening. She used his shoulder to push herself up, staring at the opposite wall. "Be right back."

Jack lifted his head to see what had stolen her attention.

Across the room, a bellhop pushed a luggage cart away, revealing an oil painting, lit by a dim overhead lamp. An exhausted Gwen staggered toward it like a zombie.

Jack followed. In the painting, a man in a red tunic leaned on a sword, standing before a fountain. His face flashed in Jack's brain, superimposed over a bust he had seen on Gwen's Archivipedia page. "That's him," said Jack, coming up beside her. "That's Paracelsus."

Gwen looked over at him with red, squinty eyes. "I know." She threw out an arm, pointing at a brass plaque, printed in three languages. "It's labeled."

PHILIPPUS THEOPHRASTUS PARACELSUS.

ALCHEMIST AND DOCTOR OF GREAT RENOWN.

A BAND OF LOCAL APOTHECARIES, SHAMED BY

HIS SUCCESS TREATING PATIENTS AT

ST. WOLFGANG'S CHURCH, BEAT PARACELSUS TO

DEATH IN THIS VERY ROOM.

Jack studied the alchemist's face, repeating the first line of his final words. "'Once I held a treasure worth the fortunes of pope and king.'"

"Perhaps he meant the sword," mused Gwen. "A treasure can be anything. If I was getting beaten to death by an angry mob, I'd wish for my sword too."

Her theory drew Jack's attention to the sword, and a pit

opened in his stomach. The weapon indeed looked like a treasure, with an ornate silver blade and a golden hilt. But it was the pommel that caught his eye, partially visible beneath the alchemist's hand. "It can't be."

"Can't be what?" asked Gwen.

A suspicion had been growing in Jack's mind since their meeting in the Cellar. According to Sir Drake, his grandfather had died to keep the Mind of Paracelsus out of Gall's hands. During the fight over Genghis Khan's rubies, Tanner had said the same thing about the zed.

And then there was the tailor's story.

"Herr Arnulf told me a messenger boy brought him a package from Grandpa, and asked him to send it to John Buckles."

Gwen scrunched up her nose. "Your grandfather sent a package to himself?"

"That's what I thought. But *all* the trackers in my line share that name, right?"

She had the answer before Jack could spit it out. "John Buckles the Eleventh didn't send the package to himself; he sent it to his son, John Buckles the Twelfth—your dad."

"Exactly. And inside that package was a sphere." Jack

shifted his gaze back to the painting, nodding. "The treasure isn't the sword, Gwen. It's *on* the sword."

She studied the weapon for several seconds, then smacked Jack's arm with the back of her hand. "The pommel is a *red sphere*. That's the zed, Jack! The zed *is* the Mind of Paracelsus."

·———· Chapter Twelve ·———·

THEY ATE BREAKFAST IN the hotel sunroom—
cheese, cold cuts, and boiled eggs with hard rolls. Shaw ate
three times as much as Jack and Gwen, but only twice as fast,
forcing them to wait.

A muted newscast played on a TV hanging in the corner.
Something had blown a hole through a museum wall in
China. Men and women in hardhats picked through smol-
dering rubble under the harsh glare of mobile floodlights.

Shaw lifted a pretzel made of salami from his plate.

Gwen scrunched up her face. "Whoa. Is that a meat pretzel?"

"Yes it is." The warden moved the plate out of her reach and
popped the treat into his mouth. "And it's a fing of beauty,
innit?" He polished off two more and pushed back from the

table, belly threatening to burst through his waistcoat. "So the 'otel's a bust, eh?"

"Yes," said Jack.

"Not at all," said Gwen at the same time.

Jack shot her a look. They hadn't told Shaw about the painting. If he found out Jack's family had the Mind-slash-zed, he would immediately call Mrs. Hudson to declare victory. She would make them come home and fork over the artifact, and Jack would never find the evidence he needed to put Gall away.

Shaw's eyes narrowed, nearly disappearing behind his plump cheeks.

Gwen recovered nicely. "We found a plaque that told us Paracelsus treated patients at Saint Wolfgang's Church." She leaned forward to flick a speck of salami off Shaw's sleeve and looked toward a church bell tower across the street. "That's where we're headed next."

If Saint Wolfgang's interior designer was aiming for creepy, he or she had scored big-time. Icons sculpted from dark wood stood on black marble stands, wearing sad expressions. Gilded angels, stern and peeling, glared down from the rafters. And every memorial seemed unnecessarily macabre— dozens of them, hammering Jack's overactive vision.

Skull.

Pile of skulls.

Skull with bat wings.

Skull with a snake coming out of its eye.

Life-size zombie holding an hourglass, standing on skulls with snakes slithering out of their eyes and climbing up its legs. "Oh, come on!" Jack said out loud.

Gwen turned to scowl at him. "Shhh!"

He shrugged. "These people had a messed-up way of comforting the living."

Gwen gave him a frown and followed Shaw up the center aisle. "Remember the clue, Jack. 'It rests on high beneath the seasick saint.' Look for boats among the sculptures and paintings."

"How can anything rest on *high* and still be *beneath* a saint?"

A priest walked down the aisle to meet them, spreading his hands. "*Guten Morgen.* Did you say you are looking for a saint?"

Shaw folded his arms. "Yeah. One that'd toss his chips on the barmy sea."

The priest looked perplexed, if not a little scared. "I am sorry. Mein English ist not especially good."

"Neither is his." Gwen shouldered her way past the warden

and shook the priest's hand. "What my apelike colleague means is we are looking for a saint related to ships or sailing."

"Ah. *Sailing*." The priest's confusion melted. "You seek Saint Bartholomew, patron saint of fishermen." He thought for a moment and added, "Und farmers, und hospitals, und shoe makers." He bobbled his head. "Und also milkmaids."

"So . . . Saint Bart is pretty popular," said Jack, squeezing past Shaw as well.

"Oh yes."

"And do you have any statues or paintings of him?"

"Sadly, no. There is, however, a Saint Bartholomew's Church not far from here. For centuries it was one of the primary hospitals in all Bavaria."

"A hospital?" Gwen slapped Jack's arm, right in the spot where she had backhanded him the night before. "We're in the wrong church."

Not far was a relative term. Jack had pictured something a few streets over. But, as the priest had admitted, his English was not especially good. Getting to Saint Bart's required a train ride.

And a passport.

The *clickety-clack* of rails pulsed beneath their feet as the train steamed through snow-white hills, heading into the mountains. Saint Bartholomew's lay twenty miles away on a large alpine lake known for its fishing industry. To get there, they had to cross into Germany.

"A fishermen's hospital." Gwen pounded the faux-wood table between their seats, upsetting a stack of Jaffa cakes that Shaw had procured from the dining car. "Saint Bart is the saint for the sick of the sea, not a seasick saint. It's a case of lost in translation."

As the warden finished off his cakes, the train plunged into a tunnel, emerging moments later on the northern rim of the lake valley. Jack pressed his forehead to the glass, trying to see what lay ahead. Ice extended far to the south—a frozen fjord slicing between rocky peaks, with villages on both shores.

The station was small, hardly more than a timber platform. As the train pulled away, Jack raised a hand to shield his eyes from the glare coming off the frozen lake. He could see the church a good mile or more away.

On the other side.

"This can't be right." Jack tugged at the sleeve of a passing gentleman. "Excuse me. How do we get to Saint Bartholomew's?"

"In ze sommer you would take ze boats." The man thrust an elbow at a stack of rowboats on the shore, strung with icicles. "In ze winter"—he snorted, nodding toward the vast white expanse—"you walk."

Clouds of snow swept across the lake from north to south, at times reducing the visibility to zero. By the time Jack and the others climbed the rocky shore on the far side, they looked like a polar expedition team—faces, coats, and spiked walking sticks frosted on one side.

None of the townspeople gave them a second look.

Moments later, they stood melting inside the empty cathedral. Sculpted angels smiled down from alabaster domes, looking far more welcoming than those in Saint Wolfgang's.

Gwen, however, did not like them. "Those angels are baroque," she said, chewing her lip. "Same with the paintings. It's all seventeenth-century artwork, a hundred years after Paracelsus." She lowered her voice, whispering to Jack without moving her lips. "I might actually have been . . ."

"Been what?" asked Jack, knowing what was coming and dying to hear her say it.

Gwen turned her back to Shaw. "Wrong, okay? I might have been wrong."

"Maybe." Jack strolled past her, heading for a low-hanging balcony carved from blue marble, the largest piece of solid stone in the church. "And maybe not."

Gwen caught up to him, reading his intentions. "A spark won't help us, Jack. Even if Paracelsus came here, the current building is too new."

"Yeah. I get that." Jack pulled off a glove. "But we're not really looking for Paracelsus, are we?"

He laid his hand on the pillar and dropped into a shadowed memory of the cathedral. Swirls of gray whooshed away as he landed. Jack watched dusty striations of color drift past him in the gray, catching the light from the windows. There must have been some copper in the marble.

He heard the distorted warble of explosions. Silhouettes in shadowy helmets ran up the aisle. Jack had dropped into World War II. Stone always took a tracker straight to its most terrible memory. And on the train ride to the valley, Gwen had told him that Hitler's Eagle's Nest was close by—a prime target for the Allies. He pushed with his mind, rolling the years forward.

Priests came and went. Congregations filled the pews and vanished in an instant. Ghostly Christmas trees rose, fell, and rose again until finally one lonely silhouette stood still amid the roiling shadows, flashing in and out.

Jack slowed the vision. The silhouette stared up through a high window, one hand resting on a cane, the other holding a trilby hat. After what seemed like an age, it turned, looked Jack's way, and gave a single nod.

Grandpa.

Jack backed out of the spark and speed-walked between the pews, heading for the same window. "I saw him. I saw my grandfather."

"You couldn't have." Gwen was right on his heels. "Do you know the odds?"

"He must have stood there for hours, Gwen, day after day, to mark the spot—like dog-earing a page in time. He left a breadcrumb for another tracker to find."

The window framed a mountain, all ice, snow, and jagged rock. A bronze plaque with multiple translations hung below the sill.

ST. BARTHOLOMEW AND THE ICE CHAPEL

FOR MORE THAN A MILLENNIUM, PILGRIMS

CLIMBED MOUNT WATZMANN TO VISIT

ST. BARTHOLOMEW'S SHRINE, SET ON AN
OUTCROPPING ABOVE A COLLECTION OF ICE
CAVES KNOWN AS THE ICE CHAPEL. THE SHRINE
IS LOST TO TIME, BUT THE CAVES REMAIN AS
A TESTIMONY TO THE INTRICACY OF THE
CREATOR'S HANDIWORK.

"The treasure rests on *high*," muttered Jack, "*beneath* the seasick saint. Paracelsus kept a stash *above* the church but *below* the shrine, somewhere in those ice caves. That's the answer to the riddle." He stared out through the window, studying the mountain for a long time.

Gwen leaned close and whispered, "What are you doing now?"

"Memorizing the terrain. We have to get up to those ice caves."

"Or we could do this." She snapped a picture with her smartphone and started for the door. "Think outside the box, Jack."

The trailhead lay a few hundred meters up the road. A steel gate barred the path, secured with a heavy chain and a sign that read LEBENSGEFAHR: LAWINE / DANGER: AVALANCHE. Jack and Gwen stomped through the drifts on either side and continued on.

"Oi," said Shaw, staring at the sign. "Where're you two goin'?"

"Outside the box," Gwen called over her shoulder.

"Yeah." Shaw pushed into the drifts to follow, grumbling so that Jack could barely hear him. "But sometimes the box is there for a reason, innit?"

—— · Chapter Thirteen · ——

THE SNOW HUNG HEAVY in the pine boughs, falling in clumps whenever Shaw's big shoulders brushed their lower branches. But the pines, at least, made the trail obvious. That bit of help ended soon enough as the three breached the tree line. Jack's world became a steep, sloping uniformity of deep snow and rocky crags.

Gwen used her photo and a compass hidden beneath one wing of her cobalt owl to pick the most likely path to the ice caves. They were looking for a shallow valley that ran up the mountainside.

Zzap.

The noise was so faint that Jack might have imagined it. He had heard it before, and seen the tiny yellow-orange lightning bolt it caused in the corner of his mind. He had seen it every time the thief who had framed him for the theft of the Crown Jewels used a phase-jumping device.

A patch of darkness shifted at the edge of the pines. Jack paused his march, waiting for another glimpse. Nothing. "Shaw," he said, slogging through the drifts to catch up to the warden. "Hang back and keep an eye out, will you? We don't want any trouble with the locals."

Shaw doubled over, resting his hands on his knees and panting. "Good . . . idea. I'll wait 'ere . . . Keep an eye out . . . Like you said, eh?"

Gwen pointed up the mountainside with her cane as Jack caught up to her. "This is it. This is the valley. We've been on the edge of it since we left the trees."

Another hundred yards up the slope, the ice chapel came into view, partially masked by the snow. Era after era of wind and meltwater had formed a network of caves in a permanent mass of ice. The openings were stacked among the mountain outcroppings like doors and windows in a church.

Jack and Gwen climbed up to the mouth of the largest, sixty feet wide and eighty high. Walls of translucent blue towered above them, filtering sunlight like stained glass.

"Now we know why they call it an ice chapel," said Gwen,

leaning on her stick. "Of course, no one should ever enter an ice cave. They're notorious death traps."

Jack dug his spiked cane into the drifts and kept going. "We don't have a choice."

In the shelter of the cave, the snowdrifts dissipated, giving way to a gravelly slope. Freezing winds whistled and howled through countless side tunnels.

"Where to now?" asked Gwen, raising her voice.

Her photo had gotten them this far. The rest was up to Jack, but at that moment his tracker senses felt useless. The extreme cold numbed all feeling and suppressed all scent. The wind masked all sound.

"Jack?"

He held up a hand. "Just . . . give me a sec." He closed his eyes.

Frozen air: a white sheet covering the data like the snow covered the mountain.

Smell of ice and rock: stale and gray, hardly scents at all.

Howling wind: a half dozen streaks of pink and red, ripping across a white background, glittering with gold and silver flecks.

Glittering?

The sound of wind had never looked metallic to Jack. He

focused on the streaks and realized only one was glittering. With his concentration, the white of the cold faded. The pink and red faded as well, leaving a lone ribbon of gold and silver. It pulsated in sharp, steady waves—a mechanical noise, riding the wind like leaves on a river.

Jack let out a laugh and took off at a brisk hike, chasing the trail. "Follow me."

A series of lefts and rights took them deep into the maze, where the glowing blue walls darkened. Gwen flipped on a light—the eyes of her owl. "Slow down, Jack. We won't know how to get out."

"Trust me."

Another left, another right, and there it was, a titanium disc mounted on a knee-high post. Three counter-rotating blades turned within, sending out their pulsating whine.

Gwen gasped. "A *whinger*." She rushed over and crouched beside the device, holding her fingers close to the fans. "I've read about these in the *Quartermaster's Guide to Gadgets*. Trackers use them as markers."

"Grandpa left it here. And that means the alchemist's stash must be close."

Gwen flipped off the owl's eyes, engulfing them in a thick, blue darkness.

Jack frowned. "Hey!"

"Outside the box, Jack. Remember?" She pulled him into a crouch beside her. "Let your eyes adjust. Tell me what you see."

A few seconds later, he understood. Without the owl's artificial beams, he could sense the sunlight reaching down through the ice. The walls glowed a deep blue—all but one. "Over there," said Jack, pointing. "That has to be the mountainside."

Using Herr Arnulf's torches, Jack and Gwen melted random spots until they found empty space. Soon they had uncovered a low arch in the rock wall. A rough-hewn staircase led up to a furnished cave much brighter than the chamber below. At the opposite end, the afternoon sun streamed in through a cluster of icicles. The place was trashed. A wooden workbench lay overturned. A rusty iron stove sat crumbling in one corner. Rotting shelves had fallen from the walls, littering the floor with shattered beakers and brass instruments.

"This cave wasn't Paracelsus's stash," said Gwen, lifting a brass ladle and shaking off the glass. "It was his lab."

Jack peered out between the icicles covering the mouth of the cave and saw nothing but blue sky. "We're pretty high up, maybe on a cliff face." He knelt and touched a black smudge at his feet. Streaks of soot formed a radial pattern. "Are these scorch marks?"

"A bad sign," said Gwen. "And so is that." She pointed with her owl toward globs of ice spreading out from cracks in the ceiling. "Ice has infested the rock, Jack, breaking it up. This whole place could go at any moment."

At the center of the scorch marks, Jack found an iron spike stuck into the floor. He pried it loose and held it to his nose. "Gunpowder. A bomb. This is the evidence we need. Gall laid a trap for my grandpa." He tossed the spike to Gwen. "That's the obvious deduction, right?"

Gwen turned the spike over and back, chewing her lip.

"Well? Isn't it?"

"You're not making a deduction, Jack. You're jumping to a conclusion. We haven't got one shred of evidence that Gall was ever here."

"Then we'll find some." Jack stood, ripping off his gloves and heading to the only group of shelves still hanging. He picked up pots and crucibles at random, slamming them down again.

"Be careful, Jack."

He didn't want to be careful. He didn't want to go slow.

He was sick of delays and dead ends. "Careful of what?" He thumped an astrolabe down on the shelf, earning a *crick* and sending up a small cloud of dust.

Gwen took a big step backward.

With an unbearable *creak*, the shelf collapsed, taking out the one beneath it. Beakers, flasks, and all manner of instruments crashed to the floor. Dust filled the cave.

"Of that." Gwen waved a hand in front of her face, coughing. "I told you—" She stopped, eyes shifting to the center of the wreckage. "Oh, Jack. Look."

One of the ruined shelves had been hiding a secret drawer. Amid shards of wood and tatters of red satin, a silver blade gleamed—the sword from the painting. The golden hilt terminated in an eagle claw, spread wide as if to catch its prey.

Jack gingerly lifted the weapon from the wreckage. "Do you have it?"

"Need you even ask?" After a bit of rummaging in her pockets, Gwen produced the zed, still wound in a strip of silk from Genghis Khan's tomb. It had turned white after the battle with Tanner, as if some evil had been banished from within.

Jack held up the sword, and she placed the sphere in the claw.

The talons snapped closed—a perfect fit.

"That's it, then. Theory confirmed." Gwen thumbed a catch on the hilt and the claw snapped open again. "The zed is definitely the Mind."

She offered the artifact to Jack, but he shook his head. "Put it away, please."

Jack turned away to right the overturned workbench. "So that's one answer found, but what about the scorch marks? What about the evidence against—"

A flash of yellow-green caught his eye. The crashing shelf had blown the dust off a walnut-size jewel lying in the corner. Trackers used such gems for training or passing messages across time. Forgetting to put his glove back on—forgetting the dangers such gems posed—Jack picked it up.

———·Chapter Fourteen·———

JEWELS OFFERED A TRACKER the ultimate in sparks. The hard, clear, crystalline structure held memories for centuries, perhaps millennia, with images and sounds so perfectly preserved they took on a life of their own. That quality made large gems infinitely useful.

It also made them infinitely dangerous.

The rocky floor evaporated into smoke and Jack dropped into darkness. He did not panic. This was nothing like the spark at the trial. He was not standing on a podium in front of Gall, the Royal Arbiter, and the whole of the Elder Ministries. Gwen would look out for him. And this spark might give him much-needed answers.

A gloved hand peeled away, as if from a camera lens,

revealing a haggard face. The grandfather Jack had never met looked up with a weary smile, eyebrows frosted. He must have set the gem on the shelf a moment before. "Son," he said, brushing snow from the arms of a bombardier's jacket, "relay this message to Alistair Drake. Tell him I found the Mind."

The older John Buckles glanced toward a sunlit ledge at the mouth of the cave. The icicles had not yet grown in. Worry creased his brow. "I took too long surveying the mountainside. Gall is nipping at my heels. If I don't make it back, bring Drake's men and uncover what remains of this lab." His gaze drifted to another shelf with a collection of mismatched artifacts—an obelisk, a Chinese fan, a piece of clay tablet, and others. "Paracelsus left us more than just the Mind."

Uncover what remains of the lab. The phrase stuck in Jack's brain. What did his grandfather mean? The lab had no fallen shelves or upturned tables, and no cracks or scorch marks—not yet.

The alchemist's sword lay on the workbench along with two wrinkled squares of brown wrapping paper, a cane with a pewter bear for its handle, and two halves of a titanium sphere.

Jack's grandfather held up the Mind. "*This* is what Gall

wants, and what he must never get." He wrapped the artifact in a square of paper and drew a canted Z on top, pressing it all into the bottom half of the sphere. "I've made an arrangement with a village boy. With any luck, you'll have both the Mind and this message within—"

Jack heard a scraping of stone.

His grandfather heard it too. "Someone's coming." The older John Buckles shoved the sword back in its drawer and snatched up the second slip of paper. He made a grab for the jewel, but only succeeded in knocking it to the rocky floor. The impact smashed into Jack's brain like the cracking of thunder.

The vision tumbled. There were shouts, a scuffle. Jack saw not one but two pairs of legs and little else. The workbench, still standing, blocked his view.

A simple spark was a lot like looking through a telescope, offering only one narrow perspective. Getting out could be as simple as backing away from the lens. But once a tracker pushed beyond that observation point, into the memory, all the rules changed. Pushing into a vision was risky. One wrong move might leave him trapped in the jewel's memories forever.

Jack made the leap anyway. He needed to see.

With the mental equivalent of heaving open a trapdoor,

Jack forced his way up from the floor. His grandfather had backed up to the sunlit ledge, one hand behind his back, holding the bear cane like a sword in the other. The intruder calmly reached up and lowered a hood trimmed with fur.

Gall.

The spook looked two decades younger, with neither the clockwork monocle nor the clockwork arm. Those injuries, it seemed, were yet to come. "Hand it over, John," he said, taking a step forward. "Let us be friends, you and I. We could be powerful allies."

"I don't think so." Jack's grandfather stabbed the air in a fencer's lunge to keep Gall back.

Spike or not, the cane did not intimidate Gall. He stood his ground. His voice deepened, reverberating in Jack's head. "Give me the Mind, John."

"No." John Buckles grit his teeth, fighting to get the word out. He turned, straining as if moving through molasses, and hurled the titanium sphere into the sunlight.

"Don't!" Gall reached out with an open hand, but spinning blades popped open and the copter scout flew away, vanishing into the glare.

The tracker gave him a grim smile. "Give it up, old boy. You don't have that kind of reach."

"Don't I?" Gall shifted his hand, and John Buckles lurched forward, boots scraping along the floor. "You're going to tell me exactly where that scout is going." The spook's other hand flicked open. A blue flame hovered at his palm. "You know what I can do."

"Yes." The tracker stabbed his cane down into the rock to stop his momentum. "I know. But let's see if you're more powerful than gravity." He pushed against his makeshift anchor. His feet inched back toward the ledge.

For a fraction of a millisecond John Buckles the Eleventh looked toward his grandson, or perhaps the jewel, and smiled. Then he threw his arms back and plunged into oblivion.

"No!" Jack and Gall's voices merged into one.

A cloud passed over the sun, and Jack saw the cane, still rigid, without its master. The eyes of the pewter bear flashed red. A steady beeping filled the cave, growing faster by the second.

Acting on instinct, Jack dove to the back of the cave. Gall was right behind him. The spook knocked over the workbench to use as a shield, but he wasn't fast enough.

The bear exploded.

A black cloud of sound rumbled across Jack's senses, with a yellow-orange bolt at its center. The bolt looked familiar, but Jack had little time to consider it. Immediately after the explosion, the walls and floor took on a green, crystalline sheen. His mind was becoming trapped. He heard a distant boom. The ground shook. He had to get out of the memory. Fast.

He knew how. Tanner, of all people, had taught him. Find an exit and think of nothing but escape. Jack broke into a run and leaped from the same ledge that had claimed his grandfather.

"Jack!"

A bright light.

A ringing in his ears.

Another boom, distant and gray.

"Wake up, Jack!"

The light shrank to become the mouth of the cave. The icicles had broken away. He was back, and Gwen was dragging him across quaking ground. Jack tried to gain a footing and tripped, smacking his wrist on the floor. The jewel skittered off into the debris.

Gwen hauled him up again. "We have to get out of here!"

The cave shook. A long crevice split the floor, racing between Jack's feet. Snow tumbled past the ledge, glittering in the sunlight. Chunks of rock fell from the ceiling.

"It's an avalanche!" shouted Gwen, trying to break through his confusion. "The cave is breaking up."

Something in the present had started an avalanche. And Paracelsus's lab, weakened by the explosion and two decades of encroaching ice, would not survive. If he and Gwen did not get out of there, they would not survive either.

The two rushed out onto the ledge. Looking up, Jack could see a great cloud of snow rolling down the mountainside. They had seconds. Maybe.

Gwen drew out the pillbox and tossed Spec into the air. He hummed away.

"You're worried about the drone?" asked Jack, covering his head as more snow fell past.

Instead of answering, Gwen clutched the front of his jacket and pointed to an outcropping twenty yards away. "Use your cane!"

His cane. By some miracle, Jack was still clutching it in his left hand. He aimed and fired. The spike shot out, trailing its microfilament wire, and stuck in bare stone. "Grab on!" The two leaped out over the ice and snow. Rock and dust billowed out of the cave behind them.

They swung into a crusted snowdrift, landing with a hefty *crunch*, and scrambled up into the shelter of the outcropping.

A white cloud enveloped them, accompanied by an unbelievable roar.

"Stay close and swim to the top!" Jack knew what to do in an avalanche. Every kid raised in Colorado did. He wrapped an arm around Gwen's waist and clung to the cane with all his might, fighting to keep them both close to the rocks.

He failed.

Overpowered by the torrent, Jack and Gwen tumbled away from their shelter. Snow and ice poured over them like dirt poured over a grave.

———·Chapter Fifteen·———

JACK AWOKE WITHIN AN icy cocoon, not sure if he'd been out for a millisecond or an hour. Herr Arnulf's amazing shirt had activated, turning all his previous kinetic energy into heat that kept him from freezing. He tried to call out, but the snow muted his voice to nothing.

Nevertheless, a blue light appeared, filtering through the grainy gloom. It began to spin.

Spec.

Snow pelted Jack's face, followed by a burst of sunlight as the drone burrowed through. Spec floated down and *booped* him on the nose.

"I'm . . . okay. A little stuck is all. Thanks."

The drone's engines flared in victory. It raced around the rim, widening the hole, and shot out again.

"Well, don't just leave." But Spec was long gone. Jack sighed. "Drones."

He wiggled out of his cocoon onto a powdery field, and saw Gwen's hand poking out a short distance away. Spec hovered over her, LEDs flashing red and yellow. There were rocks in the snow. The drone was having trouble reaching her.

"Relax. I've got her." Jack crawled over and dragged Gwen out, and they collapsed side by side, coughing in the freezing air.

The coughing turned to a long fit of laughter, until they both gasped at once. "Shaw!"

Perhaps Jack didn't look quite as hard as he should have. So it was Spec who found the warden—pinned against a tree trunk and buried up to his armpits. Shaw glowered at the drone circling his head as Jack and Gwen came trudging through the drifts. "I'd like to go 'ome now, eh?"

They spent another night at the White Horse Inn and took another ride in coach class the following day with Shaw snoring, big shoulders deep in Jack's personal space. And when they arrived at Heathrow, a senior clerk drove them into London and ushered them straight to a conference room on the Keep's Baker Street level. She wouldn't tell them the reason for the rush, only that an urgent matter had arisen.

Mrs. Hudson waited at the far end of an absurdly long mahogany table inlaid with bronze. And she was not alone. An Asian boy with ice-blue eyes stood a short distance behind her, wearing the gray overcoat and red scarf of the Ministry of Dragons.

"Do I know you?" asked Jack.

Mrs. Hudson did not give the boy a chance to reply. "Welcome home, Mr. Buckles. Miss Kincaid. Shaw." She gestured for the three of them to take their seats and raised her spectacles. "How was your first mission?"

Jack sank into the chair closest to her. "Mrs. Hudson, we—"

"Botched it? Bungled it? Mucked it all up?"

So she knew. Jack shouldn't have been surprised.

Gwen sat down beside him. "Not exactly. You see, Jack and I—"

"Ignored a regulation Bavarian Parks Authority warning sign? Provoked an avalanche? Destroyed a *prrriceless* historic site and buried all its secrets?"

Shaw remained standing, arms folded. "Yeah. That's about the size of it."

Mrs. Hudson turned her stern glare on the warden, letting

her spectacles drop. "And yet I'm sending you out again."

"What?" said Gwen.

"Really?" asked Jack at the same time.

Shaw raised a hand. "In that case, I'd like to req'isition some snowshoes."

"I fear I will regret it," said Mrs. Hudson, "but we've been given a chance at redemption—a mission of the highest urgency favored by the Crown." She reached over her shoulder, curling a bony finger to call the drago over. "This is Mr. Liu Fai, an emissary between our own Ministry of Dragons and a sister organization in China. He will explain."

Liu Fai gave Mrs. Hudson a curt but respectful nod and addressed the other three. "Artifacts precious to my government have gone missing, all relating to the First Emperor, Qin Shi Huang, who unified China more than two thousand years ago." He narrowed his eyes at Jack, voice casting a pronounced vote of no confidence. "I am tasked with asking *you* to help us."

Jack met the boy's steely gaze and snapped his fingers. "The Thieves' Guild. That's where I saw you, working on the docks as a magician. You made a rose out of ice."

The emissary's flat expression cracked for the first time. He glanced down at his hand, twisting an emerald ring around his finger. "I am afraid you are mistaken."

"Why is the Ministry of Dragons involved?" interjected Gwen. "This sounds like a matter for the Chinese authorities."

Liu Fai's whole torso turned as he shifted his gaze. "We do not feel the police are . . . equipped . . . to handle this case. Unusual sightings have accompanied each theft."

"Yeah?" asked Shaw, raising his chin to look down his bulbous nose at the boy. "What sort o' sightings is that?"

"A huge metal dragon."

Jack shut his eyes, failing to block out the nightmare those words evoked. Fire flowed from steel jaws. He felt heat at his palm and whipped it down to his lap. "We can't help you."

Mrs. Hudson leaned forward and folded her hands over a bronze falcon. "*What* did you say?"

Aside from the sudden and all too coincidental revelation of a clockwork dragon, Jack wasn't ready to give up on the Gall investigation. The jewel was gone, but it had banished all doubt from his mind that the spook had killed his grandfather, or at least given his grandfather no choice but to sacrifice his own life. The evidence was out there, somewhere. "I'm not going. I'm not finished with the Paracelsus mission."

Mrs. Hudson's knuckles whitened. "Yes, you are, Mr. Buckles. And that is an order. *Sic biscuitus disintegratum.*"

"Um . . ." Jack had learned some Latin during his time at

the ministry. The younger clerks and agents had school and everything when they weren't on a holiday break, or when Jack wasn't on trial for being an abomination. But that was a new one. "Sic bisca-what?"

"A phrase in schoolyard Latin. It has been the ministry's unofficial motto ever since the dragos began calling us crumbs two hundred years ago." Mrs. Hudson straightened. "You wanted to be a real tracker with real assignments. The new one trumps the old. *Sic biscuitus disintegratum*, Mr. Buckles. *That's how the cookie crumbles.* Get used to it."

As Jack opened his mouth to argue, the door at the end of the conference room opened. Sadie stood in the frame, dwarfed by its height, wearing her favorite green flouncy dress and sparkly shoes. A wave of joy and excruciating sorrow flooded Jack's mind.

Dad.

He was out of the chair and halfway to his sister before he even knew his body was moving. "Sadie? What is it? What's happening?"

Her eyes were puffy. A tear rolled down her cheek. "He's awake."

Chapter Sixteen

I CAN'T SEE HIM. *He's awake, but I can't see him.*

The thought slammed into Jack's mind over and over as he and Sadie hurried down the Great Stair. The utter sadness of it gave him vertigo. He had to steady himself against the wooden wall. "Use your voice, Sadie. Your thoughts are too strong."

She took his hand. "He's awake, but I can't see him."

"Yeah. I got that part. Why not? Did someone stop you?"

Sadie pulled him down the steps, increasing her pace. "It wasn't supposed to be like this."

They raced across the cobblestones to the underground cul-de-sac, to the second house on the right. Mrs. Hudson met them both at the door.

"How did you—?" asked Jack.

"Never mind that." Mrs. Hudson allowed Sadie past, but she took Jack gently by the arm and led him to the family's leather couch. Jack had never seen her face so gray.

Ash came down the stairs, holding his newsboy cap in his hands. "I'm sorry, Jack. I'm sorry it's gone this way."

"What way?" Jack tried to stand, but Mrs. Hudson held him. "Let me go!"

She sat him down again. "Jack, you've survived a good many trials in the last year. You're as tough as they come. But some trials are harder than others."

Jack could hear shouting from the floor above, the jostling of furniture. "I don't understand."

Mrs. Hudson took a step back. "Be brave. For your mother. For Sadie. Be ever so brave." She nodded at the dark wood stairs. "Go on now."

None of the terrifying thoughts that rushed through Jack's mind as he ran up the steps could have prepared him for what he found in his father's bedroom. A flood of unnerving data hit his senses all at once.

An overwhelming scent of sick: a wave of yellow-white sludge that made Jack wretch.

Sadie crying into their mother's arm: "I can't see him. He's awake, but I can't see him."

Black, percussive thumps: the bed jostling around under his father's thrashing.

His dad shouting in the raspy voice of a year's sleep: "The king, the mountain hermit, the figures in the cloud!"

A warden, so big he could barely fit between the floor and ceiling timbers, held John Buckles down, and still could not stop the thrashing. The doctor barked orders at a pair of nurses. One was fighting to lay a fresh sheet on the bed. Another cleaned up a puddle of sick beside it.

The doctor saw Jack and came striding over. "He nearly choked to death on the feeding tube when he woke up. Now he won't settle down. The standard sedatives are useless."

Jack hardly heard him. He dodged the doctor and rushed the warden, punching with both fists. "Leave him alone!" He might as well have punched a brick wall. Still, the warden let go, and his dad convulsed until Jack caught his hand.

John Buckles settled, staring straight ahead, eyes bulging and bloodshot. "The fan. The key. The rivers and stars."

"Dad, it's Jack. You're not making sense. What are you trying to say?"

"Jack?" His father turned the bloodshot stare Jack's way but stopped a few degrees short, the way a blind man might. He squeezed Jack's hand so hard it hurt. "Child of ice, child of flame. Castle crumbles, forms your grave."

"Grave?" Jack tore his hand free and backed into his mother's arms. His father started convulsing again. Another nurse rushed into the room with a huge syringe on a silver platter. The doctor jabbed it into the IV line.

Whatever was in that shot did the trick. John Buckles settled back into the pillows, his urgent shouts shriveling to whispers. "The first king knew, and though he tried, you must join to win the maiden's life."

Jack glared at the doctor. "What did you do to him?"

"Give me a little credit, Jack. He was my friend long before he was your father." The doctor returned the syringe to the nurse's platter. "I gave him a sedative, the strongest I dare. I can't risk sending him back into the coma."

"I saw him," said Sadie, sniffling. "For a split second, I saw him."

"What was that, Sadie?" The question came from Gwen. She stood in the doorway, and by the pallor of her skin, Jack figured she must have been standing there awhile.

Sadie wiped away a tear and tried to answer.

Jack's mom interrupted her. "Out. All of you," she said,

dabbing her eyes with a handkerchief. "You too, Arnold. Everyone but family."

The doctor raised a hand in protest. "Mary, I shouldn't—"

"I said out!"

They all obeyed. The doc—Arnold—was the last to go. He nodded at Gwen. "After you."

"She stays."

The doctor glanced over his shoulder. "Mary, you said you only wanted family."

Jack's mom balled the handkerchief in her fist. "Gwen *is* family."

Jack found the room much quieter once Arnold and his nurses had gone, and much larger without the warden taking up half the space. His dad's muttering continued. "Through forest green, through planet's core, the fire inside will light the way."

"He's been talking like that for over an hour, ever since he woke up." Mary Buckles collapsed into the chair beside the bed. She paid no notice to the burn marks. "Stars and kings, forests and maidens—Arnold thinks he's recalling old missions, reciting old clues." She held out a hand to Sadie, giving a subtle nod for Gwen and Jack to join them. "Sweetie, tell me what you meant when you said that you saw your dad."

Sadie shrugged one shoulder, poking the floor with her toe. "I just . . . saw him."

Gwen gave it a try, kneeling beside her. "Do you mean that you saw him the way you sometimes see Jack when he's far away, the way you saw Jack in the Thieves' Guild when Ash was looking for him?"

Sadie leaned to one side, looking past Gwen to her father. "When he held Jack's hand, I could see him. I could feel his heart. And then he was gone again."

None of them had yet grasped the rhythm of Sadie's Merlinian inclinations, least of all Sadie, but Jack had learned to take them seriously. Gwen pulled him aside. "I think your dad is in there, flirting with the edge of consciousness." Her hand moved toward her pocket. "Tanner said the Mind could save him. Perhaps if we—"

Jack caught her wrist. "Not until we know more about it. The doc was right about one thing. I don't want to risk sending him back into the coma." Cautiously, afraid to hear more about castles crumbling on his grave, he returned to the bed and took his father's hand.

Nothing happened.

The four pale fingers remained limp in Jack's palm. "Eight figures on a fan will save you from the ghostly thief."

Jack sighed. The Mind of Paracelsus might be his only chance to help his dad, but he wasn't ready to use it. "We need to talk to the one person besides Gall who knows something about all this." Jack looked up at Gwen. "We need to see Sir Drake again."

—— · Chapter Seventeen · ——

JACK WAITED FOR GWEN in a shadowed alley near 221B, having made his own way out of the Keep. She had left him at House Buckles hours before, with the promise that she would arrange the meeting.

Spec arrived first, coasting down in a sliver of moonlight, camera twitching as if scoping out the scene. He settled at eye level, paused a moment, and switched on his high-powered LED.

"It's me, Spec," said Jack, shielding his eyes. "Who else would it be?"

Spec seemed to consider this, then switched off the light and zipped away.

A few seconds later, Gwen peeked around the corner. "Sorry. He gets a little overzealous at times."

Jack blinked away the spots still swirling in his vision. "Did you arrange the meeting?"

"I told you I could get Will's number if I wanted to."

"You talked to Will?"

"Naturally. He's the adjudicator's clerk and a member of Fulcrum." Gwen pulled out her phone. "He'll call any moment now with the location."

"Which means you gave him your number too." Jack rubbed the back of his neck. "I really didn't think this through."

Gwen giggled far too much for a clandestine call received in a dark alley. Near the end of it, she twirled a lock of hair around her finger. "Of *course* I'll be there." Another giggle. She pulled down on the curl and let it bounce back up like a spring. "He can't go *anywhere* without me."

As she put the phone away, Jack folded his arms, not liking her wistful smile one bit. "So where is this meeting?"

Gwen didn't answer. She walked past him, checked the street, and turned south onto the sidewalk. "This way."

He followed. "You know, the only reason I can't go anywhere without you is you never tell me where we're going."

They took the Tube from Baker Street Station, surfacing

at Westminster, and found Will waiting beneath a lamppost across the Thames. He gave Gwen a hug.

"What? None for me?" asked Jack.

"Sorry. Didn't take ya for the 'uggin' type." Will spread his arms, calling the bluff.

Jack backed away. "You're right. I'm not."

"Ahem." Gwen clutched her lapels against the evening chill. "Could we . . . gentlemen?"

"Yes, miss." Will inclined his head toward the Eye. "Up there, and be quick about it, yeah? Sir Drake's car'll reach the platform soon."

Gwen cocked her head. "You're not coming with us?"

"Someone's gotta play lookout." Will took on an *I'm-so-good-looking-it-hurts* smirk and winked at her. "But you'll miss me. Right, miss?"

"Oh, please." Jack took Gwen's elbow and led her past.

London's giant Ferris wheel slowly turned, letting out deep metallic creaks in the quiet of the night. Jack spied a solitary figure in one of the glass capsules. Will hadn't been joking. The car would soon pass the platform, and he got the feeling that if they missed it, the meeting would not take place. He took Gwen's hand, and the two ran up the ramp and hopped on board.

"Good evening." Sir Drake sat on a bench, raising a silver claw-foot mug to his panting guests. "I brought some hot chocolate. Want some?"

The golden spires of Parliament came into alignment as the capsule climbed out over the Thames. Jack took Sir Drake up on the offer of refreshment, turning a key on a copper dispenser until chocolate fell gloopy and steaming into a silver mug. He raised it to his lips. "No brambleberry juice in this stuff, right?"

"No, but it is made with moose milk. That's what makes it so creamy."

Jack coughed, forcing himself to swallow. "Of course . . . it is."

Across the river, a few late-night tourists still milled about at the base of Big Ben. Overzealous runners jogged along Victoria Embankment. "To be honest," said Jack, "I'm not sure a glass bubble is the best choice for a secret meeting." He took another sip. Moose milk or not, the chocolate *was* incredibly creamy, with just the right amount of sweetness.

"On the contrary. I often find the best place to hide is in plain sight, where people rarely look. Now, suppose you tell me why we're—" Sir Drake stopped, lowering his mug. "Oh. You've found the Mind."

The thought had formed at the forefront of Jack's brain, so close to speech that it had betrayed him. He didn't bother denying it.

"Turns out we had it all along," said Gwen, helping herself to the last silver mug.

"And now you want to use it to help Jack's father."

Jack nodded, turning to face the glass. Beyond his reflection stretched all of London, rooftops brushed gray by the moon.

"Hmm." Sir Drake lowered his mug to his knee. "That may be a slippery slope. Many believe Paracelsus found a way to sink his knowledge into the stone—to draw from it as he pleased. But your grandfather feared the Mind was something more."

"It is," said Jack. The Mind had sliced away at him for a year, and when he had finally sparked into its memory, he had found a sliver of his father trapped inside. "I think Paracelsus wanted to push his consciousness into the stone. That's why he called for it at the White Horse. He was dying."

"A path to immortality." Sir Drake gazed out at the night. "Witchcraft in the alchemist's time. Yet today, many scientists are pouring their lives into the same pursuit. They call it the singularity, transferring a complete mind onto a hard drive." He returned his eyes to Jack. "This is a cold and terrifying path. The transfer of a mind reaches beyond questions of life into questions of control. If you can transfer the data out, you can transfer other data in."

"And become a prime minister," said Gwen, sitting down beside him.

"Or the head of a corporation," added Jack.

"Thankfully, Paracelsus left us no answers on how this might be achieved."

Jack choked on his chocolate again. "Um . . . Maybe he did." He told Sir Drake about the jewel and the spark. "Grandpa meant for that message to reach my dad. And Dad was supposed to give it to you. He was supposed to say that Paracelsus *left us more than just the Mind.*"

Sir Drake considered this for several seconds. "Did you find any evidence to corroborate that assertion?"

"There were artifacts, stuff from all over the globe."

It was Gwen's turn to cough. She lowered the mug and wiped her chin. "What artifacts? You didn't tell me about any artifacts."

"Yeah, well, maybe I don't tell you everything, like when you don't tell me where we're going or what you and Will are giggling about."

"I . . ." Gwen turned away, muttering into her chocolate. "I wasn't giggling *that* much."

Sir Drake's mug landed on the tray with a pronounced *clank*. "A little focus, please. Paracelsus traveled the world in his search for immortality—as far south as Alexandria, and as far east as China. The artifacts Jack saw might hold the answers you're looking for."

"But they're gone," said Gwen. "There was nothing left but cracked beakers and broken instruments."

"Which means . . ." The arbiter looked expectantly from one to the other. When neither of them offered an answer, he sighed and rephrased. "Who, besides you two and Jack's grandfather, has been in that lab in the last five centuries?"

Jack smacked his own forehead. "Gall."

The capsule entered the lower quarter of its rotation, and Sir Drake spread his hands like a therapist. "I'm afraid we're out of time."

"Wait," said Gwen. "If Gall has the artifacts, how do we get to them? We can't get caught breaking into the Mobius Tower again."

"No. You can't. But do you really think Gall would keep artifacts like those in his own office?" Outside, the platform drifted up to meet them. Sir Drake stood, picking up the tray and the copper dispenser. "I should start with the Ministry of Secrets Collection—in the Archive."

"We've seen the spook collection," said Gwen as the Royal Arbiter collected their mugs. "All the shelves were empty."

The doors opened with a pneumatic hiss, and Sir Drake placed his burdens in Will's waiting hands. "Don't be so certain. You're talking about an agency founded by pure-blood Merlinians, Miss Kincaid. And Merlinians are masters of illusion."

Chapter Eighteen

JACK HEARD NO MORE about China from Mrs. Hudson. And he did not ask, for fear she might press him to go. He and Gwen left for the Archive the following afternoon on the pretense that they were searching for a cure to his father's new mental state.

A swipe of Jack's platinum tracker card unlocked the big bronze doors at the rear of the Archive Ministry Express station. They parted, casting a shaft of yellow light into a giant well. Once a drago stronghold cut from the mysterious dark stone known as dragonite, the Archive now held the compendium of the ministries' joint knowledge. Shelves filled with books, scrolls, and leather-bound parchments were carved into the circular walls, spiraling down into the bottomless black. Unfortunately, those who made them had neglected to carve out any stairs.

Gwen leaned out to peer down into the well. "The Archivist should have come up by now."

A spherical balloon, purple with golden ropes and a broad gondola, floated idle a good distance below. Lanterns hanging from its brass railing cast a warm glow across the books. Gwen cupped her hands to her mouth. "Hello? Archivist?"

"I don't think she's on board," said Jack.

"Well, we can't just leave."

"I didn't say we should." Jack wasn't going back to his dad's bedside empty-handed. He glanced up, checking the wooden door to the Tracker Collection and the gold-plated door to the Ministry of Guilds Private Library. Both remained shut, flush with the shelves. In the shadows far below, the iron door to the dragos' insane dragon caves looked closed as well. Only the door to the Ministry of Secrets Collection, where the balloon waited, stood open—dematerialized, as was the nature of many spook doors.

Gwen tried again. "Archivist! Are you there?"

Her shout earned a *Shhh!* from the guard at the turnstiles behind them. Elder Ministry regulations demanded utter silence in the Ministry Express stations.

Jack gave him an apologetic cringe. "The Archivist is always here," he whispered to Gwen, "waiting for us when we arrive. Always." He cast a wary glance back at the guard, who had returned to his newspaper. "Something's wrong. I'm going down."

"What? How?"

"I'll climb." Jack crouched down and put a foot over the ledge. "This is nothing but a big set of bookshelves, right? Didn't you ever climb bookshelves when you were little?"

Gwen crossed her arms, looking away. "No."

"Liar." Jack slipped his other foot over the ledge and found a foothold. "I'll climb down to the Ministry of Secrets Collection. If she's not there, I'll bring the balloon back to get you."

"Have you ever flown a hot-air balloon?"

"No." The answer came out as a grunt. Jack tried not to imagine his toes rubbing the bindings off priceless historic texts as he lowered himself to the next shelf. "How hard can it be?"

The climb went smoothly until Jack made the mistake of looking down. The bottomless dark climbed up the walls to claw at him, and the balloon looked farther away than when he'd begun—a lot farther away. He swallowed hard and focused on the strange titles that passed his eyes as he descended.

On Sphere Making by Archimedes

The Book of Fallacies by Euclid

Inventio Forunata: King Arthur, the North Pole, and the Islands of the Great Whirlpool by Nicholas of Lynn

That last one sounded interesting.

Three-quarters of the way down, nowhere near close enough to the balloon to jump, Jack's forearms were screaming. Sweat slickened his fingertips. He glanced up at Gwen. "Um . . . I'm not actually sure I'm going to make it."

"Then come back up."

"Right, because that's so much easier than going down."

One hand slipped under the strain. Jack grappled for a hold and caught a thick volume with two fingers. The book fell away, fluttering down into the well, and his whole body swung out.

"Careful!" Gwen covered her mouth with both hands.

The memory of the rope snapping on the obstacle course flashed in Jack's mind. He swung back and clung to the wall. "Don't start a fire. Don't start a fire. Please, don't start a fire."

"Are you okay?"

"Do I look okay?"

Scritch. As if prompted by its leaping literary companion, another book inched out from the shelf. *Scritch.* It moved another inch.

Jack furrowed his brow. "What the—?"

Scriiiitch. The book slid all the way out, bounced off his shoulder, and dropped.

Gwen's hands went to her hips. "All right. Now you're tossing them on purpose."

"That wasn't me."

Scritch. The book directly in front of Jack's face inched out.

He crossed his eyes, trying to read the title. *The Stories of Charles Perrault.* Not particularly suicidal.

Scriiitch. The book scooted out another two inches.

To keep from getting blamed for another lost text, Jack head-butted it back into place.

Scritch. Scritch. The book pushed out with new fervor, squishing Jack's nose sideways until it passed him by and dropped into oblivion. He watched it fall.

Brrrowwl.

His eyes snapped back to the gap. A pair of yellow eyes glowed in the dark. "Oh. It's you."

Brrr-brrrowwl. An orange-and-white paw reached out and playfully batted his nose.

"Please . . . don't . . . do that."

"Don't do what?" called Gwen.

"Not you. The Archivist's cat. He's in a passage behind the shelves."

Gwen let out a gurgling *Ugh*. She and the cat had never gotten along. "Can you get in there with him?"

"The gap's too small."

"Hang on. I'm sending Spec down."

Hang on. Jack could not have laughed if he tried. "Good one."

"Good what?"

Brrrowwl? The calico poked its head out through the gap, whiskers tickling Jack's nose.

He grimaced, puffing to drive it back. "No. Bad kitty. Stay."

Cats don't stay. It crawled out onto the shelf, fluffy tail running under Jack's nose until his eyes watered. And then, as if the situation wasn't bad enough, Spec arrived.

The calico and the nano-drone became the best of instant frenemies. Spec shined a red light in the cat's face, the cat countered with a swipe, and Spec dodged, shooting into the gap between the books. The cat gave chase, grinding a hairy flank over Jack's nose.

Staring through the gap while holding back a potentially

fatal sneeze, Jack saw Spec descend into view, then cat paws come up, then Spec again, then whiskers, then Spec, then the cat, and so on, as if the nano-drone had a calico yo-yo.

"If you're not too busy . . . ," he shouted up to Gwen.

"The video is a *little* jumpy, but I think the opening is big enough. You'll have to move a few books." She paused, then added, "Push them *in*to the gap if you don't mind."

Jack would have liked to argue that he wasn't dumb enough to pull the books out, or that his life was more important than books, but he had a new problem. His muscles had gone rigid. He could barely cling to the wall, let alone lift a hand to move the books.

Aching and burning faded to terrifying numbness, leaving one remaining sensation—heat. Jack could feel it seeping up his arms.

Dragonite, charcoal gray and streaked with opalescent rivers of red and blue, had always transferred heat through Jack's senses. He had never learned why. It was commonly noted in the ministry that no tracker could spark off dragonite, making it unique among stones, but no one ever mentioned the heat thing. Did it have something to do with Jack's drago tendencies?

The warmth countered the fatigue. Jack closed his eyes,

sinking his nerve endings into the stone the way he sank them into a spark. Within seconds, he had the strength to lift one hand and ease a book inward, back into the calico's secret passage. He rested a moment, and tried another.

Book after book dropped until Jack had made a gap big enough for his shoulders. He pulled himself up and scrambled through, collapsing onto a set of steps on the other side.

The calico's whiskery face appeared, upside down above his eyes. *Brrrowl?*

"Thanks for the assist." Jack lifted a hand for a feline fist bump, but the cat rubbed its face across his knuckles instead, leaving a gooey line of kitty-cat goobers. He wiped it off on his jeans. "Thanks for that, too."

—— · Chapter Nineteen · ——

JACK REPLACED THE FALLEN books, know-
ing he would not hear the end of it from Gwen if he didn't.
He had fallen onto narrow steps, lit only by the glow of
Spec's LEDs. "Where's the Archivist, kitty? We could really
use her help."

The calico answered with a mournful *Mew*, but no real
explanation.

The stairs led up along the outer rim of the well, with more
than one side passage leading away. At the top, Jack pushed
open an iron door and found he had come out in a nook at the
edge of the Ministry Express station. A wall of chocolate-brown
tiles painted with gold script hid him from the guard's view.
Gwen waited at the ledge where he had left her.

She ran to him, having seen herself on Spec's video feed. "Oh, thank goodness."

In the stairwell behind Jack, the nano-drone lowered itself to within range of the calico's paws, then shot up again, drawing the cat into a futile leap—what Jack now called the yo-yo game. He thrust a thumb over his shoulder. "Is 'Spec' short for anything?"

"It's an acronym. Surveillance and Protection Electrodynamic Companion. Uncle Percy made it up."

"That would be SAPEC, wouldn't it?"

"Don't overthink it, Jack."

The calico let out a sharp *browl* and abandoned the yo-yo game. It padded away down the steps, leading them past levers and peepholes, and finally down a low side passage. It stopped before an arched door of blue marble, sat down, and looked up at Jack, waiting.

Gwen eased the door open a crack and peeked inside. "This is the spook collection." She bent down to pat the calico's head. "Well done, you."

The cat let out a threatening moan at her touch.

"Oh, learn to take a compliment."

The three crept out from behind a swiveling fireplace burning with cold green flame and entered a black marble antechamber with velvet furnishings. A columned archway bounded by Egyptian statues led out into the main library.

The Ministry of Secrets Collection looked exactly as Jack remembered it from his last visit—walls and ceiling cut from the darkest blue marble, a hissing gas chandelier above. At the center stood a table made of copper shapes fit together like puzzle pieces. The model of London on top was copper as well, oiled and gleaming. Jack gave it a wide berth. The last time he had touched that model, know as the Map, it had shown him seventeenth-century London drowning in flame.

The calico ran off, disappearing around a corner.

"Where's he going?"

"Litter box, I imagine." Gwen inclined her head toward the balloon, hovering driverless at the door. "Where's the Archivist? Do you think Gall took her?"

"Or she's working with him." Jack gave her a hard look. "Remember what Mrs. Hudson said about our incident in the Drago Collection? The spooks chasing us couldn't have unlocked the dragon cages. The Archivist controls the key, and only a drago can compel her to use it. Those doors should never have opened, unless—"

"Unless the Archivist chose to use the key on her own."

"Exactly." Jack pressed his lips together. "Sir Drake said

battle lines were being drawn. Maybe she picked her side."

"We can't worry about that now. We have bigger issues." Gwen gestured at the marble shelves. "Empty, just as I said. What sort of library has no books?"

Jack stepped closer, brow furrowed, nose mere inches from the marble. The shelves looked as normal as dusty-cobwebby-shelves-in-a-mysterious-chamber-with-a-hissing-gas-chandelier-and-a-dangerous-copper-map could look. "Sir Drake said Merlinians are masters of illusion. What if the books are . . . hidden?" He blew out a breath. The cobwebs quivered.

"Talk to me, tracker," said Gwen. "What are you onto?"

Jack cocked his head. "Say that again."

"You mean 'What are you onto?' I don't see how—"

Jack raised a finger, cutting her off, which earned him a dour look. The echo of Gwen's voice—ghostly greenish-white waves in Jack's senses—hadn't looked right for empty marble shelves. The waves had come back muted and broken. He knew of only one thing that caused such an effect. Jack let out a mystified chuckle. "Books. They're in there somewhere."

Gwen pressed a hand into the empty shelf, and her eyes widened. She drew it back, clutching a leather-bound text titled *On Non-Existence*. She wiggled it at Jack and grinned. "Abracadabra."

The moment he saw the book, the air grew thick in Jack's vision—wavy, like a mirage above hot sand. This was a hologram, but more—an illusion of the mind. Gwen's simple act of reaching through had cracked its power. Jack scrunched his eyebrows together and glared at the empty shelves. "I. Don't. Believe in you."

The shelves lost their depth. The cobwebs lost their quiver. The whole scene became as flat and two-dimensional as a photograph. Jack puffed out another breath and the empty shelves dissolved in a black cloud. What remained were real shelves full of real books. He cast a smile Gwen's way, waiting for a similar reaction. She made none. "Don't you see it?" he asked.

"See what?"

Set near the center of the shelves like a friendless bookend was a stone pyramid with sides so black they absorbed the flickering light from the chandelier. On a hunch, Jack tried to pick it up. He couldn't lift it, but the pyramid did turn on its base. He turned it farther, all the way around, until he heard Gwen's gasp.

Now she saw it. Jack pumped his eyebrows. "Alakazam."

He showed her the pyramid. "It's some kind of mental projector—way more high-tech than a hologram."

"And yet a little older, I think." Gwen examined the device through her magnifying glass. "Thought projection. Incredibly dangerous." She lifted one eye to look at Jack. "I think Gall wants to take this sort of tech to the next level."

"And if that same tech extends his life indefinitely, he'll have plenty of time to use it for no good." Jack took a step back, folding his arms and surveying the books. "Now what?"

"Think like Gall. If you were a power-hungry psychopath-slash-alchemist searching for immortality, where would you stash your darkest secrets?"

A hodgepodge of script and symbols from the book bindings floated across Jack's brain. Most were in Latin or Spook Script, the special hieroglyphs of the Ministry of Secrets. One name in Latin letters stood out. *Paracelsus*. He found the book and beckoned to Gwen. "I'd stash my secrets with the alchemists I admire."

Jack slid the book out and heard a *click*. He stopped, leaving it half-out, and glanced around. Nothing else happened. "Um . . . Tell me the name of another alchemist."

"Nicholas Flamel, Zhao Zheng. Oh, and Gilgamesh."

More floating text. Hieroglyphic eyes and one-legged birds. Another name. Jack walked three steps over and crouched down. "I've got *The Epic of Gilgamesh*." He pulled the book out halfway. Another *click*. Nothing else. "Give me one more."

"Saint Germaine?"

He looked up at her. "How do you say that in Latin?"

"*Sancti Germani*." Gwen pressed her lips together. "So, pretty much the same."

Sancti Germani had tumbled across his vision earlier, but from where? Jack stood and sidestepped to the center of the shelves. "Right here, below the pyramid." He tried sliding the book out. Nothing. He tried pressing it inward instead.

Squeak.

A secret panel opened above the top shelf. An old leather journal dropped into Gwen's open palm. "Hello, mysterious little book," she said, winking at Jack. "What secrets might you be hiding?"

Unfortunately, she chose to open it on the copper map table. Jack hung back several paces. "Maybe we could look at it somewhere else. That black velvet furniture in the room with the creepy Egyptian statues and the impossible green fire looked kind of comfy."

"Oh, don't be a baby." Gwen tugged at his sleeve. "The Map won't hurt you."

"Last time it showed me dead people."

"It did no such thing."

"You're right. It showed me live people from three hundred fifty years ago in the process of becoming dead people."

"Jack."

"Fine." He gave in, careful not to let any part of his body graze the copper.

Most of the journal was written in Spook Script, but they did find a few recognizable sketches—the Mind of Paracelsus, for instance, and the same triangular emblem that had led them to the tomb of Genghis Khan two months before.

Gwen paged slowly through until she came to an odd map. Hand-drawn fragments of locations around the globe were squeezed together like a nearly finished jigsaw puzzle. Symbols and sketches filled the spaces between. She ran a finger over the drawing. "These are all key astronomical sites. Jaipur, in India. Arcetri, the home of Galileo." She stopped on a fragment that bridged the divide between the two pages. A single dot, almost lost in the crease, marked the location. "And this is London, specifically the Royal Observatory at Greenwich."

"What makes you think that dot is the observatory?"

Gwen shifted her finger to a sketch in the margin. "This is a telescope house. And this"—she traced a line of longitude that bisected the fragment—"is the Prime Meridian."

—— · Chapter Twenty · ——

JACK AND GWEN TOOK a Thames river bus to Greenwich, the safest boat ride Jack had experienced in a year—and the funniest. The young skipper had a pun or a snide comment for every historical point on the waterfront.

"You don't have to laugh at *all* his jokes," said Gwen. "They're the same on all the river buses, on every trip, a thousand times a day."

Jack laughed as the skipper, who had just pointed out the obelisk known as Cleopatra's Needle and added that Cleopatra's Thread, Spool, and Thimble could all be found in a very large room at the British Museum. "Maybe, but I'm hearing them for the first time."

She looked away. "A year later, and you're still *such* an American."

The setting sun outpaced them in the long trek across Greenwich Park, descending into the barren trees. By the time Jack and Gwen reached the top of the observatory hill, the gates to the seventeenth-century complex were closed. Gwen tried the lock.

"Sorry, miss," said a boy coming over to the fence. "No new entries. The last visitors for the night are already passing through."

Gwen snapped her fingers at Jack.

Jack presented his platinum card.

The boy jumped to attention. "Apologies, miss," he said, rushing to unlock the gate. "Right this way. Anything you need, just ask. Khalil's the name."

With Khalil standing off at a respectful distance, the two paused in the observatory courtyard and opened Gall's journal. The spook had drawn a couple of recognizable symbols in the space around the map fragment. One was an octagon.

"I'd say that represents the Octagon Room"—Gwen thrust her chin at a brick tower with tall windows—"built by Sir

Christopher Wren. It was *supposed* to be this magnificent chamber where the royal astronomers would designate the Prime Meridian."

"Supposed to be?" asked Jack as she took off, striding toward its steps.

They pushed through a glossy black door and hurried up a narrow stair to an octagonal room with twenty-foot windows. A family of four, the last of the day's tourists, was taking turns at one of three antique telescopes. Jack and Gwen waited for them to move on.

"Supposed to be?" whispered Jack, repeating the question.

"Wren fouled it up. None of the windows face the correct chunk of sky." Gwen nodded at a few grand paintings of royalty and snickered. "The astronomers brought the money men here to look through the telescopes, but the real observations were made from the garden outhouse."

Unnerved by the whispering pair, the family left. Gwen opened the journal again. "According to Archivipedia, Paracelsus believed in the alchemical power of astronomical alignments. Perhaps Gall does too."

"Which means?"

"He does experiments here." She glanced around the

room. "And Gall's not fool enough to play the mad scientist in front of all these windows. There must be a second chamber."

They checked the journal. Not far from the octagon sketch, Jack found a sphere with a curving arrow, like a rotating globe. Neither of them knew what it meant.

"It's tracker time," said Gwen.

Jack blanched at the phrase.

"Too much?"

"Definitely."

He let the quiet of the tower settle over him.

Scent of oiled wood: the wainscoting was well taken care of.

Click and whir of the clocks: there were five—three set into the wall on either side of the door and two grandfather clocks between the southern windows.

Shadows: slow and drifting, marking the last, vanishing rays of the sun. But odd.

Jack zeroed in on the darkest corner of the room. The window there was set back from the wooden wainscoting instead of flush, creating a hidden alcove—an illusion of Wren's design. That meant empty space behind the walls.

Could it be a coincidence that the grandfather clocks were placed on either side?

"The clocks," said Jack. "One of those grandfather clocks is a door."

The clock to the right didn't look like any Jack had ever seen. The face was a mash-up of compasses, with a big dial around the outside, a medium-size dial at the high center, and a small window of tick marks off to the right.

"Three hundred sixty degrees of longitude," said Gwen. "This clock measures time by the earth's rotation."

"The earth." Jack took the journal from her hands, searching the notes. "That explains the rotating sphere. This is the door, but how do we unlock it?"

"How else?" Gwen opened the winding hatch and turned a crank. All three compasses rotated backward. "You can read this clock as time, but also as location. You know. Longitude. And what famous longitude are we standing on?"

He slapped the journal closed. "The Prime Meridian."

The clock reached zero, zero, zero, and a heavy *clank* sounded within. Gwen pumped a fist and then swung the case away from the wainscoting. She disappeared behind it.

And immediately let out a squeal.

"Gwen?" Jack stuck his head around the corner to find her straddling a well, face pale.

"It's nothing more than a manhole and a ladder," she gasped.

"What'd you expect? Some fur coats and a forest? You're up against an exterior wall." A flutter of gray skittered across Jack's brain. He recognized the sound as rapid footfalls. "The stairs. Someone's coming." He squished into the tiny space with Gwen and pulled the clock-door closed.

They stood in the dark, nose to nose, feet pressed into the two-inch lip on each side.

"Well, this is awkward," whispered Gwen.

Jack said nothing, trying not to meet her gaze.

She crossed her eyes at him. "What?"

"Your hair has a certain . . . scent."

"So? What's wrong with it?"

Nothing. Long ago, the pinkish-purple strawberry haze of Gwen's hair had become Jack's favorite scent amid the flood of sensations in his world. Of course, he couldn't tell *her* that. "I mean, is it a shampoo? Or a hairspray or something?"

Her eyebrows scrunched together. "Shut up and go down the ladder."

At the bottom, Gwen drew a monstrous flashlight—what

James R. Hannibal

she called a torch—from her pocket, illuminating a chamber like a small section of railway tunnel. Wood shelves and iron tables were strewn with instruments, powders, and bones. Endless scrawls of red chalk marred the brick—symbols both pagan and mathematical. Gwen followed a string of them to a crisscrossed circle at the ceiling's apex. "These are formulas."

Jack picked up a ceramic crucible and sniffed the white residue inside. He cringed at an acrid scent, like a thousand yellow razor blades, and set it down again. "What kind of formulas?"

"I think we could hazard a guess."

Her light fell on a broad copper pedestal at the far end of the room. Three objects rested on a jade platter—a broken clay tablet, a folded Chinese fan, and a black obelisk with a jeweled crane on each side, rising in progression. "Those are the artifacts from Paracelsus's lab," said Jack, rushing over.

"Are they, now?" Gwen snapped a picture with her phone.

"What are you doing?"

"Feeding them into Archivipedia." Her thumbs flashed over the screen. "Starting with the obelisk."

Jack watched her slide the picture into the search box. He shook his head. "How do you even have a signal down here?"

"It's all about the right data plan."

A half second later, Archivipedia coughed up a result. "'The Obelisk of Bennu,'" read Gwen. "'Whereabouts unknown.'" She raised an eyebrow. "Not anymore, right? According to this, Bennu is the Egyptian phoenix, and the obelisk is a relic of Heliopolis, bearing Ra's recipe for the scarabs he fed to the immortal bird."

Jack shrugged. "Okay."

The tablet was next, and Archivipedia tagged it as a missing fragment of *The Epic of Gilgamesh*, said to hold the elemental formula for a life-giving plant. "'Gilgamesh learned of the plant from Utnapishtim,'" read Gwen, "'a Sumerian immortal.'" She panned the flashlight across the walls, with their jumbles of red symbols. "Some of these look Sumerian, and others Egyptian. I think Gall's been taking bits and pieces from all these artifacts. It's an alchemical mash-up."

"With some Chinese mixed in. Try the fan."

Gwen snapped a picture and frowned. "No result. But perhaps if we spread it out." With ginger movements, she carefully opened the fan, revealing the painting on the silk folds. She drew a breath, never taking the picture. "It can't be."

"Can't be what?" Jack leaned in to see. The artist had painted a beautiful scene in gold, ivory, and blue. Eight robed figures floated in the clouds, some playing instruments, others lounging in long wooden boats. It was pretty, but not enough to get that kind of reaction—not out of Gwen. "I don't get it."

Gwen held the light below her chin, illuminating her face. "Eight figures, Jack. *Eight figures on a fan.*" She slid the artifacts into her pockets. "We need to get back to the Keep. Your dad's rantings aren't as random as we thought."

Chapter Twenty-One

THE TWO ARRIVED AT House Buckles to find Jack's dad still mumbling away, with Sadie at his bedside and Jack's mother watching from the high-backed chair. As they entered the room, a nurse poked the IV with a syringe, thumb resting on the plunger.

"Stop!" said Jack, waving his arms.

Doc Arnold did not bother looking up from his clipboard. "It's only a sedative, Jack. Your father needs to rest if he's to have any chance of recovery."

"Yeah? Well, I need him awake." Jack glanced at his mom, using his *help-me* eyes. "And . . . alone."

His mom didn't hesitate. "Out. The lot of you."

"Oh, not again." Doc Arnold lowered his clipboard. "Mary, please."

She stood, waggling her hands at the nurses and the poor warden, whose head was canted against the plaster between a pair of ceiling timbers. "I'm sorry, Arnold, but I insist."

"Never in all my years . . ." Doc Arnold hung the clipboard on the end of the bed and marched out, his small entourage following after.

The moment they were gone, Gwen laid the three artifacts on the comforter. "Mr. Buckles, can you see these? Do you know what they are?"

Jack's dad kept mumbling. "Am I the answer? Can I destroy the monster that still haunts the boy?"

"The artifacts, Dad." Jack raised his voice, even though he didn't mean to. He joined Gwen and picked up the clay tablet and the obelisk. "Have you seen them before?"

"Stars above that never wheel, hide the truth from mortal man."

Sadie looked at the three of them, then backed away to stand beside her mother.

Gwen sat back on her haunches. "It's no good."

Desperate, Jack opened his dad's hand and placed the tablet in his palm.

John Buckles frowned. Without the slightest glance at the artifact, he tossed it away.

"No!" squealed Gwen, watching the priceless piece of history fly across the room.

It landed in Sadie's waiting hands.

Gwen laughed. "How did you—?"

"Any reaction is a good reaction, right?" said Jack. He tried the obelisk, curling his dad's fingers around it.

Mechanically, his dad brought the obelisk up to his ear and lobbed it at the door.

Once again, Sadie had positioned herself to intercept. Jack and Gwen gave her questioning looks. She set both artifacts down on a shelf. "What?"

"Never mind," said Gwen, shaking her head. "One thing at a time." She unfurled the fan, exposing the scene with the eight figures, and gave it to Jack's father.

"Wait," said Jack before she let go. He checked on Sadie. She hadn't moved. "Um . . . Okay."

The second Gwen let go, John Buckles snapped the fan closed, gripping it hard and speaking fast. "Eight figures on a fan hide the truth from mortal man. The first king knew, and though he tried, he took the pills and so he died."

"It's . . . a poem . . . ," said Jack's mom.

"Oh, brilliant!" Gwen snatched up the clipboard and ripped off Doc Arnold's chart, holding a pen poised on the blank page beneath. "The lines were all jumbled up before, but giving him the fan has fixed one of the stanzas." She recited the line as she wrote. "'Eight figures on a fan hide the truth from mortal man—'"

"The first king knew and though he tried, he took the pills and so he died," answered Jack's father, staring into space.

"Well done, Mr. Buckles. Well done!" said Gwen, writing the second half down. Her pen slowed. "But what does it mean?" After a long stare at the fan, she gently pried it away from Jack's dad and laid it open on the bed to snap a picture.

"Well?" asked Jack.

Gwen shook her head. "Still not in the database. I'll need *you* to tell me its origin."

"And how am I supposed to do that?"

She closed the fan and pressed it into his hands. "You know how."

Jack did know, though he didn't want to admit it. Gwen had often told him how cool his tracker abilities were—how amazing it must be to look into the past simply by touching stone or steel. Experience had taught Jack better. Nearly every spark went horribly wrong. He'd woken up from his last in the middle of an avalanche. And he doubted that a mysterious artifact they'd stolen from the lair of a maniacal villain would prove any safer.

But this was for his dad. Jack sat back on his heels, reaching with his senses into the cold hard jade.

Chapter Twenty-Two

JACK LANDED WITH A thud on scorched dirt, sending clouds of mist billowing out in all directions. Mounted riders surrounded him, wearing armor of silk and painted leather. Given his elevated perspective, Jack, or at least the person with the fan, seemed to be mounted as well.

The mist covered everything, obscuring his view, but down the hill at the intersection of two rivers, Jack could make out a city, walled with timber and stone. Thousands of men with dozens of war machines camped before it on burned and blackened ground. Jack had dropped into a siege.

Murmurs drifted through the ranks of the army, nothing more than the grumbles of a large crowd. There were no battle cries. The war had grown quiet.

Odd.

Usually the first spark brought Jack to the most terrifying or deadly moment in an object's history. He thought perhaps the mist had something to do with the muted mood, until he noticed its green tint. He focused on the drifting vapors. Some passed right through the men and machines. The horses left trails of gray-green particles, their hooves and flanks indistinct. The mist was not a weather phenomenon. It was a trick of the jade, clouding the vision.

What was the fan doing at a battle, anyway? Did the owner carry it as a good-luck charm, like a rabbit's foot?

The ethereal white streak of a long whistle drew Jack's attention to the sky. An arrow the size of a lamppost drilled through the mist, heading right for him. He let out a cry of surprise and jumped out of the way as it buried itself in the dirt.

The sound of Jack's own voice caught him off guard.

"Great," he said out loud, half in protest and half to confirm his suspicion. The ability to speak during a vision meant only one thing—Jack had stepped away from the safety of the fan's observation point, putting his mind at risk of getting stranded in the memory. He had chosen the same risk at the alpine cave. This time it was an accident—unnecessary and much more dangerous.

The only way out was to find a physical exit, as he had done by diving out of the cave. But this memory took place outside, and there weren't a lot of *exits* outside.

A mounted man with black-and-gold robes over his armor had shifted his horse out of the big arrow's way. The men around him aimed crossbows at the wall to return fire, but he waved a calming hand and spoke in a language Jack assumed was a form of Chinese. The men lowered their weapons.

With a subtle change in his voice, the commander—the king, Jack decided—issued an order. A rider immediately shouted and waved a tall black flag. Matching flags answered from camp. Bells rang. The army pulled up stakes and backed away from the city. Shirtless warriors whipped oxen to drag the war machines up the slope, trailing green clouds as they went.

A confused buzz of voices rose from the wall, and then a cheer.

Had it been that easy? Was the king giving up merely because an archer had almost skewered him? As he wondered, Jack turned from the retreating army to see the king galloping toward the crest of the hill, the fan bouncing at his belt. The other riders turned to follow.

The last time the events of a vision had separated Jack from an artifact—a famous ruby from England's Crown

Jewels—the whole vision had gone crystalline, threatening to trap his consciousness. Jack looked down. The soft black dirt turned to cloudy green stone and began creeping up his legs. He closed his eyes. "Not again."

"Aaaggh!" With a shout, Jack broke free of the jade and sprinted after the nearest rider, grabbing hold of the bridle. His heels bounced across crystalline formations growing out of the soil, inches from the pounding hooves. Grunting and growling, he clawed his way up the rider's back, until he finally hauled himself into a semi-stable position behind the saddle.

Neither rider nor horse acknowledged him. They were part of the memory, their every action predetermined by history.

As they closed in on the king, the crystalline formations retreated, leaving Jack's consciousness safe for the time being. And then the rider crested the hill. "Whoa," said Jack.

He wasn't talking to the horse.

Thousands of men, a second army, labored in a giant trough—a canal, ending at an earthen dam on the bank of a river that led down to the city. The riders slowed and Jack slid down, walking a little way along the hilltop to see around the king's pavilion. The mist obscured the beginning of the canal. It had to be miles away.

The king issued another command through his flag-waving subordinate, and the men dropped their tools and clambered out of the trough. An archer launched a flaming arrow into the sky. Moments later, a second arrow answered from the distance, the fire tinted green by the jade.

Jack heard a murmur. Not the brownish murmur he had heard from the army, but a gray sound—gray and growing. The murmur became a rumble and then a roar. Churning, mint-green water rolled into view, surging through the canal. It obliterated the earthen dam, and the combined waters of the two rivers rushed down the valley to smash the city. The wall collapsed. Cheers turned to screams. The army surrounding the king chanted his name.

"Zhao Zheng! Zhao Zheng! Zhao Zheng!"

The king pointed at the ruined city, and every man raced down the hill to take it.

Jack did not want to see what happened next. Cities were not filled with armies. They were filled with families, women and children. The next few minutes would hold the trauma that had brought him to this point in the jade's memory. He looked for an exit. The flap of the king's pavilion snapped in the breeze. He raced through.

"Zhao Zheng!" Jack was back at his father's bedside. He

stared at Gwen, his normal vision still coming into focus. "A man named Zhao Zheng owned the fan."

"Yes, I know. You were kind of chanting it."

Jack blushed. "Sorry. His men were celebrating. The king diverted a river to destroy an enemy city. It was tactical genius, but thousands must have died."

Gwen did not seem to hear that last part. "The king," she muttered, chewing her lip. "Zhao Zheng the king. Oh, we've botched it, Jack. Totally botched it. We should have gone with him."

"Gone with who?"

Gwen frowned at him, as if Jack should have understood. "Remember the names I gave you in the spook library."

Jack connected the dots, despite the speed at which Gwen kept moving them. "Zhao Zheng was one of the alchemists you mentioned."

"Yes." She took the fan and slipped it into her coat pocket. "More importantly, he was a king—the *first king*, Jack, like your father said. Zhao Zheng became the first emperor of China, taking the name *Qin Shi Huang*."

A whirlwind of remembered phrases spun through Jack's brain. *Qin Shi Huang. The First Emperor. Artifacts going missing.* He saw a placid face, the boy with the blue eyes. "The clockwork dragon. The Mind of Paracelsus. It's all related. Everything leads back to—"

"Gall," said Gwen. "If we're going to stop him and save your family, we have to find Liu Fai." She took his hand, helping him to his feet. "Jack, we have to go to China."

—————· Chapter Twenty-Three ·—————

"WHERE IS IT, JACK?"

Zzap.

Jack tossed and turned in a half-sleeping state, unable to wake from the delirium. Fire swirled. Gwen screamed. A shadow moved between Jack and the scene—fleeting and dangerous.

Zzap.

The shadow was beside him again, hissing in his ear. "Where *is* it?"

Jack bolted upright. "Raven?"

Only silence and darkness answered. Jack rubbed his eyes, trying to recover his memory of the evening. His mom had made up the guest room, but Gwen wouldn't leave his father's side. Jack had drifted off in the high-backed chair while she scribbled away, writing down every rant and mumble. Now she was gone.

He left the house, grabbing a handful of stale tea biscuits for breakfast, and found Mrs. Hudson in the Keep's Botanical Artifact Conservatory—what Gwen called the Dodgy Plant Vault. She had often warned Jack to keep clear.

He passed through an ironwood door into four open stories of trees, vines, and shrubs. Fountains trickled down from walkway to walkway. Clouds of steam poured from copper pipes.

The place didn't look dangerous, until the great oak at the center tried to *eat* a passing QED. The big tree curled its leaves into fangs and snapped at the drone. The QED ducked low and flew on, as if that sort of thing happened all the time.

"Kite-eater," said Mrs. Hudson, appearing from a path overgrown with ivy. She wore bright orange gardening gloves that clashed horribly with her gray dress, and she carried a set of pruning shears in a holster at her hip. "*Chloromehlnes czarus* in the Latin. Nasty breed. Usually feeds on paper and string, but this one acquired a taste for drone." She raised her spectacles to her eyes and glanced around.

"Where is Miss Kincaid? Doesn't she normally accompany you on these unscheduled and unannounced visits?" She pronounced unscheduled as *unshheduled*.

Jack had the urge to correct her. He suppressed it. "Gwen was up late . . . taking notes."

As the two rode a wooden elevator to the next level, a hanging vine snaked over the rail. A steel sign behind it read STRANGLERVINE (*HEDERA GAROTTUS*). The plant whipped out, going for Jack's arm.

"Oh no you don't." In one quick motion, Mrs. Hudson drew her shears and snipped. A wiggling appendage fell to the floor and shriveled.

Jack kicked it over the side. He cleared his throat. "About that China mission, I've—"

"Had a change of heart? Reconsidered? *Flip*-flopped?" The lift bounced to a stop at the third level and Mrs. Hudson stepped off onto a stone path.

"Sort of." Jack strode after her, awed by the depth of color around him. Plants and flowers in a hundred shades grew beneath showers of mist. Each had a small steel sign such as INKWEED (*PRINTEX LIBELUS*) or WHISPERING IVY (*RUMEX VULGARIUM*). A red root stood apart on a marble pedestal marked BLOOD-DRAKE (*MANGRADORA SANGUINOUS*). The head turned to follow them, cute and puppetlike. Jack reached out to pet it. "Actually, Gwen and I—"

"Realized you had left a whole country in the lurch? Finally felt the weight of your *rrr*esponsibilities?" Mrs. Hudson smacked his hand away as she trilled her r. The blooddrake gurgled in disappointment, toothy spikes fading back into its hide.

Jack held his hand to his chest, eyes wide. "Yeah. Sure."

"I see." Mrs. Hudson made an about-face. With a sharp nod, she sent a QED humming off toward the exit, and it dodged the rustling branches of the Kite-eater on the way. "So the two of you want to help Liu Fai now. Is that it?"

Jack nodded.

"And what about your father?"

"We believe catching Liu Fai's dragon may be the best way to help him."

Mrs. Hudson stared down at him through her spectacles. "Intriguing." She said nothing else.

Jack blinked. "So . . . can you tell Liu Fai we're ready to go with him?"

"I'm sorry, Mr. Buckles. He's gone." She walked on, snipping the occasional leaf.

Jack stutter-stepped to catch up. "Gone?"

"*You* turned down the China assignment, didn't you? And after your father woke up, I assumed you'd want to stay with him." She stopped, throwing out an arm to stop Jack as well, and looked up at a scraggly tuft of green hanging from a stone bridge. Little clusters of conical flowers grew among leaves. She lowered her voice. "Beware the *viscum projecticalus*."

"The what?"

"The *missile*-toe." Mrs. Hudson shoved his head down. With a series of light *pops*, the conical flowers shot out in all directions, trailing smoke. Miniature explosions lit up the path. When it was over, Mrs. Hudson sniffed and continued under the bridge. "Mr. Liu was your escort, your transportation, and your visa. To visit China without him, you'll need paperwork."

Jack should have guessed. Paperwork was Mrs. Hudson's favorite pastime. "Sure. Whatever it takes."

"I thought you'd say that." As they emerged from under the bridge, the QED reappeared, weighed down with a stack of paper as thick as a Victorian novel. Mrs. Hudson made a flourish with a bony hand. "Visa application, customs declaration, statement of intent, medical history, shot record . . . and a postcard for the Foreign Minister's private collection—"

The QED dropped the stack into Jack's arms.

"—in triplicate. The copier is on Sublevel Two."

Jack glanced down at the multicolored pile in his arms. "This will take us all day."

"A trifle in the grand scheme. Processing alone will take three to six weeks." The stranglervine crept out of the bushes, snaking across the path toward Mrs. Hudson's ankles. She stomped it into the pavers. "Give it up, Nigel. It's not your day."

The vine slithered away.

Three to six weeks. Jack shook his head and held the stack up for the QED to take. "Thanks, but I can't wait that long."

The drone looked taken aback. It swiveled, pointing its camera at Mrs. Hudson. She nodded and it sagged slowly down to recover the papers. On the way out, the frustrated QED forgot to dodge the Kite-eater. The mutant oak snatched it out of the air, repeatedly crunching its bronze frame with spiky leaves. Frantic, the drone managed to escape, but left the forms behind. A shower of confetti rained down on the topsoil.

Mrs. Hudson watched the whole affair with a flat frown. "We'll call that recycling, shall we?"

Another lift returned them to the first level, and on the way out, Jack spied a crop of purple-and-white blooms on four-foot stems. They waved in a nonexistent breeze, demanding his attention. Their sign read LOOK-AT-ME (*LOOKATUS LOOKATUS*). Jack hugged the other side of the path, remembering the blooddrake. "What's the deal with these? Do they spray poison or something?"

"Not at all."

"They why are they here?"

"Why does anyone keep flowers, Mr. Buckles? They're pretty."

Jack left Mrs. Hudson to tend her pretty flowers and headed for the vault door, held open by a warden.

"There is one chance," she called after him.

He turned, surprised by the helpful tone in her voice. "What chance?"

"Mr. Liu had other business before returning to China. I'll offer no guarantees, but"—she snipped a pepper from a nearby vine and it splatted on the pavers, melting a hole right through the stone—"you might still find him at the Ministry of Dragons."

─────·Chapter Twenty-Four·─────

JACK AND GWEN HAD permission to leave the Keep, but they had no access to the headquarters of the Ministry of Dragons, known as the Citadel. For that, they needed a drago, such as Liu Fai, who was already in the Citadel—making for a sort of which-came-first-the-drago-or-the-egg dilemma.

"Why are we taking the regular Tube?" asked Jack, perched on the edge of a plastic seat upholstered in an obnoxious triangle-confetti motif. "Can't we get into the Citadel from the Temple Ministry Express station?"

Gwen gave him her *you're-such-a-tremendous-wally* look from across the aisle. "One does not simply *walk* into the Ministry of Dragons, Jack, not through the front door.

Besides"—she pulled the collar of her sweater away from her neck, scrunched up her nose, and let it snap back again—"I need to stop by the flat for a change of clothes."

They left the Tube at King's Cross and walked to a drab brick apartment building. A bearded man sat huddled under a blanket in the open stairwell. Gwen dropped a coin into his cup.

"Wow," said Jack. "The ministry posted an undercover guard at your flat."

"Nope." Gwen yanked open a sticky door on the second level. "That's just Albert."

Jack walked through the door straight into a giant hug from Gwen's mom. While Gwen ran off to change, her mom plopped him down on a faded denim couch and shoved a bowl of crisps—her word for potato chips—into his hands, along with a purple juice drink that desperately needed whatever sugar the makers had removed.

The place was small and clean, though it was cluttered with books and the smell of books—the bluish-gray glow of ink and old paper. Jack suspected that was Gwen's touch.

Mrs. Kincaid retreated to the kitchen, all of three paces, and sat down on a stool, smoothing out her skirt. "So," she said in a Welsh accent far thicker than Gwen's. "Gwenny tells me the two of you are headin' off on ministry business. Where to this time?"

"Uh . . ." Jack forced down a half-chewed crisp. Gwen hadn't prepared him for an interrogation, however congenial. "China?"

"Ooh. How lovely. Nice dark teas in China." Gwen had the most easygoing mom on the planet.

Gwen reappeared before Jack had finished the crisps. She looked much the same, although he noticed a stronger scent of strawberries. With another hug from her mom, and another tasteless purple drink for the road, they were off again, taking the Piccadilly Line to Holborn.

"If we can't go through the front door of the Citadel," asked Jack once they had surfaced again, "then how do you propose we get in?"

Gwen waited for a light to change, then started south. "Trust me. I have a plan."

A few blocks later, Jack saw the *plan*, seated at the base of a bronze statue on the Strand. He did not like the plan one bit. "Please, Gwen. Not him."

"Play nice. Will knows a back way into the Citadel."

"Sure he does."

"'ello, miss." Will met Gwen with a hug, as always, giving Jack a sly wink in the process. "Lovely to see *you* again."

Jack took Will's *you* to mean Gwen, not him. He nodded. "Consider the feeling mutual. Where are we going?"

Will turned, allowing Gwen to take his arm, and started across the street. "A place of mystery and wonder, Jackie Boy. Mystery and wonder."

He led them to a covered alley, hidden behind the black timber porch of an old pub. And after a confusing jumble of lefts and rights, they emerged in a world set apart. He hadn't lied about the mystery and wonder.

Jack looked up and down a cobblestone lane of Victorian buildings. Grand arches at one end were carved with griffins and winged horses. It felt as if the last century hadn't touched the place. "Where are we?"

"The Temple." Gwen let Will escort her through another short passage toward a colonnade that bordered a long courtyard, forcing Jack to walk behind. "Two of England's four Inns of Court are headquartered here. The lawyers have had it for centuries, but this compound once belonged to the Templar Knights, who were of course—"

"Dragos," said Jack.

All three came to a halt at the edge of the courtyard, and Gwen let go of Will's arm. "Correct, Jack. High marks for you. The Citadel lies directly beneath our feet."

"Great. So how do we get in?"

They both looked at Will, whose normally confident expression cracked.

Jack lowered his chin without releasing the boy from his gaze. "You do know how to get in, right? Otherwise, why are you here?"

"I know where the entrance *is*." Will's gaze shifted to a cathedral that sat lower than the main courtyard, as if resting on far more ancient ground. "Over there, in the Temple Church."

"You could have told Gwen that much over the phone."

"I wanted to tag along, yeah?" He cast a sideways glance at Gwen.

She blushed.

Jack rolled his eyes and headed for the church. "Of course you did."

Inside, huge marble pillars supported a many-arched ceiling. The plush box pews all faced the center aisle, rather than the altar, like two armies of worshipers squaring off.

"The Middle Temple barristers use the pews on the left," said Gwen. "The set on the right is for the Inner Temple barristers. I shouldn't sit down in either. Bit of a rivalry between them. You might find a thumbtack in your cushion."

She turned to Will. "If you can't tell us how to get through the secret door, then what *can* you tell us?"

"I 'eard about the back door while on reconnaissance for Fulcrum, watchin' two dragos in a pub. The older chap says to the younger, 'There's an entrance 'idden in Temple Church, brother.'"

"Yes, we know that part," muttered Jack. "Maybe you should skip a bit, *brother*."

Gwen slapped his arm, right on the bruise. "Go ahead, Will. What else?"

His expression darkened, as if contemplating a puzzle. "The older chap looks all cryptical and says, 'The door will only open in the round when one drago's gaze meets another's.'"

Jack slumped down into a pew, ignoring Gwen's warning about thumbtacks. "So we need a pair of dragos to help us sneak into drago headquarters? Why am I not surprised?"

"You and I *are* dragos, Jack," said Will. "By blood, yeah?"

"Well, I'm not gazing into your eyes, if that's what you want."

"The Round." Gwen stepped between them, touching their shoulders. "I know what that is. You two muffins can stay here and stare into each other's eyes, or you can follow me."

Six more columns stood beneath a central dome at the far

end of the cathedral, forming a small chapel. Life-size effigies of knights lined the floor—medieval Han Solos trapped in carbonite. Jack scooted between them to catch up to Gwen, careful not to let any part of his body touch the slabs. He had a thing about dead people.

"The Knights Templar called this the Round," said Gwen, turning in a slow circle. "They built it to mimic the Church of the Holy Sepulcher in Jerusalem."

"Okay." Jack sidestepped another Han Solo. "But what about our romantically gazing dragos?"

Gwen left the center and walked along a rounded wall sculpted with figures, mostly grotesque tormented faces. She patted the head of a rat-lizard gnawing on a man's ear, then smiled at a pair of dragons above the chapel's rear door. "Will, are you certain you heard that old gentleman correctly?"

Will dropped his eyes to his Italian leather shoes. "They were meetin' in a pub. It was loud."

"Dragons," said Gwen with a little laugh. "Not dragos. The old man said the door would open when one *dragon's* gaze met another's." She frowned at the sculptures. "But these dragons are both looking down."

"Maybe we can turn the heads." Jack started toward one of the dragons.

Will caught his arm, glancing at a vicar in the main cathedral. "Wait. Let me." He made a curving pass with three fingers of each hand, and the heads of the dragons noiselessly turned. Dark red beams like rays of shadow shot from their eyes and crossed to form an X in the doorway. The air shimmered, and with a low *whump*, the intersection of shadows grew into a burgundy portal filled with stars.

Gwen laughed. "Excellent, Will." And the two of them walked through.

"Hey, turning the heads was my idea." Jack flopped his hands against his sides. Why had he bothered? There was no one left to hear him. He held out a hand, wincing, and pushed through.

Chapter Twenty-Five

WHUMP.

Jack had teleported before, using the phase-jumping device the jewel thief had carried—something called the Einstein-Rosen Bridge. This felt far more natural. Pushing through the red shadow felt like pushing through gelatin, without the wet and sticky bits.

He emerged in a mirror image of the Round with its pillars and dome carved from a dark metallic stone. In place of the grotesque faces at the periphery, there were suits of armor. He glanced back at the portal. "How did we—?"

"Looks like the spooks aren't the only ones with secret tech," said Gwen, pushing a finger into the gelatinous shadow and watching it wiggle.

Will snorted. "Telekinesis, telepath, teleport. All in the same family, yeah?"

As the clerk turned away from the portal, Jack stepped in front of him, blocking his path. "You've done your part. Now go back through and let us do ours."

"What? Not a chance."

"Gwen and I are *real* agents of one of the four secret societies." Jack shrugged in a mock *so-sorry* motion. "You're not. If we're caught, we have protection from Mrs. Hudson, but who knows what the dragos might do to you?" He lowered his voice to a whisper. "They keep dragons here."

"Thanks." Will pushed past him. "But I can take care o' myself."

Beyond the circle of knights, they found a long bridge over an open chasm, running straight into sheer black ramparts. The high walls disappeared into the dark to the left and right.

"A castle," said Jack as they crossed the bridge. "Why would you need defenses like this down here?" He peered down over the edge into a fathomless mist. "What sort of monster were the dragos worried about?"

At the far end, they passed between a pair of statues as tall as the giant wardens back at the Keep—a man and a woman, both in armor. "Look." Gwen slowed, nodding at a reptilian creature poised at the woman's heel like a hunting dog. "She has a dragon."

A long passage led past wooden doors and spiraling stairwells. Sconces flickered with smokeless yellow flame, casting their light across tapestries of knights in battle. Sometimes the knights fought dragons, but not always. In a few scenes, the dragons fought alongside them.

The passage ended at a switchback staircase that descended into a grand hall. Giant cauldrons burned at the four corners. The dark floor was polished to a high shine. The three ducked behind the railing. There were many dragos— all wearing their gray coats, trilby hats, and red scarves—but there was no sign of Liu Fai.

"Well, that's a new 'un," whispered Will, staring straight out into the open air instead.

Jack could not disagree with his assessment. A silver knight on horseback floated high above the floor, battling a winged dragon. By what art the two-piece monument remained suspended, Jack could not say.

"Come on," said Gwen, starting down. They kept low, hiding behind the solid stone railing, but Jack peeked over once in a while to keep an eye on the opposite wall, where the stone facades of ancient houses took up every inch.

Columned doorways and paneless windows opened into empty space. A few of the houses pushed out far enough to have a gabled porch. Others were recessed deeper in.

As the three reached the last switchback, a spout of flame lit up a window. A creature roared. Someone cried out in pain. Another someone grumbled impatiently.

Jack caught up to Gwen. "That's not good."

She waved him off, whispering in her Encyclopedia Kincaidia voice. "Article twelve, directive fourteen of the Dragon Code: 'All agents above the level of squire will train with live dragons.' I'm guessing those sounds are routine for this place."

Jack peeked over the rail. Gwen was right. Not one of the dragos showed any concern over the roar or the cry. "The Dragon Code?"

"The Code of the Order of Dragons. The *coodos*, if you like."

Jack raised a skeptical eyebrow.

Gwen stopped at the bottom step and shrugged. "Most just call it the Dragon Code."

The implication that Gwen had memorized the drago regulations did not surprise Jack in the least. She had a thing for rules. She also had a thing for breaking them.

"Train with live dragons?" Will—rather sensibly—had fixated on the content of the rule instead of the code's title. "Sounds like they're begging for grievicious bodily 'arm."

The three snuck along a shadowed arcade, and soon Jack felt a tingling in the back of his neck. He looked out across the hall, then up. In the same window where he'd seen the spout of flame, he saw a man staring right at him. A second later, a girl on the polished floor stopped, turned, and stared as well. Then another drago stopped and stared, and another, and another.

"Um . . . I think the dragos can sense my presence." Jack tugged at Gwen's sleeve. "I'm endangering the mission. I shouldn't have come."

"Why does that sound so familiar?" asked Will.

More dragos appeared in the empty doorways. None looked happy, and Jack's tingling became a hot, hostile burn. "Time to go," he said, pulling the other two into a run.

He took a right into a passage, and then a left, checking over his shoulder for men and women in gray coats. "You'd think one or two of them would make a different fashion choice."

"Article seven, directive six," said Gwen, panting beside him. "All dragos must wear their armor at all times."

"Armor?" Jack checked the doors on his side of the passage, looking for a place to hide and rethink the plan. If the wrong crowd caught them first, they might get ejected from the premises, without ever finding Liu Fai. "What armor?"

Gwen tried an iron door, broader than the rest. It opened. "You don't think they wear those ridiculous secret-police coats for the looks, do you?" She pushed the door wide and waved the others through.

Instead of a room, they found a stairwell made entirely of dragonite. Jack could feel the heat of it as his fingers grazed the wall. Outside the Archive well, he had only encountered that much of the rare mineral in one other place—the Drago Collection, where the Ministry of Dragons kept a number of . . . "Live specimens." Jack breathed out the last two words.

"What was that?" asked Will

Jack couldn't answer. His head buzzed, invaded by a deep voice.

The flame.

New blood.

Doesn't know.

Jack stumbled down the last few steps into a chamber lit by bubbling white sconces. A dragon the size of a school bus blocked their path. It had deep yellow scales and horns and talons like uncut amber. Coal-black eyes drilled into Jack's brain.

Yes! New blood.

Show me the flame!

Jack crumpled, throwing up his arms and turning back toward the stairs.

Will backed up beside him, pulling Gwen. "Good call, Jackie Boy. Let's not go this way."

Unfortunately, retracing their steps did not help. A small gray army poured into the passage as the three burst out of the stairwell. Gwen and Will, surging ahead, took the first turn they came to. Jack rounded the corner a few paces behind, waving his arm. "Keep going!"

Perhaps to answer him, or to check his progress, Gwen glanced back, and the motion spoiled her balance. She bumped into a wall sconce, which tilted ninety degrees without losing its yellow flame. Will steadied her, and together they ran onward between a pair of pewter dragon statues.

They never saw the dragons move.

Jack did. And try as he might, he could not stop his momentum.

The pewter dragons turned on their bases and opened

their jaws. Dark beams shot out, slamming together in a roiling ball of red shadow.

Whump.

The passage around Jack vanished as he stumbled through gelatin—without the wet and sticky bits. He managed to spin around once he passed through, but the portal evaporated, leaving a set of high silver doors, inches from his nose.

Jack heard the squeak of a chair far behind him. Sharp heels clicked on stone. A melodious feminine voice said, "Hello, Jack. I was wondering when you'd finally stop by."

Chapter Twenty-Six

JACK SLOWLY TURNED, MIND reeling. Gwen was out there somewhere. Alone. No. Worse than that. She was out there somewhere. *With Will.* He blanched at the thought.

The portal had brought him to the Citadel's throne room. And yet a simple oak desk and a coat rack sat atop the stepped dais where he'd expected to see a big golden chair. A tall woman in a white blouse and gray skirt walked down the steps. Jack remembered her from the tribunal. He remembered her ice-blue eyes. And now that he saw them again, her eyes reminded him of another set he had recently seen.

"Come here, Jack. Don't be shy."

Jack walked the thirty meters or so to the dais, passing

dusty shafts of sunlight on both sides. He had to wonder how the dragos had managed that so deep underground. "You're—" Jack's throat had gone dry. He swallowed to wet it. "You're the Minister of Dragons."

The woman put a finger to her lips. "Outside these walls, I am the Marshall of the Citadel or the Countess Ravenswick. My true station is a secret, but"—her eyes flicked down to Jack's hands and back up again—"I'm quite certain you can keep a secret, can't you, Jack?"

"Sure . . ." Jack realized the woman had casually slipped in the fact that she was nobility and added, "My lady."

"No need for such formality here." A chair flew in from the edge of the room at breakneck speed, halting right behind him. "Have a seat. I have been *so* looking forward to this meeting."

"You knew I was coming?"

She laughed. "I'm no Merlinian, if that's what you're asking. But I knew you'd come to us soon enough. I'm quite familiar with your heritage, Jack. *Quite* familiar." The countess walked around the chair. Long fingers traced the line of Jack's shoulders. "Your father and I were close before the incident with the Clockmaker."

The way she said *close* sent a cold trickle down Jack's

spine. He didn't think his mother would like it either. But it occurred to him that if his dad had cozied up to the Minister of Dragons, then it had probably been part of his work with Fulcrum, on the orders of Sir Drake.

Lady Ravenswick took his silence for disbelief and strolled over to the hat stand, where her coat, hat, and scarf hung alongside a sword and scabbard. She peeled back the lapel of her coat, showing him the shimmering green lining beneath. "Recognize this?"

"Dragon scales." Jack sat forward in the chair. "My father wore a similar lining when he faced the Clockmaker."

"A gift he asked me for"—she lifted the fabric to her eyes, as if looking for a flaw—"one I had hoped would better protect him."

"Why?" Jack hardened his features. "Why would a drago countess help a Buckles? After all, we're nothing but crumbs and commoners."

"Oh, but you're not so common as that, are you?" Lady Ravenswick let the coat fall back into place and returned to the front of her desk. "Your father showed Arthurian tendencies too, Jack. Nothing like yours, of course, but some—a little heat in a handshake, an inclination toward fire. When he married a girl from another tracker bloodline, I knew that you"—she nudged Jack's heel with the toe of her high-heeled shoe—"would be special."

Her gaze was like a tractor beam. Jack bailed out of the chair.

Lady Ravenswick didn't let him off that easy. She closed the distance between them. "I can help you, Jack. I can take your abilities further than you ever dreamed."

She spread her hands, and a flame sprouted from each palm, one white, one blue. With a thrust of her palms, they merged into a fireball that whipped past Jack's ear, growing in flight until it crashed into the silver doors. The brassy ring of a gong filled Jack's senses.

"Now you," she said, folding her arms and sitting back against her desk, crossing her ankles. "Show me."

"I . . . Uh . . ." He didn't want to, even if he had known how. "I can't."

"Pyrokinetic stage fright?" She sighed. "Nothing to be ashamed of. Happens a lot to boys your age. But fire is just the beginning." The chair tipped onto one leg all by itself and began to spin. "Our ability is telekinesis, Jack—all about motion. Fire is instinctual. We create it by exciting air molecules. But the best of us can do much more."

Dust streamed to her palm from the shafts of light and

coalescing into a perfectly smooth sphere. "In times gone by, the most powerful dragos raised the earth from the battle-field to hem in their foes. They spun the rain into whirl-winds." She lowered her chin, cocking her head slightly and raising her eyes to meet Jack's. "They made their enemies burst into flame."

Jack knew she wanted a reaction, some confirmation that he had done exactly that to Tanner. He held his poker face, but the questions remained. Had he caused the fire inside Tanner? Had the roof of the tomb fallen on its own, or had Jack brought it down to crush the man?

What kind of person did that make him?

"Oh, Jack." The chair settled onto all four legs, one at a time. Lady Ravenswick tossed the sphere out into the room, and it burst into dust, filling up the shafts of light once more. "Don't look so glum. You ought to be thrilled. I'm offering you freedom."

"Freedom?"

"You and your family are prisoners of the Keep and the whole Section-Thirteen-Section-Eight thing. I can put an end to all that, and to this thing with Gall." She wiggled her fingers as if *this thing with Gall* were a spat between neighbors over ugly lawn furniture and uncut shrubs. "The crumbs don't *want* you. You *know* that. You're a black mark on their prim and perfect record. Come to the Citadel, Jack. Join your true family. This is where you belong."

The room seemed to tilt on its side. "You want me to be a drago?"

"You *are* a drago, Jack. You've felt it in Ministry Express stations. It's the reason you stood no chance of sneaking through the Citadel unnoticed." She bent forward and touched his arm, pushing a hot, tingling sensation into his muscles. "Dragos with the full measure of the gift unconsciously excite the air. And they can feel that energy from others like them."

Jack's eyes drifted. *"That's* why they stare at me."

"They recognize one of their own, lost out in the cold. Let us bring you in where it's warm."

Warmth. Belonging. He had to admit it sounded nice. "But I don't have the pedigree."

"That won't be a problem." Lady Ravenswick walked to the other side of her desk, thumbing through an old ledger that just happened to be sitting out. "There are extinct titles within my discretion, family names waiting to be reborn." She paused at a yellowed page and looked up. "The Baron Buckland, I think, in honor of your history. How does that sound?"

She was offering him knighthood, a noble title. A pit—
small but deep and screaming *Danger!*—opened in Jack's gut.
He ignored it. "What about my parents and Sadie?"

"They'd be welcome here, free to come and go as they
please. The Ministry of Dragons doesn't care one whit about
tracker regulations. We're talking a clean slate here."

A clean slate. No more Section Thirteen. No impending
Section Eight trial hanging over his parents. Jack would
lose his family name, but he'd have a new one. And clean
slates were all about change, weren't they? "What about Mrs.
Hudson? And Gwen and Ash?"

"Jack." The corners of her mouth turned down in an admon-
ishing smile. "To be honest, most of us in the Elder Ministries
believe the crumbs are an anomaly that has outlived its time—a
three-century fad that suited a royal fancy. I can protect *you*
from Gall, but I can't protect our whole ministry."

Amid the thoughts churning in Jack's brain, one stood
out—something Mrs. Hudson had said. He looked down at
his shoes, muttering the phrase. *"Sic biscuitus disintegratum."*

Lady Ravenswick chuckled, nodding. "Just so, I'm afraid.
Now, what do you say?"

Jack was going to say he'd have to think about it, but he
didn't get the chance.

One of the silver doors swung open with a long, pitiful moan that spilled across Jack's mental vision like yellow goo. He turned to see Gwen come walking through. She looked utterly surprised to see him, as did the boy with her, who wasn't Will.

Liu Fai, the Chinese emissary, scrunched his ice-blue eyes into a suspicious stare. "Mother? What are you up to?"

Chapter Twenty-Seven

LADY RAVENSWICK STRODE PAST Jack, arms wide. "Hel-*lo*, Stephen. Thank you for bringing Miss Kincaid. You've saved me all kinds of trouble."

Jack tried to pick his jaw up off the floor. "*Mother?*"

Gwen looked equally stunned. "*Stephen?*"

Lady Ravenswick clasped Liu Fai's shoulders, kissing him on each cheek. "That is my son's English name: Stephen Corvus, Earl of Ravenswick."

Jack let out a laugh of disbelief. "Really? Can I call you Steve?"

"No."

Long fingers caressed Jack's neck. Heat sank into his skin. Lady Ravenswick ushered him out through the open door along with the other two. "I am sorry you have to leave so soon, Stephen. But I understand the urgency of your mission." There was fondness in her smile and sadness in her voice—a little too much fondness and a little too much sadness. "Give my love to your father." She strode back into the chamber, heels clicking. The silver door shut on its own.

Without a word, Liu Fai set off down a corridor lined with pewter statues. Jack held Gwen back a few paces. "What happened to Will?"

"Your little maneuver with the portal slowed the dragos down," whispered Gwen, keeping one eye on their escort. "Will and I escaped, and we found Liu Fai in the kitchen. *Lovely* place. Twelve-foot stoves with copper pots everywhere. Biscuits and strawberry jam you would die for. The tea was—"

"*What about Will?*"

"He left before I made contact with Liu Fai—said he'd find his own way to the surface."

Jack pursed his lips. "So he abandoned you."

"Noooo." She slapped his arm, managing to find the bruise as always. "He made sure I'd be okay, then ducked out of sight for the sake of our mission. He was being gallant, Jack."

"Sure he was."

Liu Fai stopped at the edge of the grand hall. "From now on, stay close. And stop whispering. You are not exactly welcome here."

They crossed the hall beneath the silver knight and his dragon, and climbed a broad stair to a bronze portcullis guarded by a pair of large dragos. Panels of semiprecious stones formed a mural between its bars. A red garnet dragon wrestled a white opal dragon on an aventurine hill. The flickering light from the giant cauldrons gave life to the battle.

The guards zeroed in on Jack, and it occurred to him that their glares did not match the warm, come-in-from-the-cold looks Lady Ravenswick had described. Jack lifted his chin at the one on the left, doing his best not to notice the jagged scar bisecting the man's face. "Sup?"

The drago frowned, but after a nod from Liu Fai, he spun a crank to raise the gate.

The three stepped out onto the red tiles of Temple Station, on the secret Ministry Express side, and Liu Fai led them to a small empty platform.

Gwen had questions—lots of them, Jack could tell. She looked like a balloon about to burst, but she obeyed the rule of silence until they were safely inside their carriage. The moment the clamshell door hissed closed, she flopped down onto the thick green cushion next to Liu Fai, pulled her legs up beneath her, and managed to ask all her questions with a single statement. "So"—she folded her hands beneath her chin—"your mom seems nice."

Liu Fai sighed, staring out the portal at the purple light of the maglev rings. "My mother is the British Minister of Dragons and the only child of the late Earl of Ravenswick. My father, Liu Hei, is *Long Buzhang*, the Chinese Minister of Dragons." He turned to face them both. "Their courtship was a negotiation, their marriage a merger, and *I* am the disappointing product." With a note of somewhat severe finality, he returned his gaze to the portal.

Jack and Gwen shared a wide-eyed glance.

After several minutes of silence, the carriage screeched to a stop. Sparks flew past the window, and Newton's laws threw Jack into Gwen's lap. As Jack untangled himself, apologizing profusely, Liu Fai calmly stood. "Did I fail to mention that this line is . . . incomplete?"

Jack caught a hint of a smile.

The door hissed open, but only partway, jiggling a little. Jack ducked beneath it, jumping the four-foot space between the car and the platform while more sparks rained down from above. A burly man straddling a half-completed maglev ring peeled back a welding mask and shouted, "Oi! Mind the gap!" He laughed and slapped the mask down again.

"Trust between the two dragon ministries has been slow to come," said Liu Fai, steering them toward a questionable-looking elevator with all its guts exposed. "But this line will soon join Temple Station directly to our consulate. For the time being, we must walk part of the way."

The elevator let them out in a parking garage, not far from a brick pedestrian walkway and a Chinese arch with a tiered roof. Strings of paper lanterns hung above the shops and restaurants.

"We call this a *paifang*," said Liu Fai as he led them beneath the arch. "Gateways such as this have long provided a sense of coming home to our people."

A block later, in a square filled with a cacophony of scents, sights, song, and chatter, Jack heard a noise that part of him had been expecting all day.

Zzap.

He saw the yellow-orange bolt at the back of his mind.

Where is it, Jack?

Zzap.

He might have imagined the sounds, even the bolts, but not

the *thump* of the miniature blast wave that came with them.

Gwen felt it too. "Ow." She rubbed the top of her back. "Did you just pop me between the shoulder blades?"

"No. I didn't." Jack scanned the square.

Paper lanterns: jostled by a winter breeze.

Black granite lions: one guarding an ornate ball, the other tickling a cub. Jack would have to ask Liu Fai about that.

Scent of ginger: red and grainy.

Scent of roast duck: a deep, earthy green, filling his nostrils with warm smoothness.

Zzap.

This time Jack was ready for it. The orange bolt drew his eye to a stairwell beside a storefront marked PANDA'S DELIGHTS. He broke into a run.

"Where are you going?" Liu Fai called out behind him.

A shadow moved in the stairwell door—a woman, short, wearing a hooded cloak. When she saw him coming, she pulled the hood back.

Jack skidded to a stop. "Mom?"

"Hi, Jack." Sadie appeared from behind her, smiling as if they'd run into each other on the way to school or a Saturday lunch.

Jack's mom did not smile. She pulled her daughter back against her body, concern creasing her brow. "Were you expecting someone else?"

"Yeah, Mom." Jack searched the streets leading away from the square. "I was."

— · Chapter Twenty-Eight · —

JACK EASED HIS MOM and sister back into the stairwell, out of view from the rest of the street. Neither of them held the Einstein-Rosen Bridge, the device he had heard and felt. "How did you get here?"

"Jack." His mom pressed her lips into a flat frown. "I know more ways out of the Keep than you and Gwen put together."

"That's not what I meant."

"We took the Tube," offered Sadie. She never lied to Jack, and if they had used a teleportation device, she would not have looked so calm.

He sighed. "Okay, Mom. You dressed up in a cloak, broke out of the Keep, violating your Section Eight confinement, and took the Tube out to Chinatown. Why?"

Sadie bounced on her toes. "So I could come with you!"

Jack looked from his mom to his bouncing sister and back. "Uh. *No*."

His mom held his gaze. "*Yes*."

"Mrs. Buckles?" Gwen strode up behind Jack with Liu Fai in tow.

Sadie gave her a finger-wiggling wave. "Hi, Gwen. I'm coming with you to China."

"Fantastic," said Gwen.

"I don't think so," said Liu Fai at the same time.

"What he said." Jack thrust a thumb over his shoulder at the drago emissary.

Jack's mom pulled him a few paces away from the others. "I don't have Sadie's Merlinian gifts, not to the level of pushing thoughts and"—she glanced at her daughter—"the other things. But I've had . . . hunches . . . my whole life. And right now, one of those hunches is telling me that you *need* your sister on this trip."

The tightness of her grip told him she wasn't taking no for an answer. He shot her his *this-is-torture-you-must-be-the-worst-parent-ever* look as if it gave him some tiny win. "Fine."

Jack's mom pulled him into a hug. He could feel the wetness of tears against his cheek. "Find the answer, Jack.

Find the last piece of your father's puzzle. And come home safe."

"I will."

She didn't let go. And after a long time, Jack cleared his throat. "Mom."

His mom sniffled. "Yes?"

"You're kind of embarrassing me in front of the Earl of Ravenswick."

She backed away and wiped her eyes. Then she pulled her hood into place and disappeared into the crowd.

"Why are we bringing a nine-year-old girl along?" asked Liu Fai as they left the square.

"I'm almost ten," countered Sadie.

"Oh, good. That is so much better."

They arrived at a shop with porcelain cups and jars of spice in the windows. Liu Fai opened the door, unleashing a flood of deep-colored scents. "So the consulate of the Chinese Ministry of Dragons is underneath a tea shop," said Jack.

"Right next to the Fire Brigade," added Gwen, eyeing a big red truck across the street.

Liu Fai closed the door behind them. "As I said, trust has come slowly."

The proprietor snapped into action the moment she saw

Liu Fai. She spoke rapid Chinese, gesturing wildly at the customers already in the store. Most looked English, but they caught her meaning. *Get. Out.*

As soon as they were gone, she pulled a blind down the full length of the door and barked an order to her assistant. The girl put her whole body into the effort of swinging a block of teak apothecary drawers away from the wall. Liu Fai motioned to the others. "This way."

Two men in suits guarded a small foyer. A third man, seated behind a reception desk, stood and then leaned forward to look over the edge at Sadie. He asked a question in Chinese.

Liu Fai answered in Chinese, but by his tone, it sounded a lot like *Yeah. I know. But these two numbskulls insisted on bringing her along.*

The man behind the desk gave a half-chuckling reply that Jack interpreted as *Your funeral.*

"Our transport is this way." Liu Fai led them to a steel door, where he passed his emerald ring across a gold wall plate. Mist burst from the threshold as it opened.

A list of possible transports that might be waiting on the other side floated through Jack's mind—a hyperloop tube, a maglev super train like a Ministry Express on steroids, a hover jet. Jack was still waiting for someone, anyone, to put him on a hover jet.

The chamber was not unlike the tea shop, with walls and flooring of dark tropical hardwoods. Serpentine dragons writhed on wooden screens. Narrow blue mountains rose into the clouds on silk tapestries. But Jack hardly noticed the artwork.

He walked slowly to the center of the chamber, where a three-toed dragon claw hung from the ceiling, clutching a bronze sphere. The top third was mostly windows, and Jack could see leather padded seats inside. "This is the transport?"

"And this is the door," said Sadie, running a finger along a seam masked by the ornate etchings in the bronze.

"The word we use is closer to *hatch*." Liu Fai joined them, having traded his coat, scarf, and trilby hat for a black canvas jacket with a single blue stripe down each sleeve.

Gwen gave him an approving nod. "I like that look. It suits you."

"Thank you." Liu Fai eased Sadie back a step as a circular plate dropped into the floor and slid out of sight, leaving a large hole beneath the sphere. He turned a recessed handle and opened the hatch, gesturing at the darkness. "Watch your step. You do not want to fall in."

Jack lifted his sister over the gap. "We don't want to fall down the dark, scary hole, but we're climbing into the ominous sphere hanging directly over that same dark, scary hole?"

Liu Fai helped Gwen up next. "Correct." He did not seem to be big on idle conversation.

Once they were all on board, the emissary held five fingers against the glass, signaling an attendant. He lowered his pinky, then his ring finger.

"Just so we're clear," asked Jack, cinching a four-point harness as tight as it would go, "why *are* we suspended over a dark, scary hole?"

Liu Fai grinned for the first time since Jack had met him. It was not a pleasant grin. "Don't all Americans know how you get to China?" He lowered his index finger, finishing with a thumbs-up in the window, and the attendant yanked on a great big lever. "You dig!"

The claw snapped open.

The sphere dropped into the black.

——·Chapter Twenty-Nine·——

JACK GRABBED THE LEATHER bench as gravity gave way.

Gwen screamed.

Sadie threw her hands in the air, letting her body rise in her straps. "Woo-hoo!"

The feeling of his internal organs trying to escape through his mouth and nose surrounded Jack's tracker brain with a sort of maroon bubbly sensation. That was a new one. He forced his stomach down out of his throat. "You dug a hole? From London? To China?"

"Oh, Jack." Gwen slapped his arm. "That is ignorant on so many levels."

Jack rubbed his bruise and pointed. "He started it."

"This hole," said Liu Fai, keeping his eyes on a control pedestal, "is purely for acceleration." He turned a dial, and the sphere rotated upside down.

Again, Jack had to swallow his stomach. The glass panes above—or maybe below—showed him nothing but darkness. He lost all sense of orientation. The maroon bubbles surrounded him.

Liu Fai remained nonchalant. He removed a vial of blue liquid from his jacket and plugged it into a port in the roof. "A dragon door can only transport you a few meters."

"Dragon door?" asked Sadie, completely unfazed by the situation.

"The trans-spatial portals your brother and Miss Kincaid experienced when they snuck into the Citadel"—he scrunched his brow at the other two—"*uninvited*." Liu Fai flipped a toggle. Lights flickered on outside, illuminating rock walls racing past. "As I was saying, walking through a dragon door can only transport you a few meters. To cross the globe, we must reach terminal velocity."

"I don't think *terminal* is the best word right now," said Jack.

"Then perhaps *escape* is a better one." The emissary flipped up a guard covering a red button, and mashed down. The liquid from the vial shot out ahead, becoming a fine mist that ignited a millisecond later. Flames with the deep blue glow of a midnight sky swallowed the sphere.

"Whoa," said Gwen and Sadie at the same time.

Jack couldn't speak at all. Passing through the fire, he had the sense of going up, not down, into a black ceiling rippling with tiny waves. The sphere hit. Black liquid splashed down over the windows. And an instant later, they were through, slowing to a perfect stop as another dragon claw closed to receive them. Liu Fai popped the hatch.

"How—?" Gwen poked her head out, staring down at the black pool as a steel grate walkway swung into place beneath the sphere. The pool split down the middle, retracting into its metal shore.

"A deceleration trap. A sheet of ferro-carbon nano-particles so fine they behave like liquid. Their magnetic properties allow us to suspend them in midair and steer them as we please."

"'Ferro.' As in iron?" said Gwen. "You dropped us into a sheet of *iron*?"

"That *behaves* like *liquid*." Liu Fai rolled his eyes and helped her down, followed by Sadie. He let Jack fend for himself.

"You're late." A man in a high-collared suit crossed the floor to meet them at the end of the steel grate bridge. Titanium panels, pipes, and gauges merged with the natural stone in the chamber behind him. "And why are you wearing that absurd jacket? It only highlights your shame."

It occurred to Jack that he was speaking English to maximize Liu Fai's embarrassment.

They switched to Chinese, and after a few sharp exchanges, Liu Fai lowered his eyes and muttered something under his breath. The relationship between the two seemed obvious.

"So," whispered Gwen as the man led them to an elevator, "your dad seems nice too."

A deep charcoal-colored hum inside the elevator pressed in on Jack like a vise—that and the palpable strain between Liu Fai and his dad.

"My father is disappointed," said the emissary, speaking far too loud for the small space. "He was expecting the great tracker John Buckles that my mother so often described. He thinks I have returned with a collection of school pals instead."

"That is an exaggeration, *Shuang*. Mr. Buckles—*this* Mr. Buckles—came highly recommended by a far more reliable source than your mother."

"And that source was . . ." Gwen glanced up at the minister, fishing.

He wasn't biting. "You shall see." The elevator doors opened, revealing a hallway cut from brown stone, and he gestured for his guests to disembark. "She is waiting in my office."

The minister's office was not so grand as his wife's, though the double doors were still intimidating—red-painted iron, reinforced with spikes. Bladed weapons hung on the walls. The furniture was sparse, a modest desk and a few chairs. A blond woman seated in one of these turned halfway around, holding a long green skirt in place with a delicate hand. She wore round glasses so dark they were almost black. "Wonderful. I am so glad you all could make it."

"Archivist!" Gwen clasped her hand, but Jack held back. This was, after all, a woman who may have unleashed a horde of dragons upon them two months before. "What happened to you?"

"Yes," asked Jack. "What *did* happen to you?"

"An urgent journey, that is all." She held Gwen's fingers. "When I heard about the stolen artifacts and the dragon sightings, I offered my help."

"It was the Archivist who recommended I bring Mr. Buckles into the investigation," added the minister. "She mentioned that both he and his team were young." He sighed and sank into his desk chair, casting a glance Sadie's way. "She failed to mention *how* young."

Sadie looked right back at him, crossing her arms. "I'm. Almost. Ten."

"We saw the calico," said Gwen, taking the chair beside the Archivist. "He misses you."

The Archivist snorted. "That cat misses me the way a prince misses his kitchen maid."

"It is late." Liu Fai's dad rested his hands on a pile of files. "And I still have much to do. Shuang will find you food and show you to your rooms."

By *Shuang*, it seemed, he meant Liu Fai. They stopped at a kitchen, where they ate a quick snack of roasted sweet potatoes and rice-dough-cinnamon-roll things called rolling donkeys, before taking the elevator up to a moonlit walkway.

Cool, damp air brushed Jack's cheeks. Beyond the stone railing, tile-roofed pagodas linked by arched walkways hung suspended in a silver mist. "When the minister said it was late, I didn't realize how late," he whispered, unwilling to spoil the soft feel of the night with loud words.

The Archivist whispered as well. "You crossed five thousand miles chasing the moon, Jack. Didn't you expect to catch it?" She smiled and split from the group, taking one of the bridges into the mist.

Not long after, the remaining four came to an alcove with three wooden doors. "These are your rooms," said Liu Fai. "You will find water and more food inside." He raised an eyebrow at Gwen. "I must apologize, but the Wi-Fi is currently down." Jack couldn't tell if he was joking.

Gwen waggled her phone. "Not a problem. Satellite."

"Wait." Jack caught Liu Fai's arm before he could leave them. "Why does your dad call you Shuang?"

"Many Chinese parents assign nicknames to their children. *Shuang* is the name my father gave. It is *not* one of fondness." He yanked his arm free and walked away. "It means *frost*."

Chapter Thirty

"GWEN!"

Jack sat up in his bed, breathing hard and fast. He rubbed the sleep from his eyes, noticing the orange glow of the room, as if someone had lit his lamp while he slept.

But the lamp remained dark.

Deep red spikes of heat pressed down on his scalp and shoulders, sucking the oxygen from the air. Slowly, warily, Jack looked up. A ball of flame no bigger than a baseball hovered above. He let out a rueful laugh. "At least I didn't light the comforter on fire this time."

He opened his palm, and the fireball raced down to meet it. What had Lady Ravenswick said? *Fire is instinctual. We create it by exciting air molecules.* "Instinctual." Jack concentrated, pushing his senses into the fireball the way he pushed into a spark, straining until his temples bulged. At first, nothing happened.

Then the flame exploded to the size of a beach ball, blowing itself out.

Jack let out a cry and felt for his eyebrows. They were still there.

The fire had not been the only light in the room. Jack could smell the misty blue of dawn wafting in through the window. Its gray light fell across an end table, and a paper Gwen had given him the night before.

"I finished the puzzle," she had said, biting her lip. "Before we set off to meet Will."

"What puzzle?"

"Your dad's puzzle. The poem." She had shown him the paper. "The lines were all jumbled up, but I've got them sorted into stanzas. They might help us. They may even be prophetic."

Jack picked up the paper and read through the poem again. His dad had put together the first few lines for them.

> *Eight figures on a fan*
> *Hide the truth from mortal man.*

The first king knew, and though he tried,
He took the pills and so he died.

The rest remained a mystery, though Jack had his suspicions.

Child of flame and child of ice
Must join to win the maiden's life.
Fear not boys, the girl who sees
Will save you from the ghostly thief.
Beneath the stars that never wheel
Above the rivers made of steel.
In dungeon deep you'll find the key
That sets long-hidden secrets free.

And if the last few lines were prophecy instead of history, they did not bode well.

When castle crumbles, forms your grave,
The fire inside will light the way.
Then matron dies. Then maiden flies.
Then mountain hermit guides your eyes.
Off through time and space I soar
Through forest green, through planet's core.

Am I the answer? Can I destroy
The monster that still haunts the boy?

"Jack, are you in there?" His sister pounded at the door. "Hurry up. You have to see this!"

Jack cracked the door. "See wha—? Oh."

The sun had burned off much of the night's mist, but not all. The wisps that remained hung among natural pillars that rose from a forest canopy. The nearest pillars, in a variety of heights, were topped with pagodas and linked by arched bridges. Jack breathed the fresh air, and marveled at it, because his lungs had gotten so used to the secret compounds beneath London.

Liu Fai waited with Sadie, forearms resting on the walkway's stone rail, and Gwen emerged from her room a moment later, yawning. Halfway through the yawn, she gasped.

The emissary nodded. "All our visitors share this reaction, and yet the mountains are not the most impressive feature of our agency." He straightened. "Come. I will show you the rest while I bring you up to speed on the thefts." A thin white film covered the stone railing where his arms had been.

Jack raised his chin. "Hold up a sec, Frosty." He was done pretending he didn't know Liu Fai's secret.

Liu Fai said nothing, but his jaw tightened. He clenched his fists.

"Jack, don't," said Sadie. "He never wanted us to see."

Gwen looked from brother to sister. "What are you two on about?"

Jack gestured at the rail where the white film had melted into dew. "You can stop pretending, *Shuang*. You can't hide your ability. I know you're the magician I saw in the Thieves' Guild after Tanner's people stole the Crown Jewels. Admit it so we can move on."

Liu Fai growled and thrust out his hands, firing off a stream of frost. Icicles formed above Jack's head. Gwen yanked him out of the way as one fell and shattered on the stones.

"Oh, is that how you want to play it?" Jack took a menacing step forward, heat pulsing through his arms. He opened his palms. "Fine. Let's dance."

After a long, awkward pause, Liu Fai squinted at him, annoyed, a little confused, but not fearful. "I . . . do not want to dance."

Jack glanced down at his hands and sighed, shoulders drooping. No flame.

Liu Fai huffed and walked away.

They ate breakfast in a cafeteria filled with men and

women in loose robes of red, green, or blue, bound with black leather armor. Jack noticed metal studs on the leather covering their palms. He wanted to ask what they were for, but Liu Fai was still sulking, freezing slices of banana and stacking them beside his plate.

Jack found a new favorite food in the doughy steamed buns at the end of the buffet, which turned out to be stuffed with meat. He never got to finish his second round, though. Without warning, their frosty guide stood up and walked off.

"He does that a lot," said Sadie, popping one of Liu Fai's frozen banana slices into her mouth.

Jack tossed a cloth napkin down over his plate. "I guess breakfast is over."

They caught up to Liu Fai in a sloping tunnel lined with square bells, as if together the bells and tunnel formed a single instrument. Jack resisted the urge to play it.

Sadie did not. She tapped the smallest bell with her knuckle, sending a cool tone out into the morning, and laughed. She slipped a hand into Liu Fai's. "It's all right. You can trust us."

He nodded, placing his free hand on the bell to mute it. "Those you saw in the cafeteria are the *long wushi*, the dragon warriors. You may have noticed that not one of them acknowledged our presence, especially not mine." The four continued down the line of bells. "The long wushi were once like the dragos, but the fire went out of our bloodlines long ago. My father sought to reinvigorate ours with an arranged marriage."

"Your mother," said Gwen, "our Minister of Dragons."

"I was to be the *suhuifujan*, the rekindling. But I did not inherit my mother's skills—not exactly. Dragos who carry the telekinetic DNA make fire by quickening the air and drawing in dust for fuel. I was born with a similar instinct. Just . . ."

"The opposite?" offered Sadie.

"When I try to make fire, I draw moisture instead of dust. And instead of quickening the molecules, I slow them down, to the point of freezing." Their little group had entered a stairwell in the cliff face, partially exposed to the daylight. A dragon's-head fountain at the first landing fed a brook that ran beside the stairs. Liu Fai dipped a hand into the trickling water. When he lifted it out again, he held a many-faceted jewel of pure ice. He handed it to Sadie.

"Oh, it's lovely," she said.

"A parlor trick," he countered. "I am a disappointment to the long wushi. And the dragos look harshly upon a titled earl who cannot make fire." Liu Fai flicked the remaining water from his hand in a flurry of snowflakes. "For a while, I found a place at the Magicians' Guild, but once they discovered my trick was no illusion, they rejected me too."

At the bottom of the stairwell, they entered a passage filled with the burbling of the brook. "We're sorry," said Gwen. "We didn't know." When Jack said nothing, she slapped his arm.

He rubbed his bruise. "Uh . . . Right. Sorry. We"—Jack gave Gwen a shrug—"didn't know."

"How could you know? I became the emissary, wandering back and forth between my two families. Never welcome for long." Liu Fai stopped before a door carved with serpentine creatures hiding among trees. "The residents of this garden are the only creatures of either ministry who never look upon me with judgment." He tugged at a big iron ring, swinging the door wide.

Sadie gasped and covered her mouth with both hands. She dropped them to her sides and bounced on her toes. "Jack! It's like a dream!"

Chapter Thirty-One

THE BROOK PASSED THROUGH a culvert out into a garden with high stone walls overgrown with trees. Large creatures lumbered and slithered among the ponds and pagodas in apparent freedom. Scales in a host of colors glittered in the morning sun.

Jack had some experience with dragons—at the Citadel and in the Archive's Drago Collection. None of it had been positive. But Sadie forced his hand by rushing out into the open.

"Sadie, wait!"

"She is perfectly safe," said Liu Fai. "Come and see."

The other three caught up with her at a koi pond, legs swinging beneath a wooden bridge. Sadie had found the one dragon in the compound that matched her sparkly lavender shoes, though its scales were marbled with emerald green as well. The dragon lay with half its long body in the grass and half on the bridge, its giant head in Sadie's lap. The horns, branched like antlers, resembled pink granite. It let out a gurgling, contented growl.

In Jack's estimation, *perfectly safe* did not apply. A yellow-gold dragon, even larger, took interest in them. He reached for his sister. "Sadie . . ."

Liu Fai touched his elbow. "Trust me, Jack. Your sister *is* safe. Meet Biyu, our cuddle-bug, to use my mother's term. She loves people, especially girls."

"As friends, or for breakfast?" asked Jack.

"She?" asked Gwen.

"You can tell by the flamboyancy of her coloring. Dragons share that trait with humans. The females are the more beautiful of the species."

"*Yeah*, we are." Sadie scratched the dragon under her chin. "Isn't that right, Biyu?"

A koi swam out from beneath the bridge with dangly whiskers that matched the dragon's. Jack thought perhaps the two shared some heritage until Biyu snatched it out of the pond, lifted her head, and gulped it down.

"Ōi yōu, Biyu!" Liu wiped away the pond water she had slung at his jacket. He laughed and said something in Chinese, pointing away, and the dragon lumbered off, clawed feet flopping.

"She has no wings," said Gwen, watching her go.

"Not many of her family do. Biyu is a variety of *shilong*, a stone dragon."

Biyu reached a pillared alcove in the wall, shaded by the roots of a massive tree. Her scales blended with the stone so well that the moment she stopped moving, she vanished.

"Are there many dragons that can't fly?" asked Jack as the four of them left the brook.

"Who said she couldn't fly?" Liu Fai glanced over his shoulder with a raised eyebrow. "Eastern dragons lost the need for wings eons ago. Some families may have kept them for adornment, or perhaps enhanced control, but they are not a necessity."

"But if they don't have wings, then how——?"

"Fire," Liu Fai replied, cutting Jack off, but he offered no additional explanation.

The yellow-gold dragon still stalked their little group, coal-black eyes fixed on Jack, while a pair of long wushi in red robes walked through the trees a short distance beyond, keeping tabs. Liu Fai raised his voice, speaking in Chinese, and the beast crept closer. "That is Laohu, a *fucanglong*, or treasure dragon. When his flame is lit, he is like a fighter jet."

With Laohu closer, Jack could make out his markings. His bronze tiger stripes were far more subdued than Biyu's green marble swirls, and his antlers and talons were like pure platinum. The dragon stretched his head forward. Jack's head began to throb.

Fire? Flame?

The boy carries the flame?

Apparently dragon thoughts came pre-translated. Jack winced at the impact they had on his brain and pushed back. *No. The boy doesn't carry the flame.*

Liu Fai slowed. "Are you all right?"

The pounding subsided. The dragon raised his head, giving Jack a skeptical look.

"I'm fine," said Jack. "Keep going."

The emissary returned to his former pace, taking a bridge to a pagoda at the center of a pond, and the treasure dragon stopped at the shore, still watching Jack. Gwen glanced back at him. "Laohu's flame is not lit. I assume that means you deny your dragons fire, the same as the dragos."

"We deny them fire, yes." Liu Fai raised a finger. "But our

treatment of dragons is *nothing* like the dragos'." He walked up the pagoda steps, pointing out yet another dragon, nestled in the branches of a tree. She was well camouflaged, with copper flanks split and fissured like bark and green scales sprouting here and there along her legs and spine. "The long wushi keep their dragon guests grounded in the preserve for their own protection."

"The preserve," mused Jack, reaching the top of the steps and looking around the garden. "If the dragons can't spark their own fire from the stone here, then it must all be . . ." He let his fingers graze one of the pagoda's columns and felt heat seap into his skin. "Dragonite." The pagoda, the path, the walls—they were all dragonite, of a darker variety than the walls of the Archive, but incredibly similar. "Where did you find so much of it?"

"Right here. This valley was a dragon haven long before our agency discovered it. We merely joined them in their natural home." Liu Fai held a hand out over the pond, and a sky-blue dragon leaped out of the water to rub its head against his palm. "Our relationship is symbiotic."

The new dragon, much smaller than the others, widened its black eyes, as if excited by the sight of visitors. It snaked through balusters and wound around Sadie, climbing up to her shoulders before launching into the air on perfectly proportioned wings.

Liu Fai rolled his eyes at the performance. "This is Xiaoquan. He is *yinglong*, a water dragon, one of the few families with full wings."

The dragon did a backward, twisting loop and settled on a level with Jack's eyes.

"Watch out—" said Liu Fai, but too late. Xiaoquan unleashed a long stream of pond water straight into Jack's face.

"They spit."

Jack wiped the water from his eyes and flicked it away. "Thanks."

Gwen pressed a handkerchief into his hand. "Explain *symbiotic*."

Liu Fai let the water dragon curl around his waist to rest a wet chin on his shoulder. Xiaoquan matched his intense expression. "Man controls fire, and dragons offer luck and wisdom in return. The long wushi do not exist in enmity with their charges as the dragos do, seeking to vanquish every dragon from existence."

As they argued, Jack tried to return the soggy handkerchief.

Gwen waved him off. "The dragos do *not* vanquish every

dragon. Article two, directive eleven of the Dragon Code states that dragons may be *captured* as well as killed."

Liu Fai scowled, along with Xiaoquan. "I am as much drago as I am long wushi. Do not presume to tell me the regulations of my own ministry."

"Well, if you knew them, I wouldn't have to."

"Hey!" Jack shoved the wet handkerchief into his pocket, wincing at the cold, white wetness that seeped through. "Could we get on with the investigation, please?"

The other two went silent. Xiaoquan looked hurt, air-slithered out over the pond, and dropped in with a splash.

"Of course." Liu Fai softened his voice. "Three artifacts have gone missing, and a mechanical dragon was sighted leaving all three crime scenes." He shrugged. "We have learned little else."

"And that's why we're here." Gwen cleared her throat. "How about you start by telling us exactly what was taken?"

"As I said before, the artifacts were all related to Qin Shi Huang, the First Emperor." Liu Fai retreated to a bench on the other side of the pagoda. "The first two were taken together—a text with wooden pages composed by the Qin grand astron-omer, and the First Emperor's jade seal. The mechanical dragon tore a hole through the National Museum of China to steal them."

"Yeah," said Jack, eyeing Laohu, who was still watching from the shore. "I saw that on TV. And the third?"

"A moonstone chalice used by the emperor in his alchemical experiments, taken from a museum in Hong Kong." Liu Fai's shoulders sagged. "All our efforts to track the missing items have failed. We have only managed to protect those that remain, collecting Qin artifacts from our museums and moving them to our own vault."

"Wait." Gwen gave Jack a sideways glance. "You have more Qin artifacts here? Um . . . Do you mind if we take a look?"

Chapter Thirty-Two

LIU FAI SENT WORD to the Archivist to meet them in the vault and set off with the others. Laohu followed at a respectful distance. Xiaoquan followed at a not-so-respectful distance, doing loops and turns and occasionally cutting back and forth between the humans.

Jack laughed as the water dragon whipped past Gwen's nose. "You should let Spec out for a playdate. Those two would be peas in a pod."

"Perhaps later." Gwen fended off another pass of the blue tail. "Releasing Spec in a garden full of dragons is not a good plan."

The dragonite path they followed wound through a grove of trees, finally circling a deep well of pure dragonite, perhaps fifty feet across. Jack came to a stunned halt at the upper landing of the well's staircase, blocking his little sister from starting down. "Huh. That looks familiar."

"The Archive," said Gwen, stopping beside him.

There were differences. For starters, the walls of the long wushi well looked more natural, with no shelves. Rough-hewn striations spiraled all the way down, broken only by the steep, winding stair. Jack scrunched up his brow. "Did the long wushi dig this?"

"No." Liu Fai passed his emerald ring over a carbon fiber plate, and a luminescent strip lit the stairway. "The main well and its caves were here when the long wushi found the haven."

"Caves?" Gwen took Sadie's hand as she followed him down.

Jack paused on the second step. Their dragon entourage had stalled at the edge of the trees. "You fellas coming or what?"

Laohu snorted. Xiaoquan looped backward, rolled over, and disappeared into the grove.

The caves Liu Fai had mentioned branched off from the well at random, not unlike the four ministry collections that branched off from the Archive. Jack had to wonder at the connection. These, however, were not filled with books or map tables.

In the first cavern, a light green dragon with silver swirls snuggled with a larger companion, speckled gray and black. Liu Fai pointed them out to Sadie. "Stone dragons, like your friend Biyu. Many of our *shilong* and *fucanglong* wards prefer to live down here, below the surface."

The most impressive group played in the last and largest of the open chambers. A platinum dragon with coppery leopard spots clutched a pearl the size of Jack's head in its claws. Two others—a gold dragon with opal antlers and a third covered in silver scrollwork—clawed and tussled with the first, trying to claim its prize.

"I bet that pearl is worth a fortune," said Gwen.

Jack let out a quiet laugh. "But who would be crazy enough to try and take it?"

The chamber with the wrestling dragons was the last of the side caves, and still the four descended. The thumping of their steps became a rhythmic cycle of concentric brown circles in Jack's brain, like endless ripples in a muddy pond.

Sadie tugged on the hem of Liu Fai's canvas jacket. "How much longer?"

"Not far now. The vault is just . . . below . . ." His voice faded. Liu Fai stared downward, at the next turn of the stairs across the well. There on the steps, elbows on her knees, chin resting in her hands, sat the Archivist. Before any of them could call out, she put a finger to her lips.

"How did you get down here ahead of us?" asked Liu Fai once they reached her.

The Archivist kept her voice at a whisper. Her sightless gaze remained fixed on the other side of the well. "I was already here." She raised a hand to Jack.

He hooked her fingers and helped her to her feet. "Doing what?"

Gwen, who was already looking in the same direction as the Archivist, caught Jack's chin and turned his head. "Looking at that, I presume."

Recessed into the wall across the well, hidden from the stairway above was a giant cave barred with dragonite pillars. The inside was huge. At the sight of so many visitors, a massive dragon let out a low rumble—a sound Jack had heard before, way down among the lower reaches of the Archive.

At first, the new dragon looked black, with obsidian claws and horns. But as she moved a bulky, sinuous arm into the pale glow of the stairwell's luminescent strip, Jack caught a muted glint of purplish blue. The dragon tucked a full-size wing against its flank, sending a warm gust across the well to greet them.

Sadie brushed a strand of auburn hair out of her eyes. "Why is she caged?"

"This dragon is too dangerous to roam free—too powerful." Liu Fai glanced at Jack. "We believe it was she who bored the well, more than two thousand years ago."

"Oh no. Not her." The Archivist turned toward their host, contradicting him. "An ancestor, perhaps, but not this dragon. She's too young and small."

"Young?" asked Gwen.

"Small?" asked Jack at the same time.

They both gave the Archivist the same dumbfounded stare.

"Most definitely." She started down the steps. "I assume you've come down to see the Qin artifacts. Excellent. This way, please."

Two levels down, they entered a four-story chamber filled with artifacts from all throughout history. They fanned out among the shelves and display cases. Jack walked down an aisle between stone dragon skulls. He might have assumed they were sculptures if he had not seen the same minerals in the talons of live dragons. At the end of the line, he found a bronze urn with eight dragon heads sticking out on all sides, each with a ball in its mouth. A circle of gaping frogs surrounded the base. Frogs and dragons. He had no idea what that was all about.

The Archivist and Sadie had walked straight to a table set with a black velvet cloth. Laid in a rough circle on the cloth was a collection of artifacts—a polished meteorite etched with Chinese script, an iron sledgehammer, a misshapen glass bottle of red powder, and a jade disc with many geometric figures cut out.

"These are the Qin relics," said Liu Fai as he, Gwen, and Jack joined the other two. He lifted the glass bottle, turning it over so that the powder tumbled inside. "They were among the emperor's most prized possessions."

Sadie frowned. "How is red dust a prized possession?"

"This bottle contains cinnabar, a form of mercury. Time has ground them into powder, but two thousand years ago, this 'red dust,' as you say, was pills. The emperor took them every day to infuse his organs with eternal silver."

"Well, it looks like a bottle of rust." Sadie tried to lift the meteorite. "I like this one better."

"Sadie, don't—" said Jack.

Too late.

The space rock was too heavy. It slipped from Sadie's hands.

Jack lunged and caught it a millimeter above the floor.

Instantly, the long wushi vault disappeared, and Jack fell through a night sky onto a field of tall gray grass. The blades looked a lot like pumice, and waved in a jerky, rhythmless motion beside a flat black sea. The burst of adrenaline pumping to his brain as he caught the falling artifact had caused him to spark.

Jack no longer held the rock. Instead, it seemed, a rock held him. A man composed of the same conglomerate of minerals held the meteorite aloft, shouting at it—and thus, at Jack, whose point of view was confined to the artifact. Even so, Jack dared not step out into the vision on such a frightening, shifting landscape.

Streaks of visible flesh scarred Shouting-rock-guy's face. Likely these clear portions were the result of veins of nickel or iron running through meteorite. The effect was grotesque, like the tormented faces in the Templar church, yet Jack recognized him as the king he had watched during the spark from the jade fan. This was the same man, only older and wilder.

Gone was the brilliant general who had used a river to end a siege. Gone was the leader who had commanded such respect and praise from his army. Zhao Zheng had become the emperor Qin Shi Huang. He had also become a raving lunatic.

The emperor dropped the meteorite—and Jack—into the black sand on the seashore and picked up an oversize crossbow. He waded into the watery void, waving the weapon back and forth to challenge some unseen foe. As soon as he fired, other stone men rushed in to retrieve him. They dragged him kicking and snarling back to the shore and dropped him on his back in the pumice grass.

That, Jack suspected, was the end of Qin Shi Huang. With a mental cringe, he backed out of the spark. The vault—and his friends—descended around him in a rush of gray.

"Thank you," breathed Liu Fai, retrieving the meteorite from Jack's hands. "I could not have faced my father if this were damaged. The script on its face dates from the emperor's lifetime, and has remained pristine for millennia. It is a prophecy, predicting the emperor's death."

"And yet somehow I don't think it was a fortune-telling space rock that killed him." Jack cast a sidelong glance at Gwen.

Her expression told him she knew that he had sparked. It also said *we'll-talk-about-this-later*. She walked around the table to the last artifact, a jade disc a little larger than a Frisbee. "Um . . . Liu Fai, why don't you tell us about this one?"

Some of the confidence dropped from his expression. "We are not really sure about that piece. The record of the emperor's possessions refers to it as *bùxiŭ túlì*, the Immortal Key."

A half freckle bounce lifted the corners of Gwen's mouth. "The key," she said, partly to herself. "'*In dungeon deep they'll find the key that sets long-hidden secrets free.*'" She let out a little laugh. "Jack, this is it. This is the next clue your dad wanted us to find."

— · Chapter Thirty-Three · —

JACK EYED THE GEOMETRIC cutouts. "The Immortal Key . . . ," he mused. The disc didn't look much like a key. "Maybe it fits over some pegs and works like a crank."

"May I?" asked the Archivist, touching Gwen's shoulder.

Gwen stepped out of her way and the Archivist passed her fingers slowly around the disc, examining by feel. "Hmm. Is this a notch?" She kept going. "Yes. There are four such cuts spaced evenly around the rim, dividing the disc into wedges."

"Or *fans*," said Gwen, looking over her shoulder.

Liu Fai turned pale as Gwen produced the fan from Gall's cave and spread it out on the table beside the disc. His hands hovered over the silk, quivering. "The Eight Immortals. This fan is—"

"A precious piece of your nation's heritage that I've been

carrying around in my coat pocket this whole time?" Gwen patted him on the arm. "True. But let's circle back to that, shall we? I think your 'Immortal Key' unlocks a cipher, not a door." Ignoring the emissary's stunned glower, she lifted the disc and laid it on top of the fan, aligning two of the notches with the edges of the silk. In the painting, captured in the pattern of geometric cutouts, were Chinese characters.

The frustration faded from Liu Fai's brow. "It *is* a cipher key." He translated the top arc of characters. "'The formula of the elixir of life, recorded by my hand, the Emperor Qin Shi Huang, the True Man.' Incredible."

Sadie poked her head around his arm to get a look. "It's not *that* impressive."

Liu Fai's lips parted. He crossed arms, looking down his nose at her. "Isn't it?"

"Look." Sadie lifted the disc away. "You can see the writing in the painting with or without the disc. The cutouts make it easier to read, that's all."

She was right. Jack shook his head. "That's why Gall left it behind. He must have deciphered the formula long ago."

"Gall?" Liu Fai's frustrated glower returned. He cocked his head at Jack. "As in Ignatius Gall?"

"Um . . . Yeah . . . That Gall. Don't be angry—we might

know more about your missing artifacts than we've let on." Jack winced. "And the clockwork dragon."

Don't be angry had to be the worst conversation starter ever. He dove in anyway, and Liu Fai's glower deepened as Jack described Gall's obsession with immortality and brain transfers, his collusion with the Clockmaker, and his vendetta against the Buckles family.

"Hey," said Sadie, fiddling with the disc and the fan. "Watch this." She lined up the second set of notches, shifting the disc around the painting. The geometric cutouts isolated new characters. A few formed pictures, like a diagram. A square isolated a constellation of stars among the clouds. An oval and a triangle became a dish filled with blue fire.

"Those stars represent a specific location and time," said Liu Fai, shooting a final frown at Jack before turning his full attention to the fan. "And these shapes, here, form alchemical symbols. But this . . ." He rested his finger on the disc next to a red ball.

Sadie turned the disc twice more, revealing new steps in the formula. Each set of steps ended with a ball—red, white, and green.

Liu Fai pored over the script, but he shook his head. "I do not know what those are."

"We do." Gwen drew out the Mind of Paracelsus, letting its silk wrappings fall free in her hand. "The emperor created a mind transfer device to make the brain permanent, the way he wanted to make his organs permanent by taking pills to replace them with mercury. The alchemist Paracelsus acquired the fan and made his own version. It was red when Jack found it."

"But Paracelsus didn't have the key," said Jack. He grimaced, remembering the way the Mind had eaten away at his consciousness. "I don't think he got his version quite—"

A *plink* from the urn with all the dragon heads stole Jack's attention. A ball had dropped from a dragon's jaw into a frog's gaping mouth. He eyed the device. A silent boom rippled through his subconscious. *Plink.* A second ball dropped. "Um . . . What's that supposed to mean?"

There was an earsplitting *crack* from above, and great chunks of dragonite rained down, shattering glass display cases. Steel jaws and blue-green wings came crashing through the wall.

Jack's nightmare was real. "Run!"

With Liu Fai in the lead, they all made for the vault door—all except one.

Jack looked back and saw the Archivist, still at the table

with the relics. A huge dragon composed of several alloys hovered above her, held aloft by thrusters on each wing. "Gwen, get my sister out of here! I'll help the Archivist."

Liu Fai had already reached the vault door. He hauled it open, wheeling his arm as the girls raced through and calling back to Jack. "Come on! We—"

Jack never heard the rest. A massive section of the dragonite wall collapsed between them, cutting off Jack and the Archivist's escape. The echo of the falling stones blended in Jack's ears with a deep, cackling laugh. Fire filled his vision. Something hit Jack on the head, and sharp red pain seared his body. The fire and the light—all the data flooding his brain—faded to black.

Out in the well, Gwen shouted for Jack, but she heard no response.

The stairs shook beneath her feet, and Liu Fai tugged at her arm. "The entire well may crumble. We *must* go, Gwen!"

She tore at the rubble covering the vault door, fingernails scraping the stone, unable to move a single rock. "Jack and the Archivist are still in there!"

"And so we must get help for them!" Liu Fai yanked her back as fire flared through gaps. "Now, Gwen!"

Behind them, Sadie had crumpled to the steps, crying. Jack had told Gwen to get his sister out of there. Reluctantly, sharing the younger girl's tears, Gwen lifted Sadie to her feet, and with Liu Fai's help she half dragged, half carried Sadie up the winding stair.

As they climbed, Sadie mumbled the same phrase over and over. "I can't see my brother. I can't feel his heart."

Chapter Thirty-Four

DARKNESS SURROUNDED JACK. THICK.
Impenetrable. Yet even in that darkness, the deep voice from his nightmares found him.

"Jack. Lucky Jack."

He opened his eyes. The darkness remained, tinted bloodred by the pain. As consciousness returned, though, Jack found an orange sensation of heat as well. Broken slabs of dragonite lay on either side of him. He pressed his palms flat against them and pulled with nerve endings. Warmth coursed into his muscles. The pain lessened.

"Jack."

The voice called to him again—no longer deep, but soft and frail.

"Archivist?"

"I'm over here, Jack."

"I . . . I can't see." He rolled his eyes at his own declaration. What a dumb thing to say to a blind woman.

"Follow my voice. Use the skills you've learned."

She began to hum. Waves of glowing pink pushed through the throbbing in his head. The gentle tones reflected off ten thousand facets of broken stone, making the topography of the ruined chamber hard to read.

The words that belonged to the melody rose up from his memory, a lullaby his mother used to sing.

Sleep my child, and peace attend thee
All through the night.

The pink waves formed a dense center. That had to be the source, the Archivist. He began to crawl. "It's working. Keep humming. I think I can get to you."

Guardian angels God will send thee
All through the night.

Jack dragged himself across rocks and shattered glass until

finally, he touched the hand of that guardian angel. It was wet with blood.

She squeezed his fingers. "Well done, Jack. You found me."

"You're hurt." He slipped his hand free to check the area around her. Most of it was taken up by the largest drago-nite slab he had yet encountered. "And you're trapped, aren't you?"

"That's right." The Archivist had never been one to mince words.

Jack didn't know what to do with that information. He slipped his hand back into hers.

"He took the Immortal Key, Jack. I tried to stop him, but the clockwork dragon took the key—the emperor's fan, as well."

That was why she had lagged behind, to save the artifacts. "I should have seen. I should have stopped him and gotten you out with Gwen and Sadie. Why did the dragon even come? Gall didn't know about the key."

"He knew *of* the key, Jack. Surely." The Archivist let out a long shaky breath that Jack took to be a sigh. "Chances are he went to the museum where it came from and forced the curator to confess that the long wushi had been there. That was all the information he needed." She fell silent for several seconds and then squeezed Jack's fingers again. It seemed to be the only motion she could make. "I'm glad that you and I have a quiet moment to chat."

A quiet moment to chat? She was losing it. "Archivist, we—"

"We never talked about that incident in the Ministry of Dragons Collection."

Maybe she wasn't losing it. Jack wanted answers about that night, but not like this. "Did you open the cages?"

"Yes. Of course."

"Of course," Jack repeated, not understanding how the phrase applied. Her actions had almost cost him and Gwen their lives. "Um . . . Why 'of course'?"

"How else would you have learned who you really are?"

That night was the first time Jack had heard a dragon's thoughts, the first time he had created fire out of nothing—with brutal consequences. "You wanted me to know that I'm a drago."

"Has anyone ever told you where dragonite comes from?" The Archivist turned his hand over and pressed it down on the stone so that he could feel the heat. "Dragon eggs. Shells crushed and pressed together for eons. Dragonite is like a yolk, from which a dragon draws nourishment, all through its life."

It draws nourishment. Like drawing heat. Jack hesitated before asking the next question. "And . . . dragos draw from it too?"

"Not all. But the strongest, yes. Dragons and dragos are bonded, Jack, linked together in the order of creation. In that, the long wushi are correct."

Jack remembered what Liu Fai had told him. "Man controls the fire."

"And the dragons serve and protect him in return. This is an idea that the knights of the Ministry of Dragons forgot long ago. But the bond between dragon and drago is not formed entirely of flame. That bond also requires . . . It requires . . ."

The Archivist's voice faded. Her fingers went limp in Jack's hand.

"Archivist?" Jack passed his hand up her arm until he found her neck, feeling for a pulse. He couldn't find one. "Archivist!"

In that moment, it occurred to him that he had never learned her name. She had to have one. Why had no one ever told him her name?

"Archivist!"

She made no response.

Jack shouted in a raging effort to lift the slab that pinned her down. "Aghh!" It moved, which kind of caught him off guard. From what Jack could tell, the thing was six feet long. It must weigh a ton. "How—?"

The Archivist's voice came back to him. *This stone is like a yolk, from which a dragon draws nourishment.* And if what she said about dragos was true, Jack could draw from it as well. Had lying in dragonite rubble given him the strength to move a six-foot slab?

Slowly, carefully, he pressed himself up to his knees. Jack's back ached. His head still throbbed. He couldn't see a thing. None of that mattered. "I'm getting you out of here."

Their little hollow within the rubble was tighter than Jack had first imagined. He couldn't stand all the way up, but he had enough room to get some leverage. Jack slipped his fingers under the rough edge of the slab and bent at the knees, drawing heat through his arms. "Aghh!"

The slab rose an inch, then two. "Come . . . on!" With sudden acceleration, the giant chunk flipped over and fell away with a tremendous *crunch.*

"Great." Jack dusted off his hands. "I have super strength, but only when I'm completely surrounded by dragon eggs. It's the complete reverse of kryptonite."

Still, Jack could not see. No light—none at all—seeped through from the well into the crumbled vault. He sighed, then caught his breath. *Crumbled.* He remembered the poem. *When castle crumbles, forms your grave, the fire inside will light the way.*

The rubble made seeing the room through echoes impossible, even for Jack. But if he could create his own light, he and the Archivist stood a chance.

Lady Ravenswick had told Jack that dragos telekinetically excite the air to create fire.

Her son, Liu Fai, had told him dragos draw in dust for fuel.

"I'm a drago. I can do this." Jack held a palm out into the black and concentrated. "Excite the air. Pull in dust. You're a drago."

He felt the air molecules above his palm, soft and malleable. He felt the dust, fine and gritty. "Excite the air. Pull in dust." Jack concentrated on stirring the molecules, whipping his concoction up to a blinding speed.

Heat.

Jack stared at the spot where he imagined his palm to be, begging the air to ignite.

A spark.

"Yes." He kept stirring, grinding dust against dust for friction. A flash. Heat.

Flame.

A yellow tongue of fire rested in Jack's palm, and he laughed out loud, until the light showed him the Archivist's limp form.

It took an agonizingly long time to locate an exit from their chaotic cave. Finally, Jack spotted a hole—a path leading upward through a jagged tunnel of rock. He had no guarantee of an exit on the other side, but it was his only chance. Thankfully, the Archivist wasn't heavy, especially with the dragonite boosting his muscles. Jack lifted her up to his shoulder, and began the long hard trudge.

The journey wasn't pretty. At times, he had to set her down and drag her over the rocks, apologizing the whole time. Once he had to snuff out his light and use both hands to climb. He breathed a huge sigh of relief when he managed to light it again. After what felt like miles, he heard shouting in Chinese.

He shouted back.

No response—none that he could understand, anyway.

Jack pressed on. The tunnel brightened with a light of its own. The voices grew closer. He cupped his hand and called out to them. "Hello?"

"Jack!" Liu Fai appeared ahead of him, gripping the rock as if peering down through a hole.

Was Jack going straight up? Maybe. "The Archivist is hurt. She needs help!"

Liu Fai disappeared. More shouting. More hands than Jack

could count reached down to take her from him, and Jack found it hard to let her go. "Be careful!"

The hands returned, lifting him out into the light. He was in the well, on the stairs, still far from the top. Someone pressed a leather canteen into Jack's hands. That same someone hugged him tight, wrapping him in the pinkish-purply haze of strawberries.

"You're all right. I can't believe you're all right."

"Gwen?"

"Sadie is up top. She said she could feel your heart again. She told me I would find you."

A few steps above, two long wushi in green uniforms laid the Archivist on a stretcher. A woman in scrubs said something to Liu Fai, and from the look in his eyes—the way he bowed his head—Jack knew what she had said.

I'm sorry. She's gone.

Chapter Thirty-Five

THE CLIMB UP THE stair felt like a funeral procession. The long wushi guards carried the Archivist like a fallen princess on a bier, with Liu Fai and the doctor at the head and Gwen and Jack lagging behind.

"I can't do this alone," said Jack, watching the dragonite steps pass beneath his sneakers as if moving on their own.

Gwen took his hand. "You don't have to."

He knew what she meant. She would stand by him. But Jack couldn't allow that. He *was* alone. And that was a fact he couldn't escape. "You don't understand." Jack pulled his hand away. "I thought he had come for you."

"For me?"

"I was so glad when you got out of the vault. I still am glad, even though . . ." Jack glanced up at the stretcher. The Archivist's hands were folded peacefully at her waist.

"I know. It's the same for me, after watching you come out of that rubble and—"

"It is *not* the same." Jack locked eyes with her. "Gwen, this is about my nightmares."

He told her everything—the reason he had called her name in his sleep, the way she had died before his eyes night after night. "It was more than a dream, Gwen. I saw the clockwork dragon *before* we knew he existed. What if—?"

"What if you saw our future? What if you have some Merlinian in you, like Sadie?"

"Promise me you'll make yourself scarce the next time that dragon comes around."

Gwen snorted. "I'll do no such thing. We're talking about the Clockmaker. I'm not letting you face him, or whatever he's become, alone."

Jack paused on the steps, letting her walk ahead of him. "I have to."

The procession was getting farther away. Gwen came back and took his arm. "Come on. If we're too far behind, it will worry Sadie half to death."

The dragons—the real dragons—seemed to sense the

sadness. The trio with the pearl ceased their game and crept to the front of their cave to watch. Up in the garden, Laohu fell into step beside the procession. Xiaoquan plodded along behind him, as if he no longer felt like flying.

The guards and the doctor took the Archivist through the door beside the brook while Liu Fai led Jack and Gwen up to the top of the high dragonite wall. Sadie and the long wushi minister waited for them there, on wide battlements that looked west through the pillar mountains.

Sadie threw her arms around her brother.

The minister offered a short bow. "You have suffered a great loss. I am sorry. But now we must deal with this murderer. I understand the metal dragon took two more artifacts, the Immortal Key and the emperor's fan. What else can you tell me?"

Jack tried to answer, but Gwen elbowed his ribs and made a pointed look at Liu Fai. He got the gist. They were not at the Keep. This was Liu Fai's ministry, his father, and his time.

Liu Fai squared his shoulders. "The metal dragon was created by the Clockmaker, a madman that attacked London a little over a year ago, at the behest of Ignatius Gall."

"Gall." The minister narrowed his eyes. "From the Ministry of Secrets. So this is an attack by a rival agency."

"No, Father. Gall is acting for his own interest." Liu Fai glanced at Gwen and she gave him a nod. "He is seeking to complete the work of the First Emperor. He is seeking immortality."

"Preposterous. Immortality is a fantasy of the past."

"That is not what Gall believes," interjected Jack. "And he has bigger plans. He's been experimenting with mind transference, for control as much as for immortality. That is the secret of the clockwork dragon. The machine was not merely built by the Clockmaker. It *is* the Clockmaker." He shrugged. "Unfortunately, I don't know how to track him."

Sadie turned, looking out at the late afternoon. "You won't have to. He's coming back."

The other four rushed the battlements and stared. Jack thought Sadie had imagined it, until he picked up a hint of shadow within the orange fireball of the sun.

The minister saw it too. "*Shèjí tā! Shèjí tā!*" he shouted at his guards. "Shoot it down!"

Long wushi in blue appeared on the pagodas and bridges, firing crossbows. Their bolts plinked off the dragon's blue-green armor.

Jack lifted Sadie into the arms of a guard waiting at the stairwell. "Gwen! Time to go!"

"Not a chance." She stood her ground, wrapping one end of her scarf around her knuckles, and glaring at the incoming beast. "Bring it."

Red eyes flared.

Steel jaws gaped open.

"No!" yelled Jack, lunging for his friend.

As Jack shoved Gwen into Liu Fai and his father, the creature smashed into him, knocking him off the wall. He felt the sickening sensation of a somersaulting free fall. He saw the ground coming up to meet him.

Ash Pendleton had taught Jack how to tuck a shoulder and roll. But a roll couldn't save him this time, not after such a long fall. He would hit the grass at breakneck speed. Literally.

"Excite the air. Pull in dust." He spoke the mantra out loud, the way he had spoken it in the darkness of the crumbled vault.

Jack spun the air molecules over both palms and slammed particles of dust together, fighting to keep them tracking with his own accelerating fall. A spark flashed and fizzled in his right hand, then his left. He felt the air compress between his body and the grass.

Fffoomp.

The explosion cushioned the impact, but it still hurt. A lot.

Jack rolled out across a blackened patch of grass and wound up flat on his back beneath the dangling, carplike whiskers of a yellow-gold dragon.

Laohu bent his dragony nose down until it nearly touched Jack's.

The boy lied.

The boy carries the flame.

Jack jerked his head out from under the dragon and struggled to his feet. "I didn't lie. I couldn't do it before."

He saw a stream of flame coming in his mind. The sound of it formed into blue crystals tipped with gold, bursting one from another. Jack knew he wasn't fast enough to get out of the way.

Laohu was. The dragon coiled around him, dragging him out of the fire's path, and the clockwork beast flashed by a fraction of a second later.

"Jack!"

Jack and Laohu skidded to a stop side by side at the edge of Xiaoquan's pond. Jack searched for meaning in the treasure dragon's coal-black eyes. Laohu wanted fire—yearned for it—that much was clear. He could have ignited his own flame during the clockwork dragon's attack, but he chose to save Jack instead. White vapor spilled out between his platinum teeth.

The flame, boy.

Now.

"You got it," breathed Jack. What did he have to lose? He whipped open his palm to reveal a tongue of fire and pointed. "Go long."

Laohu leaped into the air and Jack tossed the fireball, lighting the dragon's trail of vapor like a wick. With a mighty *whoosh*, the flame rocketed up to Laohu's jaws and flared from his nostrils. Molten platinum poured down behind the once coal-black eyes.

The flame!

The clockwork dragon wheeled for another attack, and Laohu ducked his golden head through a serpentine turn to face the oncoming threat.

Now, boy! Fight!

———·Chapter Thirty-Six·———

RED-ROBED LONG WUSHI FLOODED the yard, while others in blue robes ran out on the walls. Those in red dipped their hands into pouches as they ran, smothering the steel studs at their palms with globs of metallic gel. With the flick of a thumb, each struck a spark and hurled the resulting fireball at the clockwork dragon. It seemed they had developed a replacement for the lost telekinetic art of making fire.

Their target, however, beat the fireballs back with its giant blue-green wings.

The blue-robed warriors fired flaming arrows from the walls. A few stuck in the monster's joints, but did little to slow it down. Steel jaws clamped down onto an arrow stuck in its wing, snapping it in half. The creature turned on the soldiers below and sprayed them with flame.

The long wushi covered themselves with cloaks. Two caught fire. These quickly shed their burning garments and retreated. The others closed ranks to protect them.

Fight, boy! Fight!

Laohu glared at Jack with platinum eyes.

Knowing what the gold dragon wanted, Jack conjured a flame the size of a volleyball. With both hands he thrust it at the metal dragon.

The fire disintegrated in flight. The enemy, occupied with its assault on the long wushi, did not even notice.

Jack could almost hear the disappointed sigh in Laohu's next thought.

Weak.

The dragon coiled and launched himself at the clockwork dragon, shooting a jet of white-hot flame. At the last second he veered off and whipped the monster with a heavy flick of his tail, sending it tumbling sideways, its blue-green armor dented.

As the monster struggled to regain stability, a stream of water pelted the back of Jack's head. He turned to see

Xiaoquan hovering over the pond. The blue dragon snapped his jaws and wiggled his tail like a puppy waiting for a treat.

"You too, huh?" Jack formed a new fireball in his palm and tossed it sidearm over the water.

Xiaoquan made a bid for the ball and missed. The dragon behind him did not.

Biyu, lying on her favorite bridge, opened her great mouth and swallowed the fireball whole, the way she had swallowed the carp. Glistening emerald liquid replaced the black of her eyes. Her lavender scales brightened to a red. Her emerald-green swirls darkened to black. Biyu rose, curling over herself as if using the slow, coiling roll to climb through the air.

Xiaoquan let out a rasping whimper, wiggling his tail, still waiting for his treat.

"Right. Sorry." Jack conjured a small yellow-orange ball and lined up for a proper overhand pitch. This time the fireball flew straight.

Xiaoquan caught it with a backward flip and dropped into the pond.

Jack waited for him to shoot skyward, trailing a glorious fountain of water.

Nothing.

"Okay . . . ," Jack said out loud.

"Lucky Jack!"

He heard a deep voice booming behind him. In Jack's tracker brain, he could see the air breaking before the huge metal wings. He saw the blue-gold spikes of fire, and dove to his left.

The clockwork dragon pulled up for another attack. "Jack!"

Jack rolled to his feet. It had an extremely limited vocabulary.

Laohu rocketed toward his metal rival, but the monster was ready for him. A line of thrusters fired along the base of each wing, spitting blue flame. It hovered, using its wings as a shield, and swung a plated metal tail to smack Laohu into the trees. It turned toward Jack.

Across the grass, Biyu curled over herself, snaking through the air on her way to defend him, but she was too far away.

Red fire glowed behind the clockwork dragon's jaws.

Jack's dodge had put him on open ground, no cover in sight. Then the pond behind him began to boil. Steam rose. A liquid hill formed at the center, and a big fat dragon broke the surface. Great wings, light blue at the roots fading to pure white at the tips, surged out of the water and thrust downward with one giant beat. In the new dragon's pale blue eyes, Jack recognized a mischievous smile.

"Xiaoquan?"

The enemy bore down from above. Adrenaline fueled the next fireball, a miniature sun glowing blue-white in Jack's hands. He pushed it away with all his might, and hit his target square.

The flash did little damage, but it surprised the monster, granting the other dragons time for a coordinated attack. Xiaoquan let out a billowing jet of steam that shot him backward like a deflating balloon.

The clockwork dragon backed out of the cloud, roaring in confusion, red eyes fogged over.

Biyu came next. She curled into a perfect circle, opened wide, and spewed lava all over the creature's left wing thrusters. The lava solidified into stone. It occurred to Jack that these dragons did not breathe fire, but the fire he gave them had activated the elements within.

Yes! Fight!

Laohu's unmistakable thoughts rumbled in Jack's head. A golden flash exploded from the treetops. A blast of white fire and the whip of a powerful tail sent the clockwork dragon spiraling to the grass.

"Yeah!" Gwen cheered from the top of the wall. "You should have stayed dead!"

Jack's world suddenly darkened. All sight and sound grew distant.

You should have stayed dead. Gwen had not spoken those words in the vault. But she had said them a dozen times before—in Jack's nightmares.

This was the moment.

Arrows flew from the battlements. Green-robed long wushi rushed out from the alcoves and converged on the beast, throwing chain-mail nets.

An ugly metallic *creak* brought Jack's senses back to full reception, and he saw the clockwork dragon slowly turning its jointed neck to look Gwen's way. The fog covering its eyes had cleared. The lava stone clogging its thrusters cracked. Chips of black rock fell to the grass.

"Gwen, get out of there!"

The shouting army of long wushi drowned out Jack's call. Just as in the dream, Gwen couldn't hear him. And just as in the dream, he couldn't reach her. Metal nets ripped and dropped away. The clockwork dragon's wings spread wide and free.

The thrusters flashed bright blue, blowing off the

remainder of Biyu's lava stone, and the monster soared over the wall, snatching Gwen with its talons as it passed.

Jack reached out with a flaming hand. "Gwen!"

The spires of the strange pillar-mountains rang with thunderous laughter. "Lucky Jack, come and save her if you dare!"

———— · Chapter Thirty-Seven · ————

JACK STARED AFTER HIS friend for the longest time, until a resounding *boom* erupted behind him. He turned to see a massive plume of black smoke rising from the well. Great, shadowy wings beat within. Laohu plunged into the smoke to follow. So did Biyu.

Only Xiaoquan remained. The formerly small dragon, now a giant sky-blue balloon animal, struggled to control his flight. One wing flapped wildly as he rolled upside down. He settled and let his head loll back to look at Jack as if to ask, *You coming?*

The other dragons had gone the wrong way. Jack pointed after the clockwork creature that had taken Gwen. "I have to go after her. I have to save her."

Xiaoquan seemed to accept this. The steam dragon flapped the opposite wing to right himself, wobbled his way through an about-face, and undulated off after the rest.

Long wushi surrounded the remaining dragons. Others rushed in with stretchers for the wounded. Fire burned in the trees. As Jack surveyed the aftermath, a few small fingers gently pressed their way into his clenched fist.

"I'm sorry." Sadie stood beside him, a little island of flower prints and sparkly lavender amid the blowing embers and acrid smoke.

"You can't be down here. It's not safe." But Jack did not let go of her hand.

"'Then matron dies. Then maiden flies.'" Sadie's voice felt distant, both in his ears and in his brain.

"What did you say?"

"'Then matron dies. Then maiden flies.' Dad's poem. The Archivist and Gwen."

Before Jack could fully process the thought, Sadie turned his hand over and pressed a silk-wrapped sphere into his palm. "She dropped this on the wall."

Gwen. Always thinking ahead. Jack tucked the sphere away as Liu Fai came walking up the dragonite path. He looked haggard, face marred with soot.

The emissary pointed at Jack. *"You.* Our well is destroyed. Half our dragons have fled. My father is furious. It is all your fault. *You* are the reason the clockwork dragon returned, aren't you? It saw you in the vault. It called your name."

Jack did not deny it. "And when it couldn't get past the real dragons, it took Gwen instead."

"Correct. So now Gall has the fan, the key, and a hostage who knows how to use them. He has everything he needs to make a sphere of his own."

"And once he does . . . ," said Sadie, resting her head against her brother's arm.

Jack swallowed back the lump in his throat. "He won't need Gwen anymore." He had failed to stop the nightmare. "We need to find her before it's too late. I should apologize to your dad, ask for his help."

"No," said Liu Fai, tapping frost-tipped fingers against his leg. *"I* will deal with my father. In the meantime, gather your things. Meet me at the delivery gate below the cafeteria."

Jack was too numb to argue. He and Sadie did as Liu Fai commanded, and barely fifteen minutes passed before the emissary had pulled up to the meeting point, driving a boxy off-road vehicle.

"Get in."

Liu Fai worked the gears like a pro, powering the jeep out of the high-mountain valley and down the ridge, never saying a word.

"Um," said Jack when the glaring silence began to eat at him. "It's kind of cool that your dad let us take this jeep . . . I guess." He'd been expecting a bit more.

"He didn't."

The answer had come from the back seat. Sadie yawned, pressing her fingertips upward into the gray-green morning filtering down through the trees. "His dad doesn't know we're gone."

Knowing his sister's Merlinian tendencies, Jack accepted the accusation as fact. "You stole a jeep?" He stared at Liu Fai. "What happened to asking your dad for help? We should be setting off to rescue Gwen with an army of long wushi instead of fleeing the scene in a half-rate rust bucket." He folded his arms and flopped back against his seat. "You should have let me do it."

Liu Fai slammed on the brakes, nearly planting Jack's face in the dashboard. A layer of ice formed on the steering wheel. "Oh yes. You would love that—the great Jack Buckles and Liu Hei, Minister of Dragons, fighting side by side. Well, I have news for you. My father *might* send one or two long wushi after the metal dragon, but you and your sister were never going to leave that compound again. I had to act fast to get us out of there."

"What are you talking about?" Had Jack managed to make his family the target of another secret ministry? "I mean, I know your dad was angry, but—"

"Angry?" Liu Fai threw his hands in the air. "You called fireballs out of thin air. A squadron of dragons obeyed your commands—"

Jack wiggled his hands. "That part was sort of the other way around."

"All while *I* stood by and did nothing." Liu Fai let out a sardonic laugh. "My father is not angry with you, Jack. He thinks fate has brought him the son I should have been. He wants to adopt you, by force if necessary."

A horrible silence followed. Liu Fai stared out the dusty windshield, while Jack drowned in a black mire of pure, unadulterated awkward. How was he supposed to respond to *that* bombshell?

Finally, Liu Fai laughed and muttered, "He'll probably marry you to one of my sisters, just to make it official. The younger one is eighteen." He cocked his head to look at Jack. "How do you feel about older women?"

"I . . ." Jack tried to swallow the golf ball in his throat.

"He's spoken for," said Sadie from the back seat.

Both boys twisted in their seats to look at her.

"What? Neither of them will admit it, but it's true."

"You know what?" Liu Fai pointed through the cracked plastic windshield toward the intersection ahead. "Get. Out. Take a left. In a half mile you'll find a bus station. You can save Gwen without me. Good luck."

Jack pushed open his door. "Okay. We will."

"Fine."

Child of fire and child of ice
Must join to win the maiden's life.

The lines of his dad's poem bloomed in Jack's mind like Xiaoquan's steam. He glanced over his shoulder at Sadie. Had she done that?

She scrunched up her eyes in confusion. Maybe she hadn't.

"We can't leave you," said Jack, closing the door.

Liu Fai dropped his head into his hands, which worried Jack. As stressed as he looked, the telekinetic-human-ice-box might give himself a deadly case of brain freeze. "And why not?"

There were only a few moments in history where anyone had the opportunity to whip out the mother of all answers to the question *Why?* Jack did not miss his chance.

"The prophecy."

Liu Fai cut the engine, making the jeep lurch. "What prophecy?"

"It's more of a poem, really," said Sadie, leaning forward.

Jack pressed her back again. "You're not helping." He looked past Liu Fai at the dwindling sunlight filtering through the trees. They were running out of time. "The poem we told you about in the vault. It turns out some of the lines are predictive. One line predicted the attack on the well. Another predicted the Archivist would die and that Gwen would be carried away."

"'Then matron dies. Then maiden flies.'" Sadie recited the lines from the back seat like a creepy Greek chorus in an elementary school play.

Jack gave his sister a *please-stop-talking* frown, then returned his gaze to Liu Fai. "The poem implies that you and I need to work together to save Gwen."

Sadie did the Greek chorus thing again. "'Child of fire and child of ice must join to win the maiden's life.'"

"Stop it," Jack growled through the side of his mouth. "You're weirding him out."

"Yes." Liu Fai rolled his eyes. "*She's* the one weirding me out."

Jack ignored the implication. "Well? Will you help us?"

"Child of fire. Child of ice." Liu Fai looked down at his palms, and blue-white crystals formed along the creases. "All right. I'm in. What else does the poem say?"

Sadie obeyed Jack's request to quit reciting the poem out loud, but he heard her whispering in his brain. *Then mountain hermit guides your eyes.*

That didn't sound likely at all.

"Do you . . . happen to know any mountain hermits?"

The question seemed to catch Liu Fai off guard. "No, I do not. But I know where one lives."

Liu Fai took a left at the intersection, and Jack noted with some ire that the bus station was a good deal farther along than a half mile.

"The hermit is well known to the long wushi." The emissary fought the wheel to keep the jeep straight on the washboard road. "We have shared this mountain valley for centuries."

Sadie pulled herself forward, a hand on each of the boys' seats. "So the hermit is—"

"Immortal, according to local legend." Liu Fai frowned at the road and then glanced over at Jack. "If one believes such bedtime stories, then it would seem the hermit has already acquired that which Gall desires most."

— · Chapter Thirty-Eight · —

LAKES, TREES, AND HILLS beyond count passed beneath Gwen, and all the while she pounded at the blue-green underbelly of the clockwork dragon. "Put me down, you mechanized monstrosity!"

The creature had her by the shoulders, talons stabbing through her coat and sweater. Gwen channeled the pain into anger and insults. "Set me down and face me like a real . . . whatever you are. I think you're a chicken. Yes, you're a great big clockwork chicken!"

To Gwen's surprise, the chicken bit achieved a result. The dragon tucked its wings and dove for the earth, picking up speed. Perhaps she'd gone too far.

With the sun half set, deep shadows shrouded the hillsides.

The dragon aimed for one of these shadows, as if it intended to smash them both to bits.

"I didn't mean it. You're not a chicken. And even if you are, that's no reason to become suicidal." The hillside rushed to meet them. Gwen threw her arms in front of her face, preparing for impact.

There was no impact.

She peeked over her arm with one eye, and found they were soaring through a cave. No. A tunnel. An instant later they flew out into a forest of tall pines.

The dragon flared its wings, and with a burst from its thrusters it slowed—just enough to drop Gwen and send her tumbling through the underbrush. She came to rest at a bend in a gurgling stream, one leg and one arm hoisted up in thorny vines in the most undignified manner.

The dragon laughed.

Gwen untangled herself from the vines, tearing her tights and cutting her leg in the process. One hand went to her scarf. "You're going to pay for that." But as she turned for the showdown, she noticed a man in a black cloak, standing in the bushes only a few feet away.

Ignatius Gall held a wooden book open in his palm—the missing journal of the Qin grand astronomer. He laid a red silk bookmark down the center to mark his place, closed the book with a *snap*, and scowled at the dragon, clockwork monocle twitching. "I told you to bring me the boy, not this bedraggled, insignificant creature."

"Insignificant?" asked Gwen. She couldn't argue with bedraggled, not after her fight with the brambles.

Gall ignored her. He picked up a lantern and approached the dragon, examining a dent in its side. "You ran into trouble."

The dragon growled, "*Long . . . woosh.*"

"The long wushi." Gall emphasized the *ee* sound the dragon had missed, like a teacher correcting a student. He touched the dent, running his fingers over the rippling imprint left by Laohu's armored scales. "Their pets, as well. Interesting." He straightened, shifting his gaze to Gwen. She hated the way his one good eye drifted from her head to her toes and back again. "You could not get to Mr. Buckles, so you brought me a hostage."

"Boy . . . cares," growled the dragon.

"True. And he confides in her. So perhaps she is not so insignificant after all." He opened the book again and stomped through the bushes to the edge of the stream, wiggling his fingers in the air. "Keep an eye on her. I'm busy."

Gall entered a strange routine of raising the lamp to the trees and lowering it to the overgrowth, consulting the wooden text and mumbling to himself, sometimes in English but more often in Chinese. He acted as if Gwen were not there, a misjudgment she would make him suffer for. Soon.

Keeping one eye on the dragon, Gwen slipped a hand into the left pocket of her coat. The object she desired, a long-handled electric torch, brushed against her fingers.

Uncle Percy had taught Gwen the proper way to ball up a fist while she was still in her pram—a child-rearing choice that had brought her mother no end of grief during Gwen's nursery school days. Percy had given her some kind of combat lesson nearly every day of her early life. At the ministry, Ash had refined her skills. Gwen knew how to fight.

But she needed to pick her moment.

The bend in the river had carved out a wide cove where the water pooled in dark, lazy eddies. Gall reached its shore and let out a victorious "Aha!" He set the lantern down and parted the overgrowth with a telekinetic wave, uncovering weathered stone blocks. Perhaps the cove was not as natural as it seemed. Intrigued, Gwen followed.

At her first step, the clockwork dragon rumbled.

"Oh, hush it," she said. "I want to see. That's all."

Gall followed the shoreline to a thick, scraggly bush, and without warning slung a green fireball from his clockwork arm.

Gwen gasped. She had learned about his pyrokinetic skills from Jack's description of the spark at Paracelsus's alpine cave, but she had never seen them in action.

The bush burned to cinders in a few crackling seconds. Gall blasted the remains away with a telekinetic push to reveal a small statue with the face of a tiger, the antlers of a deer, and ruby eyes. "A *qilin*," said the spook. "One of China's most ancient creatures. This one has waited here for millennia, ready to judge the wicked that cross its path."

Gwen snorted. "Then perhaps you should leave it alone."

Beneath its left hoof, the *qilin* held a faceted blue jewel the size of a softball. Gall brushed away the last few ashes and gripped it with his prosthetic hand, grunting with effort.

"Seriously, I wouldn't . . . ," warned Gwen.

But, as it turned out, Gall was not trying to dislodge the stone. After a short battle, it turned in place. He stood back, looking expectantly at the cove.

A *thunk* sounded from the stream, followed by the ratcheting of chains. A mossy wall split the water's surface, separating the cove from the main flow of the stream. The water inside drained away.

Gall grinned at Gwen. "It would seem I passed." He retrieved his lantern and stepped down onto an uneven, rocky stair, wide enough for even his clockwork dragon to descend. "And now the *qilin* has offered me a reward."

A putrid smell of worms and rotting plant life filled Gwen's nostrils. She watched the poor fish flopping on the steps, slowly dying. "I'm not so sure you can call that a reward."

Gall slipped his book into a leather bag at his side and pointed at the dragon. "You, stay here. Keep watch until I call for you." Then he looked at Gwen and his voice deepened. "You, come with me."

Gwen heard the voice echo in her head, and part of her knew that Gall was using his telepathic prowess to command her. She did not resist. She did not want to. If following Gall into that stinking, watery pit meant separating him from his clockwork henchman—evening the odds—Gwen was all in.

"Right. Where are we going?" she asked as the two stepped down from the stair into a long passage. Their only light was the lantern, which Gall held aloft so that its glow would reach the tunnel's high ceiling.

He made no answer. Gwen understood. She was not a person to him. She was a tool like the book in his satchel or the lantern in his hand. Gall would only acknowledge her existence when the time came to use her for some evil purpose.

She would not give him that chance.

Gwen waited until they were well out of shouting distance from the surface and then whipped the scarf from her neck, raising her big steel torch like a war hammer. "Yaa!"

The scarf froze in midair, curled for a snap that would never be.

"What on—?" She tugged with all her might, but the scarf hung there, as rigid as iron. "All right, then. Plan B." She chucked the torch at his shiny bald head.

The spook let go of the lantern, which remained where it was, hovering above him, and caught Gwen's weapon in his clockwork hand. He brought the torch around to his eyes, examined it with mild interest, and crushed the steel shaft like a soda can.

"How unfortunate," he said, turning and letting the torch fall to the dirt with a disappointed *thud*. "It will be *so* much work dragging your lifeless body the rest of the way."

Gwen's scarf recoiled on its own and wrapped around her neck, one end stretching to the ceiling to lift her off her feet. She clawed at the wool and finally grabbed the vertical portion to ease the pressure on her throat.

The floating lantern followed Gall as he approached. He gestured at the empty black walls within the circle of its light. "I intended to wait for comfortable surroundings, with a nice chair for you to sit in, some soft leather straps to hold you down." He sighed. "But you, my dear, like the rest of your generation, lack patience."

Gwen strained for every minuscule breath, arms aching, toes scratching at the floor. She tried to tell Gall what he could do with his leather straps, but all that came out was a quiet "*Ahhhgggg.*"

He nodded. "Yes. I know. You have . . . mixed feelings about me." His good hand lit up with white fire, and he reached for her head. "Yet you *will* tell me everything you and Mr. Buckles know about the Qin artifacts. And then you will be bait. You will lure your friend Jack to his ultimate demise."

The flaming white fingers touched Gwen's forehead. She felt them penetrate into her brain, bringing Gall's voice with them, a hundred questions all at once. Her hands slipped free of the scarf, letting her neck take her body's weight. The noose tightened. Her vision grayed.

"That's right," said Gall in a soothing tone. "It is time to give in."

But Gwen had no intention of giving in. While Gall remained focused on probing her mind, she lowered one hand to her pocket, stretching her fingers until they brushed against Spec's pillbox. As the gray in her eyes became darkness, she flipped open the catch.

Chapter Thirty-Nine

JACK GLARED AT LIU Fai. "Why have we stopped?"

The emissary had traded the discomfort of the washboard road for the unbearable slowness of a steep, rocky jeep trail, and they had climbed for nearly an hour. Now, in a clearing of red dirt and wild grass, they had come to a complete halt.

Liu Fai killed the engine. "The path to the hermit's dwelling is too rough and overgrown for a motor vehicle." He kicked open his door. "From here, we walk."

While Jack paced, Liu Fai lifted backpacks, bedrolls, and cooking utensils out of the jeep and piled everything against a tree. Jack expected him to secure the bedrolls for hiking. Instead, he dug out a dark wood cube. He studied its bronze inlays for a few seconds, then rotated a disk on one side until a little hatch popped open from the bottom. A tiny key dropped out into his palm.

Jack stopped his pacing. "A Chinese puzzle box."

"A 'Chinese puzzle box' is a figment of Western fancy, a souvenir for holding shiny trinkets." Liu Fai turned the cube over, inserted the key into a slot, and gave it a twist. Tight rolls of gold silk emerged from hidden chambers on all four sides. "We have our mystery boxes in China, but if you are fortunate enough to get a peek inside, you will most often find a cricket."

This caught Sadie's attention. "Is there a cricket in that one?"

"No."

Liu Fai twisted the key the other way and a spike stuck out from what was now the bottom. The cube shook and rattled in his hand. He planted it in the dirt, and the top half shot skyward on a telescoping pole, dragging the silk with it. The fabric wavered. With a sharp *whoomp*, it snapped out into the taut sides of a rectangular pyramid.

"A tent?" asked Jack, dropping his hands. "You're making camp? What about Gwen?"

"It is growing dark." Liu Fai returned to the pile of gear and picked up a bedroll. "The climb will take another half day"—he glanced at Sadie—"assuming your sister can keep up."

Sadie looked down at her toes, clearly upset by the implication that she was dead weight.

The trailhead had already begun to disappear in the fading light. Liu Fai gestured with the bedroll. "If we attempt that path in the dark, we *will* get lost. And we will spend the next week finding our way down." He brushed past Jack and tossed the bedroll through the tent flap. "Sometimes the fastest route is no route at all."

"How quaint. Did your dad teach you that?" Jack regretted the jab the moment it left his lips, but he was angry about pausing Gwen's rescue.

Liu Fai's expression darkened. He ducked into the beautiful tent. "Yes. He did."

Once the bedrolls were all set up, Liu Fai built a fire, spreading some of that long wushi fire-goo on the wood, but he could not find any matches in the backpacks. With a wince and flop of a frosty hand, he motioned for Jack to take care of it.

Jack struggled to comply. Without the adrenaline-pumping threat of getting fricasseed by a crazy metal dragon, he found it hard to make fire. After several disappointing sparks, he generated a flicker barely worthy of a candle and dropped it onto the pile of wood.

They ate a porridge of barley and dried meat rations and watched the crackling fire like a family watching late-night TV. The shifting colors, the dance of the flames and smoke, had its own music in Jack's crisscrossed senses.

"Jack?" asked Liu Fai, breaking the trance.

"Yeah, Frosty?"

"Please don't call me that."

"Right. Sorry."

A short pause.

A sigh. "Did your father's poem say anything else about me?"

Jack hadn't seen that question coming. He let the lines float through his brain, avoiding the one about Gwen and the Archivist. "Not really. Why?"

"No reason. Forget it."

Jack turned back to the fire, then cocked his head. "You know what? The poem *might* mention the three of us together." He recited the lines.

"Fear not boys, the girl who sees

Will save you from the ghostly thief."

"The ghostly thief." Liu Fai echoed the last line. "What does that mean?"

"I can't be sure, but there is this girl who called herself—"

The fire guttered. A flash of shadow knocked Liu Fai off his log. Rough hands grabbed Jack's jacket, and a concussion wave blasted through his gut. His back slammed against a tree twenty feet from the fire.

Teleportation. Violent, unnatural teleportation.

Jack grunted out the last of his answer. "Raven."

She held him against the tree, her face half shrouded by a hood. "I told you before, Jack. Call me Ghost."

—— · Chapter Forty · ——

"WHERE IS IT?" GHOST, as she preferred to be called, shook Jack, pressing him up against the tree. Her beauty, drawn from her Indian mother, had not waned since he last saw her, but it had hardened. On the left side of her face, she still bore the scars from the bomb that had killed her brother—ordered by Gall and planted by Tanner in a Moscow hyperloop station.

A ball of ice exploded against the tree, showering them both with snow. "Let him go!" Liu Fai held both hands straight out, the heels of his palms pressed together.

Ghost glanced at him and smiled.

Another blast wave punched through Jack's gut. Another

tree slammed into his back, and suddenly he was on the opposite edge of the fire's light.

Ghost pressed a hand into the left pocket of Jack's coat, digging around. "I asked you a question, yeah? Where is it?" Her eyes were sunken, the whites shocked with red. There was a time when Jack had been mesmerized by the purple of her irises, but her pupils were so wide he could hardly see them. In her left hand, she clutched a device shaped like a stopwatch—the Einstein-Rosen Bridge. Gall had gifted it to Ghost and her brother to help them frame Jack for multiple jewel heists. Back then, she had gone by the name Raven, and she'd smiled a lot more.

"I knew you were following me," said Jack. "You were in the square in Chinatown, and you caused that avalanche in the Alps."

"That was an accident. This isn't."

Zzap.

She slammed Jack against another tree. "I need that sphere, Jack."

Beyond the thief, Sadie quietly got up and wandered off into the trees. Where did she think she was going? Liu Fai moved as well, lining up another shot, but Jack waved him off. He narrowed his eyes at Ghost. "Why? You working for Gall again? The man who murdered your brother?"

"He wants the Mind. I can use it to get close to him."

"So you can kill him."

Ghost said nothing.

Jack frowned. "No. That's not how we're taking him down."

"Oh, Jack . . ." Ghost softened her expression and leaned close, pressing her cheek to his. Her lips were at his ear. "Do you really believe I care what you think?"

When she pulled back, Ghost was holding the Mind. She had slipped a hand into his other pocket, and Jack hadn't felt it despite the power of his senses. She winked. "Be seeing you, yeah?"

Zzap. She was gone, leaving nothing behind but a stir of red dust.

An instant later, Jack heard his sister's voice from the trees. "I'll take those, thank you."

Sadie came running into the firelight holding the Mind and the Bridge with Ghost at her heels. She had predicted the spot Ghost would jump to, the way she'd predicted the flight path of the artifacts their dad had chucked across his bedroom. And she had stolen them from the thief.

Fear not boys, the girl who sees
Will save you from the ghostly thief.

So that was another part of the riddle answered.

Sadie had a good lead, but Ghost was faster. The thief's hand, bent like a claw, got within inches of her shoulder.

"Look out!" Liu Fai fired a stream of frost at Ghost's legs, and she tumbled, missing the fire circle by inches.

"Oooh!" Ghost growled at Sadie, pushing herself up. "I'll tear you apart, yeah? You—"

A spout of flame torched the grass between them.

Sadie giggled—*giggled*—which kind of messed with Jack's perception of the whole situation. But then Laohu settled to the ground beside him.

Fire ready.

Good.

Watch thief.

Glancing down, Jack saw that he'd conjured up a blue-white ball. Far from the struggle he had faced trying to light a simple campfire, this flame had arisen on instinct.

Biyu coiled her tail protectively around Sadie, floppy feet hovering above the grass. The tips of her carplike whiskers floated a millimeter from Ghost's chin. She growled.

Ghost let out a tiny whimper, fist rapidly clenching and unclenching, trying to activate a wormhole device that wasn't there.

"How—?" Liu Fai was too stunned to finish the question.

"The dragons?" asked Sadie. "I called them, you know, with my thoughts. Well, I called Biyu. I didn't want to slow you down, and I thought she could help me up the mountain." She patted the dragon's red scales. "Looks like she brought some friends."

On cue, Xiaoquan floated down into the clearing, still in his oversize balloon-animal form. Two geysers of steam erupted from his nostrils, pale blue eyes smiling at Jack. A fourth dragon descended beside him, one that might easily have been mistaken for a tree after a forest fire. Her scales were like blackened bark, with an orange glow in the fissures between. She roared to announce her arrival, unleashing a windstorm of smoke and burning embers.

"The tree dragon?" asked Jack, shielding his face from the heat.

"Yes," said Liu Fai. "With her fires lit. It seems Laohu shared his good fortune. We call her Meilin."

"Uh. Jack? A little help, yeah?" Ghost could not tear her gaze from the dragon staring her down. A red glow flickered behind Biyu's fangs. "Give me the sphere and the Bridge, and I'll leave. You'll never see me again, yeah? Please, I have to avenge my brother."

Jack shook his head. "No way."

Biyu withdrew and Ghost backed away. Her hood had fallen, and in the firelight she looked so much like the ghost she wanted to become. Her jet-black hair, once streaked with red, was now tipped with white. Her neck had thinned so much that her jawline and collarbone threatened to break through her skin. The Bridge had not been kind.

Not so long ago, the Mind of Paracelsus had done much the same to Jack. "Come with us," he said. "Bring Gall down the *right* way. He took Gwen, Ghost. I'll bet you know where."

Whatever Ghost said in answer was drowned out by another roar, so much louder and deeper than the tree dragon's.

Jack's tracker senses snapped the world into slow motion. A shower of dark blue flame, peppered with stars, obliterated a grove of trees, and the massive dragon from the long wushi well dropped into the empty space that remained, shiny black claws pounding deep into the soil.

The other dragons lowered their heads and backed away. Ghost fled into the trees—scarpered, as Gwen would say.

With a twisting, sideways motion of her neck, the dragon brought her head down to Jack's level, scales reflecting the firelight in the darkest purple. Her eyes were no longer coal black. They were as deep blue and starry as a mountain sky at midnight.

A whisper from Liu Fai found its way to Jack's ears. "Run, Jack. Run now."

———· Chapter Forty-One ·———

JACK DID NOT RUN—NOT because he was brave or anything. His legs wouldn't move. The trees that had been there a moment before had not been simply destroyed—broken to pieces or reduced to ash. They had been removed from existence, along with the sod and their roots. A dark blue glow lit the scales at the dragon's throat. The heat of her breath threatened to cook Jack where he stood. And then a powerful thought shook his brain.

Friends.

The force of the word almost knocked him over. The blue glow at the dragon's throat subsided, and she raised her head to look into the clearing, right at Sadie.

Friends. We're all friends. Sadie paced forward. Biyu tried to corral her, but Sadie pressed her back with a wave—eyes never leaving the obsidian dragon, thoughts pounding the very air. *Friends. Yes?* She walked past her brother, and the dragon lowered her head, letting Sadie rest a hand on her muzzle. *That's right. Friends. All friends.*

Giant dragon and little girl remained motionless together for some time, until the creature lifted her head, let out a deep, crackling bark, and leaped into the night sky.

Sadie's hair was still blowing in the rush of the dragon's wings when Jack lifted her out of the dirt. He rushed her back to the fire. "What were you *thinking?*"

"She needed a friend," said Sadie, giving him one of her *matter-of-fact* smiles.

Liu Fai looked from one to the other. "Your family has issues."

"All families have issues," countered Jack.

"Not like these."

They settled down as best they could for the remainder of the night. Ghost had fled, but she would not have gone far. Fortunately, they now had dragons to guard the camp. All four either paced or hovered at the perimeter. Restless.

There were only two bedrolls. Jack gave his to Sadie. The

dirt beneath the silk was soft enough, anyway. He pushed himself up on an elbow to look over at Liu Fai. "So . . . What *was* that thing?"

"The big dragon?"

"Was there some other big scary thing?" Jack settled back and looked up at the black silk of the tent, decorated with creatures that bore a strong resemblance to Laohu. "I know she was the dragon from the long wushi well, but do you have a name for her?"

"We call her *Nu Jiazhang*. You would say matriarch."

Matriarch. The name rolled around in Jack's mind as sleep took him. Did a second matriarch lie at the bottom of the Archive? Or was it something else?

The first light of dawn married Laohu's floating shadow to the golden dragons on the silk. *Floating dragon.* Jack sat up with a new idea. Sadie had used her Merlinian abilities to call for Biyu, asking for her help to get up the mountain. And like any thoughtful camper, Biyu had brought enough dragons for everyone. He glanced at Liu Fai, who was already rolling his blankets. "Hey."

Liu Fai pressed his eyebrows together, clearly suspicious of Jack's tone. "Hey."

"I have a new plan."

"Of course you do."

"To your knowledge," asked Jack, grinning despite Liu Fai's sarcasm, "has anyone ever *ridden* a dragon?"

—— · Chapter Forty-Two · ——

"YEAH!" JACK BENT DOWN to snatch a leaf from the forest canopy and let it flutter off behind him, whisking between Sadie and Liu Fai.

Since Jack had first fallen in with the Ministry of Trackers, he had experienced a few nontraditional forms of flight. He had flown a gaudy airship over the Russian tundra, hung on for dear life as a quantum electrodynamic drone whipped him across moonlit London, and rocketed out of a collapsing ruby mine on ankle thrusters. But dragon flying became an instant favorite.

Laohu's flight path had an undulating quality that matched his serpentine form, as smooth and powerful as an ocean wave. Jack could steer him with thought, though nothing so cumbersome as thinking *Go left*, or *Go right*. Jack looked where he wanted to go, and the dragon followed.

Most of the time.

This thought-steered dragon had a mind of its own. Occasionally, Laohu performed an uncommanded barrel roll or veered off course to chase Xiaoquan through a waterfall.

The others followed, with Sadie riding Biyu and Liu Fai on Meilin. Xiaoquan passed over and around them, carried in the trio's draft like a balloon in the wind. They had started slow, but Jack had quickly developed an eye for the cut of the mountain path—the gaps and depressions it caused in the green canopy.

An hour later they saw a large rock formation breaking through the trees.

"That's it," Liu Fai called, fishtailing on Meilin as he tried to bring her alongside Laohu. Liu Fai's flying was not as smooth, but he did not have the benefit of a thought connection. He pointed for half a second, then clutched at her flank to avoid sliding off. "Put down over there, in that clearing. Hermits are reclusive by nature. No need to make things worse by landing on the cave's doorstep with a squadron of dragons."

After a graceful touchdown, which Jack had nothing to do

with, Jack slid off Laohu and laid a hand on his neck. "Thank you."

Boy fat.

Lose weight.

"I . . . What?" Jack caught a hint of mirth behind Laohu's platinum eyes. His shock melted into a smile. "Hilarious."

"What's hilarious?" Liu Fai removed a canteen from his pack.

"Nothing. Never mind."

The emissary shrugged and brought the canteen to his lips. He coughed. "It's warm."

"I think that's because you've been riding on a fire-breathing dragon."

Liu Fai gave him an *I-was-just-about-to-get-there* look, then waggled the canteen at Jack, covering it in frost.

Xiaoquan floated over, drawn perhaps by the motion. He listed to one side in random balloon fashion, rear end rising toward the vertical, sniffed the canteen, and then playfully snapped his jaws.

Jack recognized the behavior. "He did the same thing during the fight. He wanted fire."

"You want fire?" Liu Fai pointed at Jack. "Talk to him. I can't help you."

"That's not it," said Sadie. She pointed at the canteen. "I think he likes the frost. Try giving him some ice."

Liu Fai looked skeptical, but he pressed his hands together to form an ice ball and tossed it at the dragon.

Xiaoquan snatched the little sphere out of the air, but there wasn't much to it. He brought his tail end back to the horizontal and let out an exasperated belch, smacking his lips.

Jack stifled a laugh. "Try again, something more substantial."

On the next attempt, Liu Fai produced a ball large enough to fool an umpire at Yankee Stadium. The steam dragon gulped it down.

Xiaoquan's balloonish form narrowed. The pallor of his light blue scales darkened.

"Whoa," said Jack, walking over. "Hit him again."

Liu Fai tossed three more in quick succession, and Xiaoquan snapped them all up. A gurgle rumbled deep inside the dragon's belly. A moment later, he spewed out a flood of cold water, straight into Jack's face.

"H-hey! Watch it!" Jack rubbed the water out of his eyes, and drew a breath at what he saw.

Xiaoquan had deflated to his small, serpentine self, royal blue and rolling through the air in triumph.

Sadie grabbed the hem of her brother's shirt and pulled it

away from his chest, wringing it out. "Liu Fai's ice doused his fire."

Biyu and the tree dragon lined up next, like kids at an ice-cream truck.

Jack liked the tree dragon's transformation the best. Meilin only needed a single ice ball. The orange glow behind her charred black scales dimmed, and her flanks returned to a rich, dark bronze. She curled up in the low branches of a nearby oak, and as her eyelids drooped to closed, green scales sprouted all over her spine and legs, making her nearly invisible. Biyu, scales lightening to their original color, nestled in among a pile of boulders, disappearing as well.

Laohu, however, turned up his golden nose. He looked Jack's way.

Fire.

Mine.

"All right," said Jack, raising his hands. "Keep your fire." He would have said, *Chill out,* but he did not think Laohu would find it amusing. The treasure dragon shot up through the canopy.

"They need you, Liu Fai," observed Sadie, watching the leaves fall in Laohu's wake.

The frost faded from Liu Fai's fingers. "I would not go that far."

"No," said Jack. "She's right. The dragos and the long wushi are both obsessed with fire, and they both act as little more than dogcatchers for dragons, even if they go about it in different ways." He fixed his gaze on Liu Fai. "But look what you and I have accomplished in a couple of days. Maybe the relationship between man and dragon works best with fire *and* ice. Maybe that's how it's meant to be."

Liu Fai snorted. "Tell that to my father."

Jack answered with a single nod. "I will."

A short hike up the trail brought them to a narrow rock crevice, unadorned and unimpressive. But once they squeezed through, they found a cavernous chamber of stone and moss filled with the *drip, drip* of mountain runoff.

And that was only the foyer.

A stone bridge took them within inches of a waterfall, pouring down from high above and evaporating far below, then out into open air. There, the bridge became wood, a seamless joining into the roots and limbs of gnarled trees growing at steep angles in a cylindrical chasm.

Jack found it all quite beautiful, but he could not suppress a growing sense of unease. The place might have been empty for years. An arch carved into the chasm wall brought them into yet another cave, with thick columns of tangled roots descending from the ceiling. Shelves, benches, and tables were carved from the rock walls and floor. This one, at least, was furnished. But there were still no signs of recent activity.

Jack rapped Liu Fai on the arm. "There is an actual *mountain hermit* in your mountain hermit cave, right?"

"I made no guarantees." Hands clasped behind him, Liu Fai bent to examine a dusty line of glass containers on a stone table that surrounded one of the root columns. "The hermit lives in the mountain, but she is no prisoner. Perhaps she is out."

"*She?*" Jack could not mask his surprise.

"Yes. She," said a soft voice. A woman in a long silk robe appeared on the other side of the chamber, holding a watering can as if her guests had caught her tending to her plants.

———· Chapter Forty-Three ·———

"YOU COME SEEKING WISDOM." The woman tilted the can, letting water spill down a bundle of vines. White flowers bloomed wherever the droplets came to rest. "And in your mind, wisdom is an old man with drooping whiskers and a long wispy beard, rather than a woman. Is that why your eyes did not find me?"

Sadie turned on her brother. "Yeah, Jack. Is that why?"

"I . . . Uh . . . I mean . . ." He couldn't finish.

Their host set the can on a shelf carved from the rock, among beakers, texts, and scrolls. "Be at ease. I am not offended. Your arrival brings good fortune." She looked past Jack, toward the entrance, and he followed her gaze in time to see Xiaoquan poke his blue nose into view. The little dragon had followed them. From the water beading on his scales, Jack guessed he had stopped along the way to play in the waterfall. The woman stretched out a hand. "Come in, please, and show yourself, if that is what you desire."

Xiaoquan needed no other invitation. He zipped into the room, did a figure eight around two of the root columns, and spiraled around the hermit from her ankles up to her neck, finally wrapping his tail around her waist and settling his chin on her shoulder.

"He likes you," said Sadie.

The hermit nodded, earning a mirroring nod from Xiaoquan. "I believe he does. You may call me Dailan. I am pleased to meet you." She gestured at a circle of small boulders surrounding a cold fire pit. "Please. Sit down. Let us share some tea."

It took the hermit only a moment to size up Jack and Liu Fai, with the dragon at her shoulder matching her discerning smile, tail scratching his chin. She motioned to Jack, and he knew what she wanted, but without the adrenaline of an attacking thief or monster, he struggled to produce fire. After a few embarrassing sparks, he struck a flame, igniting the coals.

Dailan raised a kettle up to Xiaoquan. "If you wouldn't

mind?" He obliged her with a long stream of water, and she hung the kettle over the fire. "Very good. You have spared me a walk."

"Um . . . ," said Jack, eyeing the kettle of dragon spit. Sadie bumped his knee to shut him up.

"Now." Dailan balanced a tray of bowls and pitchers on the edge of the fire pit. "Tell me your tale."

Jack held nothing back. And all the while, Dailan brewed the tea, a graceful shell game of pouring, collecting, and re-pouring with the many bowls and pitchers. "So this Gall of yours seeks immortality?" she asked. "An ancient quest, to be sure, and perhaps the most selfish."

"Selfish?" Sadie's eyes tracked the hermit's every elegant move.

"Oh yes. As many quests are." Dailan passed around the smallest of the bowls. "Each life begins as a pitcher of the finest tea, sometimes bitter, sometimes sweet, with many bowls to fill." She set the last bowl beside her own knee and tipped the largest pitcher, pouring out the glittering tea. "If we pour too much into our own quests"—the tea began to overflow, sizzling and spitting on the coals—"how much will remain for those we love?"

Much to Jack's chagrin, the hermit saved enough for them

all to have a full bowl. Sadie pinched the back of his calf and he forced a smile, raising his bowl of brewed dragon spit. "You said the search for immortality is selfish, but aren't you . . ." Jack let the question trail off as he took a sip. He could taste hibiscus, jasmine, and fish—maybe salamander.

"Immortal?" Dailan's eyes laughed, much like Xiaoquan's. "The men and women of my family are long-lived, some surviving for two centuries or more. This has given rise to a legend, but rest assured, I am as mortal as you. We must all leave this sphere eventually."

"The First Emperor did not believe so," argued Liu Fai, sipping his dragon-spit-hibiscus-salamander tea. "And neither does Gall."

Dailan set her bowl down and sighed, and Xiaoquan sighed with her, chin flopping on her shoulder. "In that folly, he has killed one of your friends, and taken another."

At the mention of Gwen, Jack pushed his tea aside. No more delays. No more discussion. "You can help us get her back. You can 'guide our eyes.'"

"How your father discerned this, I cannot tell." Dailan said something in Chinese and Xiaoquan left her shoulder, curling up on a long boulder beside the fire. She crossed to the shelf where she had set the water can. "But he was right. I *can* help.

When you are lost, it is best to go back to the beginning. In this case, the beginning is the first stolen artifact."

"The journal of the Qin grand astronomer," said Liu Fai.

Dailan ran a finger along her books and scrolls. "Yes. Shi Lu. My ancestor. In his long years, he served both the Qin and Han dynasties, under multiple names and titles." Her finger came to rest on a hefty scroll made of long wooden rods with triangular cross sections. She drew it from the shelf, glancing at Liu Fai. "You may remember him as Sima Qian, the famous historian."

Jack left the fire to get a closer look. "How can you be sure Shi Lu's text, out of all the stolen artifacts, is so important to locating Gwen?"

"The answer you seek lies within the question. Shi Lu's text is the only stolen artifact that refers to a specific location. His many titles included royal architect, and he is famous for two incredible structures. The original Great Wall"—Dailan let the scroll fall open, and the flat sides of the triangular rods aligned into an etching of an underground palace—"and the First Emperor's tomb."

Chapter Forty-Four

JACK KNELT TO EXAMINE the etching. Shi Lu had drawn a cavern with rays of light shining down from the ceiling. The sprawling open palace below reminded him of China's Forbidden City. He let his fingers graze the ancient scroll. "You think the clockwork dragon took Gwen here?"

"All the clues you described point to the emperor's tomb."

The mountain hermit guides your eyes. His dad's poem had been tragically accurate so far. If it advised Jack to trust the hermit, he would not argue. And there was something else, another piece of the puzzle poem they had not solved. The etching rotated in Jack's vision, changing perspective. The narrow rays of light shining down on the palace became a constellation of stars. But the palace was underground, so they couldn't be real stars, and fake stars wouldn't move with the Earth's rotation.

Beneath the stars that never wheel. He almost spoke the line out loud.

With a little effort, Jack mentally reversed the etching, taking a bird's-eye view of the miniature peaks and valleys surrounding the palace plateau. "Are those rivers?"

"Of pure mercury," said Dailan.

Above the rivers made of steel. The etching in his mind's eye fell back into place on the wood. "That's it. We know where Gall is holding Gwen. Let's go."

"Wait," said Dailan. "There is more." With agonizingly slow and deliberate grace, she returned the tea set to its table and laid the scroll on the edge of the pit. She passed a hand along the slats, turning them all to display a new picture— rows of rigid soldiers, armed with crossbows. "There are good reasons that the emperor's tomb has never been unsealed."

With a rhythmic *clickety-clack* that poked at Jack's impatience, she turned the slats again. In the new etching, a stern-faced man raised a scepter over scores of bedraggled laborers. "A force of seven hundred thousand toiled for thirty-eight years to build the emperor's necropolis. Shi Lu picked the most ingenious among them to help him devise diabolical traps."

"If the complex is so dangerous," asked Liu Fai, "then how do you suppose Gall got in?"

"That, I suspect, is why he stole the book." Dailan scratched Xiaoquan behind the horns. "There are hundreds of bodies under that mound—concubines, ministers, engineers, and more. All were betrayed to keep the emperor's secrets, Shi Lu as well. But he designed a hidden escape route and recorded its secrets in a coded section of the text Gall stole."

"Why go to all that trouble?" asked Sadie, scooting closer so she could scratch the water dragon too. "What's down there that's so important?"

Dailan guided her hand to just the right spot, and Xiaoquan's back leg thumped the stone. "It is not what lies within the tomb that is so important. It is the tomb itself." With Sadie having taken over the job of pleasing Xiaoquan, Dailan was free to pass her fingers over the triangular slats one final time, returning them to the palace etching. But the etching had changed. A cutout view exposed a mass of pumps, gears, and pulleys beneath the palace plateau.

Jack glanced at the other two. Neither Sadie nor Liu Fai seemed surprised that the three-sided slats had managed to produce a fourth image.

"Qin Shi Huang never intended to die," said Dailan. "Thus,

the tomb was never meant to be a tomb. Under the emperor's guidance, Shi Lu and his laborers created a massive engine of clockwork and mercury, designed to imbue the one sitting on its jade throne with the gift of eternal life." She rolled up the scroll. "At least, that is what the emperor believed. And now this Gall of yours has inherited his madness."

"He is not *our* Gall." Obeying a gesture from the hermit, Jack returned the scroll to the shelf. "But we *will* bring him down. Without Shi Lu's secret passage, how do we get into the tomb?"

With none of the effort that age often requires, Dailan moved the dragon's head from her lap and stood from her place at the fire. She reached and drew a flat piece of black jade about the size of Jack's palm from the folds of her robe and presented it to him with a bow. "If you intend to brave the dangers of the tomb, you will need this."

Jack accepted the object with a hesitant bow of his own and held it closer to the fire's glow. The jade, smoothed by time, had been carved into the silhouette of a rearing horse.

"This black horse belonged to Shi Lu," said Dailan. "It is my family's most precious heirloom. Use it well."

Jack cast her a sideways glance, not wanting to be rude, but not knowing how else to ask. "For what?"

"You will know when the time comes."

——— · Chapter Forty-Five · ———

DAILAN GUIDED JACK, SADIE, and Liu Fai back to the mountain trail, and once the other two had started down the path, she offered Jack a final word of advice. "Qin Shi Huang was mad, for certain, but he was also a genius who experimented with animating the inanimate—a key piece of his quest for immortality." She paused to whisper something to Xiaoquan, sending him curling and somersaulting up into the trees, then returned her gaze to Jack. "In addition to Shi Lu's traps, there may be creatures in the necropolis the likes of which you have never encountered. And they may be quite difficult to dispatch."

By *dispatch*, Jack supposed she meant kill—if you could kill something that had never been alive in the first place.

He answered with far more confidence than he felt. "We can handle whatever Gall and the tomb throw at us. We'll have to."

Laohu had returned at Sadie's call, and after firing up Biyu and Meilin, the three set off to find the tomb. Xiaoquan did not accept a fireball, preferring to remain in his sleeker form so that he could weave and loop in and out of the formation. They had not gone far before Jack steered Laohu into a turn. "Did you hear that?"

Liu Fai shook his head, although staying mounted on his dragon seemed to absorb his entire focus.

Sadie pointed to the forest canopy. "Down there."

A sniffle. A whimper. Jack recognized the voice—the shape of it, the hint of bitter yellow in its color. The trees became translucent in his mental vision and there she was, walking no discernible trail. "Ghost."

"No," said Liu Fai, anticipating what came next. "Absolutely not."

Sadie pleaded with her eyes. A thought pulsated in Jack's brain. *You can't leave her.* And before he had made any conscious decision, Laohu had brought him down through the trees.

Ghost's hood had fallen. A leaf was caught in her hair, a tangle of thorny vine on her sleeve.

As Laohu alighted in the brush, Jack reached out a hand. "Come with us."

Ghost took a step toward him.

The look in her eyes made Jack curl his fingers back. "But we do it our way. This is a rescue, not revenge."

She lifted her hood into place and let Jack pull her up onto Laohu's back. "Sure. Whatever you say, yeah?"

Laohu curled his snout around to give Jack a skeptical growl.

Danger, boy.

Much danger.

Ghost wasted no time in proving the dragon right.

She held Jack tight as they soared down the mountainside, pressing her chin into the crux between his neck and shoulder. "I can't look."

But Jack knew Ghost would never be frightened by something so mundane as flying bareback on a speeding dragon. Cautiously, he let go with one hand and checked the right pocket of his leather jacket, only to find that space already occupied by the thief's searching fingers. He laughed. "I don't have them, so you can quit looking." Expecting an ambush at the camp, Jack had entrusted both the sphere and the Bridge to Liu Fai. "Besides, you can't use the Bridge anymore, Ghost. It's killing you."

"Like I care, yeah? I was just keeping warm."

"Right. Sure."

They avoided roads and hugged the treetops, for obvious reasons, and nearing midday, the trees gave way to a long, glassy lake. Laohu dipped down to soar an inch above the water and let his tail skim the surface, leaving a trail of steam. Seconds before they reached the shore, he shot out a burst of fire. Jack shouted with delight as they ripped through the flames.

Hours later, as the sun dipped down below the western hills, Liu Fai pointed. "There!" He turned Meilin toward a green pyramid near the meeting of an isolated mountain range and a wandering river. "See how the land between the Weihe River and the mountains curves into the shape of a dragon? The emerald tomb of the emperor, twice as wide as the Pyramid of Giza, forms the eye."

By *emerald*, Jack assumed he meant the evergreens that grew all over the pyramid. A sprawling complex of walls and gardens surrounded the mound, but he saw no obvious entrance. He circled Laohu in a holding pattern. "So how do we get in?"

Dailan had told Jack that without knowledge of Shi Lu's secret passage, his little team would have to enter the tomb the old-fashioned way, through a gate sealed for more than two thousand years. But when Liu Fai pointed out its location, Jack realized the situation was far more difficult.

"That's a modern building. With armed guards." Men in black uniforms milled about, carrying what appeared to be rifles.

Liu Fai did not seem surprised. "Our people have known about this site for countless generations, Jack. Did you think our archeologists would not secure the entrance?"

He had a fair point.

"What about the secret passage?" asked Sadie, eyes boring into Ghost. Jack could tell she was listening for more than the thief's verbal reply.

"Gall never told me."

Sadie glanced at Jack with a look that told him Ghost was telling the truth.

He nodded. "It's all right." His gaze shifted to Liu Fai and Meilin. Smoke trailed from the tree dragon's nostrils. "I have a plan."

As the sunset became twilight, they landed in a maze of sculpted hedges near the secure facility. Jack dismounted and appraised his four dragons, crammed awkwardly together among the bushes. He couldn't hang on to them much longer, not all of them. "It's time."

Laohu came forward, bending his golden head close to Jack's.

Miss the boy.

"I'll miss you too. But if you return to the long wushi compound, I'll come and visit you." He shrugged. "Assuming I survive."

The dragon made the slightest bow and backed silently into the maze.

Fight well.

Biyu followed, with Sadie trailing her fingers along the dragon's scales as she went.

"Don't let 'em go," whispered Ghost. "A dragon's pretty useful in a pinch, innit?"

Liu Fai knelt beside her, building a stack of ice balls. "A tomb means tight spaces. They might get stuck or trapped."

"The big ones, maybe. But the blue one's plenty small."

"Not for long," said Jack. He checked on the building, where a guard was fumbling with a set of keys, preparing to lock the steel doors for the night. The air sparked at Jack's palm. "You ready, Xiaoquan?"

The water dragon clamped his jaws shut like a dog refusing to take his pill.

Jack frowned. "Look. I need you—the steamy you—and Liu Fai is making you a stack of icy treats so you can go back to normal when it's over."

Xiaoquan considered the pile of ice balls, and lowered his head, relenting. He opened his mouth, deep blue tongue lolling out. Fire sprouted from Jack's hand.

The explosion of lithe little water dragon into balloon-like steam dragon set off a cracking and crunching of hedges that Jack had not foreseen. Their cover was instantly blown. Three guards came rushing their way.

"Go!" said Jack, grabbing his sister's hand.

Xiaoquan braced his wings against the bushes and blew a billowing mass of white fog at the building. Meilin added a storm of smoke and ash, and the two whirled together into a rolling smoke screen.

Jack ran, pulling Sadie along, and when Ghost or Liu Fai began to drift off course, he reached out a hand to reel them in. The shouting of the guards gave him all the sight he needed. Blue-gray echoes defined the angles and contours of the facility, with the brightest portion guiding him to the steel doors like a harbor lighthouse. He ushered the others inside and threw the lock.

"That won't hold them," whispered Liu Fai. "They have the key."

Jack sparked a flame in his hand and pressed it against the steel. The lock glowed red. But try as he might, he could not pump in enough heat to melt it.

Child of flame and child of ice
Must join to win the maiden's life.

Jack blinked. He nodded at the door. "Your turn."

Liu Fai took his meaning and poured out frost. There was a crackling within the lock, then a tiny *clink*.

Jack checked the bolt. Jammed. "That oughta hold 'em for a while."

"Um . . . guys?" Sadie had wandered a few feet ahead, to a stairwell of pitted black stone, as broad as the building. The whole facility seemed to be nothing but a cap for those steps.

Jack walked slowly to his sister's side, wary of whatever had drained the color from her cheeks. Below, he saw a sealed gateway with aged copper doors. A rounded lattice of red-glazed stone on either side gave the entire thing the look of a near-perfect circle.

Sadie took hold of his wrist. "There are things poking through the lattice. White things."

A small fireball appeared in Jack's free hand. He added fuel to make it brighter, and he felt Sadie's grip tighten. "Those white things are hands," he said, unable to raise his voice above a whisper, "dozens of skeletal hands."

—— · Chapter Forty-Six · ——

LIU FAI FOUND A flashlight on a rack of equipment, and Jack doused his fireball.

Ghost strolled past them. "Great plan, yeah? Now we're trapped between a tomb and armed guards. How long before they cut through Frosty's broken lock and arrest us?"

"Don't call him Frosty," said Sadie. "He doesn't like it."

A gridwork of stakes and strings marked the dirt walls on either side of the staircase, and the floor at the bottom was littered with tools—signs of archeological work, still ongoing.

Sadie kept staring at the bony hands reaching through the lattice. "Why haven't they done anything about the skeletons?"

"They could not simply pull the arms through." Liu Fai steered her away, toward the center of the gate, and crouched down in front of her. "It is unwise to disturb the rest of the dead."

"They were trying to get out," said Jack.

"'Course they were trying to get out." Ghost pursed her lips at him. "They'd been locked up with a dead king in a tomb filled with traps."

"The question is," said Liu Fai, "how do *we* get *in*?"

Jack examined the seal on the gate—a square copper plate, perhaps a meter on each side, with a slightly smaller square in the middle, made of a black alloy he could not identify. The black square was cut into seven angular pieces that fit together, each with a peg sticking out. "Is this a puzzle?"

"That is a *chin-chiao pan*," said Liu Fai, pushing Jack aside to get a better look. "You would call it a 'tangram' or 'seven-piece puzzle' in English. To solve it, one must slide the pieces around in two dimensions, making a *chin-chiao pan* the ideal face for a—"

"Combination lock," said Sadie, finishing for him.

"Correct. A *chin-chiao pan* has infinite solutions. The pieces may form any shape one can imagine, and only one will open the lock."

An alarming *clank* sounded above.

Ghost glanced up the stairs. "The guards have gone to work on the doors, yeah?" She rolled her eyes at the others. "Rank amateurs, the lot of ya. Now it's a race. We've gotta open our door before they open theirs."

"I told you," said Liu Fai. "This lock is unsolvable. To even begin, we would need the key—a drawing, or perhaps an object. A silhouette of the desired shape."

"A *silhouette*." Jack patted his pockets until he found the horse that Dailan had given him.

You'll know when the time comes.

He held the black jade carving up beside the seal, and he could see how the same general shape might be made from the squares and triangles. "This is it. Dailan gave us the key."

Another *clank*. Jack saw more depth in the noise than before, more movement. "The doors are failing. We have to go." He stepped aside, giving Liu Fai room to work. "Can you solve it?"

"In China, *chin-chiao pan* are used in mathematics competitions." Liu Fai cracked his knuckles and rolled his shoulders, as if walking into a boxing ring. "And I hold the record for all of Hubei province." He took hold of a peg, sharply sliding a triangular piece aside, and added under his breath, "Not that my father ever noticed."

Several triangles, a square, and a rhombus—Liu Fai slid them all out to the limits of their tracks and began building the horse, piece by piece. The shapes could shift, rotate, and switch from one track to another, allowing too many configurations for Jack's comfort.

Clank. The guards shouted to one another outside. Jack couldn't understand what they were saying, but he could tell there were more than three. They had brought in reinforcements.

"Any time now, yeah?" urged Ghost as Liu Fai shifted two small triangles into place. He changed his mind and replaced them with the square. "Quiet, thief. Let me work."

The shouts grew louder, and with a final *bang*, the doors swung wide. Lights flipped on.

"Got it!" Liu Fai threw his hands up, as if signaling a judge to stop a clock.

Jack heard a sound like water flowing. The left side of the gate swung inward. He cast one more worried look at the skeletal hands and then shoved his ragtag rescue squad into the tomb.

They grunted all together, pushing the heavy copper door closed again.

"How do we lock it?" asked Ghost.

The door answered with the distinctive *shink, whir, shink* of the puzzle returning to its locked configuration. Jack let go and stepped back. "We're safe."

Liu Fai's flashlight gave a ghostly glow to the skeletons piled against the lattice. He picked up a torn section of clothing. There were claw marks down the center. "*Safe* is precisely the wrong word."

"Shhh." Jack raised a finger. "The guards are coming down the stairs. What are they saying?"

Liu Fai pressed an ear to the door. "One of them swears he saw the tomb closing. Another says he is imagining things, that they should leave well enough alone."

Jack noted a third voice, harsher than the others. "What about that guy?"

"He is their lieutenant," said Liu Fai, turning to meet Jack's eye. "He says it does not matter if thieves entered the tomb, because they will never come out again."

Chapter Forty-Seven

JACK AND THE OTHERS wandered deeper into the tomb, following a wide pathway of the same pitted black stone used for the stairway. Soon, the sharp scent of fuel reached Jack's nostrils. He traced its wavering green line to a brazier as tall as Sadie. "Hang on a sec." He opened his palm and concentrated on making a spark. "I think I found the light switch."

"Wait." Liu Fai held up a hand. "You might set off a trap, or alert Gall."

"Or both, yeah?" added Ghost.

Jack rolled his eyes. "The whole place is a trap. And Gall knows we're coming. Relax. It's just one torch." The argument gave Jack the little boost of adrenaline he needed to spark a fireball. He tossed it in, and with a hefty *whoomp*, orange flames leaped up. The fire crackled. Aside from that, there were no other sounds. "See? Nothing happened."

Whoomp . . . Whoomp . . . Whoomp, whoomp, whoomp. More flames sprang from dozens of braziers along a sloping path leading off into the distance.

"Just one torch, yeah?" said Ghost.

"I . . . How did they . . . ?" Jack flopped his arms. "Sorry."

Sadie walked out in front of him. "I like it."

The braziers illuminated an underground park. Shrubs made of green opal lined the path, with flowers of many-colored jasper. The columns supporting the roof were carved to look like oaks. Conical jade pines dotted the landscape between—a forest of flickering shadows that faded to darkness on both sides.

In the distance, Jack could see the occasional arched footbridge, implying that a stream meandered through the stone trees. "What is this place?"

"A *shendao*." Liu Fai walked beside him. "A spirit way. If this is anything like the tombs of later dynasties, this road should lead us north to the central mausoleum."

Interspersed among the bushes were statues, like the terracotta soldiers Jack had seen on TV. These still had vibrant color in their paint—red, yellow, purple, and green, with flesh-colored faces and a hint of rose in their cheeks. The soldiers were not alone. There were women in silk gowns, ministers in round hats, and animals of all kinds. A few of the figures stood well off the path, as if wandering in the woods.

"Look at this one." Sadie had found a creature made of silver, rather than pottery—something between a tiger and a Doberman.

"We call that a *pixiu*," said Liu Fai, nodding at the tiger-dog-thing. "They have guarded the wealth of homes and tombs for thousands of years, farther back than even the Qin dynasty."

"He's cute," said Sadie.

Jack did not agree. He would have preferred a tiger-dog-thing that guards tombs to be made of pottery like the rest of the animals. The creature's silver claws and fangs looked sharp. "What's that in its mouth?"

Liu Fai cautiously touched a white ball trapped behind the statue's fangs. It moved freely. "The ball represents the wishes of the statue's master, fiercely guarded."

Sadie tried to get closer, but Jack held her back. His eyes drifted down to the claws, curled back and raised above the black pavers. There were three, exactly like the rips in the cloth

Liu Fai had found beside the skeletons. "Let's . . . keep going."

They had a long march ahead to reach the next section of the tomb, marked by a two-tiered gateway with tiled roofs. The wicked look of that pixiu statue made Jack nervous. He took the lead, guarding every step. Any paver might shift beneath his weight and bring arrows flying or a boulder crashing down. More than once, he thought he saw a statue out in the jade woods creep closer.

Eventually, his imaginings became reality.

The sound began softly in the distance. *Scritch, scritch*. Jack could see it with his tracker senses—catlike footfalls on the hard stones, bearing the sheen of a metallic ring. He glanced back, checking on the pixiu, and his mouth went dry.

The silver statue no longer stood on its pedestal.

Chapter Forty-Eight

SCRITCH. SCRITCH. THE METALLIC footfalls quickened.

"We have to move," said Jack in a hoarse whisper, reaching back for his sister. When the others failed to react, he shouted the command. "I said, '*Move!*'"

Dragging his sister, Jack ran straight between the flaming braziers, hoping the path and the light might somehow protect them.

Liu Fai caught up to them. "What about traps?"

"We've already set one off!"

Scritch, scritchety. Scritch, scritchety.

Whatever was hunting them had picked up its pace, galloping beside them through the trees. The shiny tracks, appearing and fading in Jack's mind, curved toward the path.

Scritch, scritchety. Scritch, scritchety . . .

The sound went away.

"Down!"

Jack yanked his sister to the floor as the creature went soaring over them, claws extended. It clipped a jade pine, and tumbled into the shadows on the other side of the path.

"Enough of this, yeah?" said Ghost.

Zzap.

She vanished in a rippling blast wave.

Jack dropped his forehead into his palm and peered over at Liu Fai with one eye. "Seriously? You had *one* job." That wasn't true, but it sounded good.

Liu Fai lay on the pavers, patting his pockets and looking stricken.

Ghost had taken the Einstein-Rosen Bridge—and probably the Mind.

"Forget it." Jack pulled Sadie to her feet and started running again. "She's a thief. It's what she does."

The stream that meandered through the dark stone woods crossed the path ahead. Beyond the footbridge, Jack could see the two-tiered gateway. A stone wall extended from both sides. "If we can make it to that gate," he shouted, "maybe we'll live!"

"So much for that idea," panted Liu Fai, pointing.

With the heavy *thunk* of metal paws on wood planks, the pixiu landed on the bridge. It swiped the air and let out a high-pitched tin-can growl, white ball rolling in its mouth.

All three came skidding to a stop, and Jack put his hands on his hips, sucking in the stale air to catch his breath. "I'm . . . guessing that's . . . pixiu for 'You shall not pass!'"

The stream reflected the flames of the braziers with the same silver luster as the creature. Something floated out from under the bridge—something with a dragon's head. At first Jack thought it was another monster, but the head was carved from wood.

"A boat," said Liu Fai. He shared a look with Jack, making a silent plan, and then fired off a stream of frost.

Jack added a fireball, causing an explosion of steam to block the creature's view, and the three leaped for the dragon skiff. The pixiu threw its paws up on the rail and shrieked.

"Make the boat go, please!" shouted Sadie, staring at the creature behind them.

The river was stagnant, not flowing. And the pixiu had already proved it could leap great distances. It would not wait long.

Jack found an oar in the bottom of the boat and started

rowing. Silver liquid clung to the paddle. "Mercury. The hermit was right."

"Isn't mercury poisonous?" asked Sadie. "Isn't that what drove the emperor mad?"

Liu Fai found a second oar and paddled on the other side. "The emperor swallowed the mercury as pills. Do not drink from the stream—or swim in it—and you should be fine."

Their course curved away into a darkness too black to be empty space. Jack tossed a fireball into the jade treetops as a flare. The wall extending from the gateway cut all the way through the forest, but the stream passed through a culvert in its base. If they all ducked, they might have enough headroom. Jack paddled harder. "We can make it!"

"Why isn't he chasing us?" asked Sadie, still watching the pixiu.

Liu Fai nodded at the wall. "Because he has a friend."

Another pixiu crept out from behind a jade tree near the culvert. It made a high-pitched growl that quickly shifted into shrieking barks. Its friend barked back. They were talking.

The first pixiu dove into the stream.

Seconds later, Jack felt a bump beneath the boat. A wake curved out in front of them, weaving back and forth until the creature jumped out onto the shore opposite its buddy. Both pixiu bared their silver teeth in monstrous tiger-dog-thing grins.

Momentum carried the boat between them. Liu Fai shot off another round of ice to harry the one on the left. Jack swung his oar at the other, turning it like a blade. He felt a *thock* as it connected with the white ball, sending it off into the trees. Liu Fai's pixiu abandoned the fight and raced after it. All three stared as their boat floated past the first pixiu, or what was left of it. Nothing remained but a silver puddle, trickling down the bank into the stream. Jack shook his head. "Weird."

"Duck!" Liu Fai grabbed his shoulder and pulled him down. The boat sailed through the culvert.

———— · Chapter Forty-Nine · ————

THE BOAT TURNED, BOUNCING off a curved stone shore. Before Liu Fai could flip on his light, the dragon head at the bow slammed into something hard.

That something gave way, like a big lever.

Jack heard a *clink* and a grinding sound deep beneath the boat. The black mist of a sinking sensation filled his chest. "Hold on!"

The skiff slid sideways down a steep ramp and plunged into a pool. There were hisses, sizzles, and blue-white flashes. Sconces lit off one by one, burning like sparklers, lighting a gray stone shore and a broad hallway beyond. The hall was guarded.

A platoon of bronze warriors turned click by click on big

round gears to face the newcomers, and each held a crossbow with a bolt already dropping into place. A skeleton in a torn silk robe lay at the center of the hall with several matching bolts stuck in its rib cage.

Jack scrambled onto the shore. "Grab the boat!"

Together, all three hauled the skiff out of the mercury pool and flipped it over to use as a shield. The first round of bolts came fast. Jack jerked his face back as a serrated bronze arrowhead came punching through the hull.

"They're like the terra-cotta warriors," said Sadie, hunkered down between the boys. "Only these warriors are—" *Thump-thump-thump-thump.* Another round of bolts hit with rhythmic impacts.

"Clockwork." Jack spat out the word. He was beginning to hate clockwork—bugs, dragons, warriors, anything with a set of gears and an unreasonable vendetta against him.

The sizzling firework sconces gave him an excellent view of the chamber's workings. The mercury pouring down the ramp into the pool turned cranks that operated the warriors.

Thump-thump-thump-thump.

More bolts from the crossbows. Light shined through the hull in a dozen places. The boat wouldn't hold up much longer. Liu Fai turned and shot frost at the pulleys and cranks, but they were too far away to freeze.

Jack tried a fireball. It hit the pulleys and vaporized, doing no harm. "If only I could hold a flame on the ropes long enough to snap them."

Thump-thump-thump-thump.

They all ducked. Two of the bolts broke through and skipped into the mercury pool.

"Maybe you can." Sadie peeked out from under her arm, looking from one boy to the other. "Remember what Dad said? You have to work together. Fire and ice."

"Oh, that's brilliant," said Liu Fai, pressing his hands close to the floor.

It took Jack a little longer to figure out the plan, but as he watched, Liu Fai built a stand of ice next to the pool, fashioning the top into a lens. He gave a sharp nod, and Jack set to work on his part. With the bolts chipping away at their shield, he had no trouble mustering enough adrenaline to form an impressive fireball between his hands.

"More heat," urged Sadie. "It has to be brighter."

Jack scrunched his brow, drawing dust from all sides. The soot from the sconces helped, and his flame turned from yellow, to blue, to white. A beam shot from the ice lens. Liu Fai kept the lens whole and shaped it to focus Jack's ray.

Almost instantly, the first rope glowed red and snapped, then another, and another.

The last bolt thumped into the upturned skiff, and the chamber went quiet, leaving nothing but the sizzle of the dying sconces.

Jack fell back onto his rear in exhausted relief, but Liu Fai lifted him to his feet. "We can't stay here. The ramp is acting as a waterfall, filling the air with mercury vapor. Poison."

Only one route of escape lay open to them—straight ahead through a low arch carved with creeping insects. "Yeah . . . I don't like that at all," said Jack, eyeing the bugs.

Liu Fai went through first, coming to a sudden stop as the sconces behind them fizzled out.

Jack smacked into the back of him. "What's wrong?"

"The paver under my right foot. I think it gave way."

"Of course it did." Jack sighed and grabbed Sadie around the waist as a thunderous *whir* shook the passage. The floor rocketed upward, carrying the three of them with it, and stopped with a jolt. The right wall came next, knocking them sideways, followed by the wall behind. Feeling very much like a pinball, Jack tumbled headlong into dead space and crashed down onto another stone floor.

Sadie landed on top of him with an "Oof!" She rolled off

to the side and patted his aching chest. "Thank you, Jack."

He could barely gather enough air into his lungs to reply. "Don't mention it."

Stone ground against stone, followed by a deep, resounding *bang*. Liu Fai grumbled, beating his flashlight against his knee until the beam flickered to life. They had fallen into a perfectly square room with no exits or windows.

"Not good," said Jack, shaking his head. "Soooo not good."

Sadie passed her hands along the walls, pushing against random stone blocks. "There must be a way out, a hidden panel or something."

Both boys sat in the middle of the cube and watched her, nursing their bruises. Jack sparked a flame to give them a little more light. "Why?"

"Why what?" asked Sadie, planting a shoulder against the wall and grunting.

"Why must there be a way out? This room seems like a perfectly good punishment for grave robbers." Jack waggled a finger, taking on a deeper voice. "Now, you just sit here and think about what you've done, all of you, right up until you suffocate."

Liu Fai gave him a hard look, but he didn't argue.

Even after Sadie guilted Jack into passing his flame over

all four walls, he could find no gaps—no indication of secret doors. "Seriously, why shouldn't this be the end?"

His sister caught his wrist, holding it in place. "Because we won't have reached the end until you save Dad." She nodded at his flame. It guttered.

"A breeze." Liu Fai jumped to his feet and felt the wall. "Yes. Right here. Air is leaking through the seams around this block." He set both palms against the block and shoved it in like a button.

With a long *crrrunch*, the entire wall to Jack's right moved outward.

Liu Fai cautiously removed his hands from the gap left by the movable stone. "This is a mystery box."

"A mystery box," mused Sadie. "So I guess that makes us the cricket."

Chapter Fifty

JACK JOINED THE OTHER two in the search for more devices, holding his flame close to the cracks. "I think 'reverse mystery box' is more accurate."

"Oh really," said Liu Fai. "And what makes it a *reverse* mystery box rather than a *regular* mystery box?"

"We're inside trying to get out." Jack bent down to inspect a low corner. "Usually it's the other way around."

"Over here." Sadie had found a metal gear set flush with the stone. "The moving wall was covering it before."

"Step two," said Liu Fai, turning his flashlight on the gear. "Remember each step. A mystery box is solved by trial and error, so we may have to repeat them in sequence many times before we are through." He rotated the gear counter-clockwise until it stopped, and waited.

A tiny eruption of gold—the barely audible ring of metal—appeared in Jack's mind. He grabbed Liu Fai's collar, yanking him back into the limbo position as a line of grout crumbled. A long blade swung out, sliced the air an inch above Liu Fai's nose, and bounced off the corner with a spark, disappearing back into its slot.

Liu Fai let out a breath, eyes wide. "If I were but a little taller . . ."

"You'd now be a little shorter," said Jack, finishing for him.

Sadie took their arms and pulled them both into a big step backward. "I don't think trial and error is the best plan."

The gear spun clockwise of its own accord, the movable wall crunched forward, compressing the room, and the first stone Liu Fai had moved returned to flush. "Back to step one," he said.

"No. Worse." Jack pointed at the floor, tracing the lines from corner to corner. "This room was a cube. Now it's a rectangle." He counted the blocks. The floor had measured five by five. Now the count was three by five. "One step forward . . ."

"Two steps back," said Liu Fai. "Penalties for errors. Three more, and if we aren't diced or skewered, we will be squashed like pancakes."

Sadie stared at the boys, looking from one to the other.

"What?" asked both at the same time.

"You do realize that you've started finishing each other's sentences, right?"

After a long, uncomfortable silence, Jack doused his fire and knelt at the center of the chamber. "I think it's time to Google the solution"—he held his palm an inch above the floor—"tracker style."

Sadie winced. So did Liu Fai.

Tracker style had sounded cooler in Jack's head than when it came out. "Gwen did it first," he said with an embarrassed shrug. "Kind of."

The others just frowned at him. Jack let it go. He closed his eyes and pushed his hand down onto the cold, black stone.

The floor evaporated, and Jack dropped through the dark shadows of time. Stone had a long memory, but without the vibrant detail of metals or jewels. Jack landed where he had started, gray vapors spreading out from the impact, but the chamber no longer hemmed him in.

Silhouettes moved all around him, thousands of them. The

murmur of their voices blended into a uniform hum, broken by sharp, echoing commands. The one barking the orders stood near Jack, directing a mass of silhouettes in and around the chamber. He stood taller than the rest, wearing a hat with a broad flat top like an exaggerated graduation cap.

Jack concentrated on the men under Flat-cap-guy's command. He pushed away the smoke between them, fighting to bring their work into focus. They were building the mystery box.

Pushing the vision back and forth through short spurts of time, Jack saw how the box worked—most of it, anyway. The first step released a series of weights that had pulled the wall back. A clockwise turn of the gear would drop a plate into place to stop the swinging blade and raise a hidden pin, allowing three movable blocks to pop out from the adjacent wall. To avoid being crushed by the roof, they would have to push them in the right sequence.

"They work like a three-button combination lock," said Jack a few minutes later, after guiding Liu Fai through the first two steps. He pressed the three moving blocks, reciting the sequence out loud. "All the way in. Halfway in. All the way in."

Jack pulled the others to the middle of the chamber and

looked up. A single block, smaller than the rest, flipped up and out of the way.

"Air," said Sadie with a sigh. "Not exactly fresh air, but it's something. What next?"

"I . . . don't know. The vision got blurry, so I couldn't see the last step." Jack stared up at the opening. "But it's got to have something to do with that hole, right?"

Even as he asked the question, a blinding white light shined down through the opening. Jack shielded his eyes. Something bonked him on the head, clattering to the floor. "Hey!"

Sadie picked up the object. "A phone."

"Gwen's phone." Jack recognized the purple-and-black striped case. He took the device from his sister's hand. "But how—?"

A cone of light descended into the cube, and Jack saw a familiar pattern of blue thrusters. He laughed. "Spec!"

"He came to rescue us." Sadie clapped her hands and held out a fist. The drone rammed her knuckles, shaking off the impact. "Good boy!"

Liu Fai looked utterly confused. "And this is . . ."

"I'll explain later." Jack held up the phone. "Spec, why did you bring me this?"

The drone dipped down below Jack's forearm and pressed it upward, raising the phone to eye level. Then he slipped sideways and waited.

"He wants you to use his video," said Sadie.

"Can't," said Jack. "The phone's locked."

"Then figure out the password." She put her hands on her hips. "It's only four letters. What sort of detective are you?"

Jack got the feeling his sister already knew, or suspected the answer. He had a suspicion too, though he hated to admit it. He typed in the letters W I L L.

The screen quivered. INCORRECT. TRY AGAIN.

Sadie poked him in the arm. "Wrong. Try the *other* name you're thinking of."

Jack swallowed and typed it in. J A C K.

With a light *ba-ding*, the home screen appeared.

Sadie giggled. "*You* are Gwen's password."

"You know what they say." Liu Fai's lips spread into a grin. "A woman's home screen is the window to her soul. In Gwen's case, you are the key."

"Quiet. Both of you." Jack pressed a little picture of Spec, and an app opened, filling the screen with live video. Spec shot up through the hole. On the phone, Jack could see his light panning across the roof. "Good. This is good. I can see four levers, one on each side of the opening, connected to pulleys." He cupped a hand to his mouth. "Spec! Show me where those ropes lead!"

Three of the pulley systems led up to a huge vat of mercury, poised to spill down into the chamber. The fourth led to a hatch in the far wall.

"I suppose that is good news," said Liu Fai, watching over Jack's shoulder. "If we had pulled the wrong lever, we would not have been diced, skewered, or squashed."

"Yeah. We would have been drowned in quicksilver. That's so much better." Jack dropped the phone into a pocket and put a hand on Liu Fai's shoulder. "Here. Give me a boost."

Moments later, he was reaching for the opening, kneeling on Liu Fai's shoulders. "Keep it steady, will you?"

"I'm trying." Liu Fai had a death grip on Jack's calves, teetering back and forth, face contorted with discomfort. "You have incredibly bony shins. Did you know that?"

Jack squeezed his hand up through the hole and caught hold of a lever. "Got it!"

"Wait," said Liu Fai. "Are you certain you have the right one?"

"Nope." Jack jerked the lever, and the motion cost him his balance. The two boys collapsed into a heap. They heard a loud *ker-chunk*, and then a large square piece of the far wall fell open. Spec hovered there, waiting.

"Where to now?" asked Jack. "Off to rescue Gwen?"

Spec twirled in a circle and did a backflip.

"I'll take that as a yes."

—— · Chapter Fifty-One · ——

SPEC LED JACK AND the others down a sky-blue tunnel. Mythic creatures played on the walls in silver clouds unmarred by the millennia, as if painted the day before. Jack got the feeling of crossing into a heavenly realm. He imagined that was the intent. The passage ended in a regal, twelve-foot archway, inlaid with precious metals in the form of serpentine dragons.

"I guess this is the place." Jack took a step across the threshold, but Spec whipped in front of him, red and yellow LEDs spinning. The lights came together into an orange beam that traced down Jack's jacket to the pocket with the phone.

"What? You want me to open your app?"

Spec did a flip.

The other two gathered close, and Spec circled around them all to watch over their shoulders.

A jittery video played—a haphazard flight through a dark hall with Spec's white spotlight grazing bronze faces, falling axes, and flying arrows.

Jack coughed. "So . . . not that way, then."

Liu Fai glanced up at the drone. "But this is the only passage. Where else can we—" He caught himself and frowned. "Why am I talking to a drone?"

The drone answered him anyway. Spec flew to the left of the arch and shaped his light into a rectangle the size of a door, shining it on the wall.

Jack looked closer. Hairline gaps broke the smoothness of the paint along the projection's entire perimeter. He pushed. The door gave way, and an unremarkable hallway followed.

The three came out of the passage on the rounded upper landing of a gold brick stairway. Liu Fai breathed out the one word they were all thinking.

"Incredible."

The claustrophobic feeling of the tunnels vanished from Jack's senses, as if he had escaped into open air under a clear night sky. "This one room must be the size of a football field."

"Two," countered Liu Fai. "Perhaps three when you consider the width."

Below them, silver rivers snaked through jade forests and curved around jagged mountains of pure onyx. There were roads, bridges, and multistory houses. Painted terra-cotta subjects stood frozen in time, tending jasper flower gardens or looking out from pagodas, all within a replica of the Great Wall that wrapped around the entire cavern.

Liu Fai pointed at a large pool of mercury, shaped like a phoenix in flight. "That is Dongting Hu, one of the largest lakes in China, where dragon boat racing was born." He traced the line of a river to a second lake close to the wall, dotted with perhaps a hundred jade islands. "And that is Tai Hu, near the eastern sea. This place represents the whole of the First Emperor's domain."

"But where is Gwen?" asked Sadie.

"Up there." Jack thrust his chin at a plateau a good fifty feet above the faux landscape. Tiered yellow roofs implying a palace complex peaked above a high red wall. Torches burned at each tower with unnatural flames of pink, green, and blue. Spec tucked himself away in Jack's pocket, dimming his thrusters. Whatever waited for them up there, it scared the drone.

As the three climbed a winding road to the plateau, Sadie tilted her head back, gazing upward at pearl constellations and gold and silver planets. A great swath of jewel dust stretched across the ceiling from horizon to horizon, glimmering in the strange flicker of the torches. "This must be the world's largest planetarium."

"A *creepy* planetarium." Jack did not look up. His eyes kept moving from shadow to shadow. "Haunted by a psychopath and his pet monster."

His roving gaze caught a glint of silver on the rim of the plateau, headed their way. "Quick." Jack slapped the back of his hand into Liu Fai's chest to stop his progress. He snapped his fingers. "Give me an ice ball."

Liu Fai glanced down at the hand. "Tell me you did not just do that."

The familiar *scritchety-scritch* reached Jack's ears. The pixiu was coming fast, scrambling across the vertical face of the plateau as if gravity made no difference. "Not now, Frosty." Jack snapped again. "We have bigger issues."

Another *scritchety-scritch* rose up from below, and Jack glanced over the edge of the road to see a second creature galloping up a stone pylon. "Aaaannd the other one's back too."

"You can't kill them," said Sadie.

"We can try," countered Jack. "Ice ball. Now!"

Liu Fai pressed his hands together, formed a frozen baseball, and plopped it into Jack's waiting hand. "Happy?"

"Not really." Jack gauged the distance to the nearest pixiu, the one galloping up the pylon, let his tracker senses read the vectors, and dropped to a knee, chucking the ice ball straight down.

Clack! The ice knocked the white sphere through the back of the thing's soft, mercury head. The creature dissolved into silver goop.

The other one had reached the road, flying toward them in impossible leaps. Liu Fai slapped a second ice ball into Jack's hand and cast out a mist of frost to slow the creature down. Jack stepped into his throw and fired the ice ball through the cloud.

The pixiu's frozen teeth shattered. The white sphere tumbled from its mouth and the creature crashed to the ground, skidding to a stop less than two feet away. It looked up at them, utterly shocked, and then melted into a line of quicksilver, running through the gaps in the pavers.

"How did you know to aim for the spheres?" asked Liu Fai.

Jack rubbed a cold wet palm on his jeans. "They're like the creatures' brains, I think—precursors to the emperor's immortality device."

"But knocking a sphere away only slows them down." Sadie pointed to one of the white balls, bouncing through a grove of jade trees below. "Watch."

Like a golf ball on an extremely expensive putt-putt course, the sphere pinged off a jade tree, made a lazy half-circle around a jasper flower, rolled down an onyx bank, and plunged into a river of quicksilver.

Sadie held up a finger. "Wait for it."

A silver tiger-Doberman head broke the surface, and a brand-new pixiu clawed its way up the bank.

"Oh, that's just great," said Jack.

The pixiu lowered a snuffling mercury snout to the onyx and took off through the forest.

"That'll be the dog part of him," said Sadie.

Liu Fai squinted. "What is he looking for?"

The pixiu nosed something out from behind a tree.

"The other white sphere, it seems," said Jack.

The creature set one paw down beside its prize and looked up at the three invaders.

Jack shook his head. "Please don't."

With an obnoxious flick, it knocked the sphere into the river.

"And that'd be the cat part," said Sadie.

The second pixiu climbed out of the river, and Jack pressed the others into a run. "Time to go." They raced up the road and through the palace gate.

The upper compound had its own pagodas and quicksilver streams, tended by colorful terra-cotta figures. White travertine pavers gave it the feel of an eastern Mount Olympus.

With the pixiu huffing and snarling behind, the three sprinted toward the largest structure in the compound—a circular temple with a two-tiered roof of golden tiles. Serpentine dragons spiraled up its columns.

"An octagon?" asked Jack between breaths.

Liu Fai puffed beside him. "A nonagon, most likely. Nine sides."

The pixiu were right on their heels. Liu Fai supplied Jack with a pair of ice balls and the two turned to face the danger. The creatures slowed, spreading out, backing their prey into the shadow of the golden roof.

Sadie glanced up at Liu Fai from beneath her brother's arm. "Why nine?"

"What?"

"Why nine sides?"

Liu Fai kept his eyes off the shifting pixiu. "The number

nine represents the Chinese emperors. It is the last single-digit number before—"

"Ten," said a voice behind them. "The number of completion—the number reserved for immortals."

The pixiu attacked, white spheres spinning behind their fangs.

Chapter Fifty-Two

JACK HAULED BACK AN arm to throw an ice ball, but the voice behind him shouted, "Enough!"

The creatures reeled to a stop. Both sat down like well-trained dogs, and the three slowly turned around.

Ignatius Gall stood on a raised platform, forearm resting on the high back of a jade throne. The throne was occupied. Gwen sat slumped there with her eyes closed, head fallen to one side, a trickle of dried blood on her earlobe. Jack took a step, reaching for her. "Gwen!"

"Ah, ah, ah . . ." Gall held up a jade cylinder etched with Chinese script, and the pixiu sprang to life, scrambling up onto the platform to bar Jack's way. "Don't try it," said Gall. "You don't stand a chance."

"What did you do to her?"

Gall strolled to the edge of the platform, looking up at the golden roof as if he had not heard the question. "Liu Fai was wrong, Jack. This temple is a decagon. There are ten sides, instead of nine. Emperor Qin Shi Huang fully intended to walk among the immortals."

It took Jack a moment to tear his eyes away from his friend. The sight of her in that state reminded him of the way he'd found his father at the top of Big Ben. "The First Emperor was crazy," he growled. "Like you."

"Was he?" Gall pointed with his cylinder at a bronze sarcophagus behind the throne, sealed with dozens of rivets as if to make sure the occupant would never escape. It looked out of place, an afterthought that was never meant to be there.

"Qin Shi Huang was far ahead of his time," said Gall. "The effort to transfer his mind into an immortal stone was no different from the work of today's scientists, attempting to squeeze the data that makes us human into a computer and declare victory over death."

Victory over death. Something about that phrase took Jack back to the moments he had shared with a fragment of his father before the battle with Tanner. *We are more than data, son. We are spirit and soul, and nothing can imprison those.*

Gall walked to a semicircular table, red jasper, like the platform and the columns. Among the odds and ends gathered there were a wooden text, a chalice of glistening white stone, and the jade disk and fan from the long wushi vault—all artifacts stolen by the clockwork dragon. One of the stolen artifacts, if Jack remembered correctly, seemed to be missing.

His gaze drifted to the cylinder in Gall's hand. "You have the First Emperor's seal. That's how you're controlling the pixiu. They recognize its authority."

Gall dropped the jade cylinder into the folds of his robe. "It is the *only* thing they recognize, apart from each other. They are early examples of the emperor's work, not terribly clever."

Both pixiu snarled at their master.

"Oh, shut up. It's true." Gall rummaged among the items on the table, picking up parchments and beakers as if looking for something. "My studies into Paracelsus led me to believe that the emperor had made additional progress, and that Paracelsus had completed the work."

Jack picked up movement among the columns. A hooded figure ducked into the shadows. Ghost. She was still with them. He had to keep Gall talking until he could figure out her plan. "So that's why you wanted the Mind."

"An artifact your greedy family withheld from me for far too long." Gall paused in his searching to examine his prosthetic arm, turning it over and back before his clockwork eye. "After I survived your grandfather's bomb, I discovered the fan, and with its formula I made my own mind transfer device." The creases in his forehead relaxed. He lifted a small white pyramid with golden caps on each corner. "This device, in fact. Optimum experimentation required a subject with an advanced neural network, amenable to data transfer."

"You mean a tracker." Sadie scrunched her face into a scowl. "Our dad."

Gall took no offense to her tone. He seemed impressed with her ability to interpret his scientific lingo. "That's right, my dear. The Clockmaker brought him to me, but"—he held the pyramid up into the light—"our experiments together proved . . . unsuccessful."

"And now you have done the same to Gwen," said Liu Fai.

"What?" Gall looked shocked. "Oh no. I merely asked your new friend a few questions in my own"—he fixed Jack with an evil stare—"*special way.*"

The words reverberated in Jack's head in a dozen versions of Gall's voice, from the loudest scream to the softest whisper. Jack could feel the situation unraveling.

It did not get any better when Ghost walked boldly up onto the platform. She made no move to attack.

"Ah. There you are," said Gall, waving her closer. "I'll be needing the Mind now."

She strolled over and dropped the Mind of Paracelsus into Gall's waiting hand, giving Jack a sneer. She had played him.

Jack's body shook with rage. "You—"

"Thief?" asked Ghost with a mocking flick of her eyes. "Get over it, yeah?"

Gall took no interest in their sidebar. He picked up the moonstone chalice, placed both the sphere and the pyramid in its bowl, and continued with his explanation. "Your father's sacrifice was not entirely wasted, Jack. I did manage to use what I'd learned from him to help poor Robert Hubert, the man you call the Clockmaker."

"You helped him? By transferring his mind into a metal monster?"

Gall's pretense of civility fell away. "I *saved* him." He shook his prosthetic fist, squeezing so tight that Jack could hear the gears grinding. "I restored him to a semblance of life after *you* sent him flying from the bell tower."

A roar split the air, and the thing that was once the Clockmaker flew up from below, landing on the golden roof so heavily that Jack feared its weight would buckle the columns. The dragon looked his way. "Jack."

Sadie snorted. "You call that saving him?" She pointed at the pixiu. "He's just like them."

The dragon's red eyes flared. He cocked his head to look at the girl. "Ssssadie."

She rolled her eyes. "Yeah. We get it. You can talk. You're sooooo much smarter."

An ominous rumble sounded from the creature's metal chest, but Gall held up a hand. "Wait, my friend. Please. If the transfer with Miss Kincaid fails, I will still have need for the rest."

"Is that what we are?" asked Liu Fai. "Fodder for your experiments?"

"Most of you. But not all." Gall returned to Gwen. He pushed the chalice down into a receptacle at the peak of the throne and went about positioning his hostage like a life-size doll, straightening her head and shoulders and folding her hands in her lap.

Jack lowered his chin and growled. "Stop. Touching. Her."

Gall frowned at him over his shoulder. "Oh, relax. This is pure science—an experiment."

"And if the experiment fails?" asked Liu Fai.

"We start again, and you get your turn in the chair." Gall finished positioning Gwen. "And little Miss Sadie next. But not Jack. Not him." He slipped both hands into the folds of his robe. "Jack, did you know that Qin Shi Huang first came to power at the age of thirteen? Does that sound familiar?"

Jack knew what he was implying. He wouldn't play along. "I have no power."

"Oh, don't be modest. Your brain is top of the line, thanks to both Arthurian and Merlinian heritage. Think of it as a computer—from the same manufacturer as mine."

Jack swallowed. Gall had managed to make *top of the line* sound terrifying. "I don't get it."

"Don't you?" Gall held up the emperor's seal, rotating it before his eyes in admiration, and then pressed it into a receptacle on the throne. "The technology of mind transference goes so far beyond long life. He who controls such technology can be anyone, anywhere." He gave the cylinder a clockwise turn, and a clanking of bronze shook the chamber.

Mercury poured from shafts in the eastern slope of the dome, setting the rivers into motion. The platform split down the middle, and a flood of mercury rushed through a channel beneath the throne. A pillar with ornate gears, cranks, and levers rose from the floor.

"Those under my control will be prime ministers, Jack. Heads of commerce. But I"—Gall's one good eye stared at him, widening in a whole new level of nutso—"I will be you. Your powerful tracker brain will become my home for a time, and then your son's, and his son's." He spread his hands wide. "For all eternity!"

Amid the racket of the machinery and the crazy man's jubilation, Jack heard a familiar *zzap*. He felt the punch of a compression wave.

Ghost reappeared at the edge of the platform, looking as if she had never moved.

A slight shift in his own weight manifested in Jack's tracker brain—an amorphous gray mass at the bottom right corner of his vision. Ghost had slipped something into his pocket. As subtly as he could, Jack reached in and felt the wooden grip of a dart gun.

The thief gave him a subtle nod.

——·Chapter Fifty-Three·——

JACK KNEW THE WEAPON in his pocket by the dings and scratches on its pistol grip. To be sure, he pressed the heel of his palm against its copper baseplate and sparked.

Darkness tumbled around him. The weapon clattered on an iron grate platform, and the vision settled into a skewed, sideways perspective of the Tinkers' Guild hyperloop station in Moscow. Jack saw Ghost's brother, Arthur, struggling to his knees as the first orange flash of the bomb lit the platform—a bomb ordered by Gall. Arthur threw his body over Ghost's, and the two vanished in the yellow glare of the blast. Jack's body jerked as he dropped out of the vision. He blinked. Gall had returned to his work with the chalice and the control pedestal.

The dart gun in Jack's pocket had come from the Buckles armory, and Ghost had carried it for a while in Moscow. She must have reclaimed it while searching his room for the Mind. It must have seemed like poetic justice to her. Jack had been the root of her conflict with Gall, and she would make Jack end it. Her way.

"All creation is the alchemist's laboratory, Jack." Gall turned cranks and shifted levers on the pedestal at a furious pace. The light reflecting off the quicksilver rivers made the jewel-dust Milky Way flow across the ceiling. "Qin Shi Huang knew this, and he leveraged that knowledge to complete his recipe for a mind transfer stone—his 'elixir of immortality,' if you like. He built this entire chamber to replicate the earthly and the heavenly conditions required."

While Gall-slash-weird-science-guy droned on about stars, rivers, and refracted light, Jack eased the dart gun out of his pocket, hiding it behind his back.

The spook returned to the chalice on Gwen's throne, sprinkled a red powder over the sphere and the pyramid, and touched the bowl with a long match. Jack and the others shielded their eyes from a purple flash. When the smoke cleared, the objects were gone, reduced to a uniform gray amalgam.

"Recycling." Gall gave them an instructive nod. "The ingredients and proportions of these previous efforts were correct. Paracelsus and I simply set our ovens to the wrong times and temperatures, so to speak." He stepped to the side and took hold of the pedestal's largest lever, shaped as a dragon with emerald eyes. Gall paused to glance around. "Yes, yes. All is set. Here we go." He pumped his one good eyebrow at Jack and shoved the lever forward.

The throne slowly descended into the mercury channel. Gwen's shoes broke the silver surface.

"Don't!" Jack lurched for her, but the pixiu closed ranks and snarled.

Bolts of lightning jumped from planet to planet overhead. "Don't worry!" Gall shouted over the noise. "The mercury won't kill her, not instantly, anyway. But she's no tracker, able to soak up data with her bare hands." The descending throne had sunk Gwen up to her shins. "I'm afraid our best bet for success is full immersion."

"Let her go!" Jack shouted back. "Last warning."

The mercury reached Gwen's knees, spilling onto the throne's seat.

Buzzing electricity gathered overhead. Every hair on Jack's arms and neck stood on end. Gall laughed. "Or what?"

"This." Jack fired.

At the same time, thunder cracked. Lightning struck the chalice, blinding them all. When his vision cleared, Jack saw that the clockwork dragon had landed on the platform, the glow of fire ready in its jaws, but Gall held both him and the pixiu back with a raised hand.

The echo of the thunderclap faded. Jack's dart rolled off the control pedestal and plinked onto the jasper floor. Gall sighed. "Well, that was . . . pointless."

Jack had shot the dragon lever, shifting the throne into reverse. Even as he and Gall stared each other down, it rose, lifting Gwen out of the mercury. She looked no worse, aside from silver leggings and boots. And the throne looked as smooth and clean as before. The only change was the amalgam in the chalice. It had formed into a light green sphere with marble swirls of gold.

"You insolent child." Gall returned to the pedestal to check the cranks and dials. "You *interrupted* my transfer. You reversed the polarity." He scowled. "But you've accomplished nothing more than a delay."

"Maybe." Jack shifted his aim to the spook's forehead. "I have three more rounds. Want to guess where the next one's going?"

Gall let go of the cranks and slowly raised his hands. "What do you want, boy?"

"I want Gwen safe. And I want you behind bars. So why don't we all pause for a breath, and then take your secret passage out of here."

"And if I refuse?"

Jack's gaze flitted from Gwen to the dragon to the pixiu, and back to Gall. He felt the chamber air brush his skin, set in motion by the flowing mercury. He felt the heat pulsating in the clockwork dragon's jaws. Vectors rose around him in white wisps. He read all the angles. "It'll go something like this. The first dart is for you. Your clockwork monstrosity will try and roast me, but Liu Fai will stop his fire with a wall of ice—"

"And my pixiu?" A half grin lifted one corner of Gall's mouth. "What about them?"

"You didn't let me finish." Jack thrust his chin at the pixiu to his right. "The next dart is going down this one's throat. I'll use his brain like a cue ball to knock the other's loose as well." He tilted the dart gun in a miniature shrug. "You know I can do it. And in case you hadn't figured it out yet, Ghost is not on your side. The last dart will occupy the dragon long enough for her to grab Gwen and Sadie, and the four of us will zap our way back to the front gate."

"That is an impressive, Rube Goldberg–ian sequence, my boy." Gall's grin flattened. He took hold of the dragon lever. "Let's see if it works."

Jack had hoped Gall would give up without a fight, but posturing and threats had failed.

He pulled the trigger.

Chapter Fifty-Four

JACK BECAME AWARE OF four things all in the same instant.

Fire poured from the clockwork dragon's jaws, but Liu Fai had thrown up a wall of ice to block it. That's as far as his predictions had gotten. The pixiu, strangely, had not attacked. This was good, since Jack could not move his arm to fire the third dart.

He could not move at all.

Gall seemed taller than before, his shoulders broader beneath the black robe. He held his clockwork arm outstretched with Jack's second dart captured in his metal fingertips. He brought it close to his monocle, inspecting it, and then tossed it away. "That is the second time a Buckles has attempted to kill me, boy. My patience is wearing thin."

Jack still could not move. Two months before, Tanner had frozen his legs in place by using the Timur Ruby to control his nervous system. This felt different, like a force field. Jack could feel a thickness around his limbs, molecules carrying Gall's telekinetic will. The air wavered between them.

The gun flew from Jack's hand and skipped across the stone. Liu Fai dropped to a knee, arms steaming.

The pixiu parted, and in an effortless, unnatural movement, Gall leaped over the quicksilver channel to stand between them. "Your mind is special, Jack. But you cannot contend with me." He flicked both hands out at his sides. Sparks flew from his fingers, telekinetic on one side, mechanical on the other. White flame sprang up in his right hand, green in his left. "This is going to hurt us both, I admit. But it will hurt you far more. *Come. Here.*"

Jack's feet skidded across the travertine, the way his grandfather's feet had skidded in the cave. He could not stop his momentum.

Or could he?

Lady Ravenswick had spun the chair and formed spheres from dust. Will had made rolls fly. Both drew their telekinetic ability from the Arthurian bloodline, same as Gall.

Same as Jack.

He stopped straining his muscles and dug in with his senses. Jack felt the air molecules, the way he felt molecules when sparking or making fire. He prodded the layer closest to his skin, fighting to understand the power controlling it, and then he tracked that power back to its source.

As his toes bumped into the edge of the platform, Jack stopped his momentum. He raised his eyes.

The sneer on Gall's face fell away. The furrow of his brow deepened, and he pulled harder.

Jack pulled back. He took one step up onto the platform and stopped again.

Neither moved. With sweat beading at his brow, Jack put his arms out at his sides to match his rival. Blue flames sprang up in each palm. "Contend with this."

Jack and Gall each threw a fireball, and they slammed together in a multicolored explosion. With their concentration split, tracker and spook slid together like magnets, stopping as they thrust their hands down again, new flames ready.

"Watch out, Jack!" shouted Sadie, reaching for her brother.

"Let. Go." The voice echoed in Jack's head. Now it was mental. This was the Merlinian side of Gall, overpowering

Jack's will. His hold on the air slipped. He skidded so close that he could see every gear, link, and rod in Gall's clockwork eye.

The spook pushed his head forward against the little resistance Jack had left. "Not. This. Time. Tracker." His flaming hands crept together, rising toward Jack's skull.

"No!" screamed Ghost.

Zzap.

Zzap.

A compression blast like none Jack had ever felt knocked him clear off the platform.

"Huh." Sadie wiped her eyes and sniffed, looking around. "*That*, I did not see coming."

Jack's flames were gone. Gall was gone. Ghost was gone.

The pixiu attacked.

Liu Fai sprayed the creatures with frost while Jack dove for the dart gun. He rolled over on his back and fired two rounds. Each struck a white ball, sending them rolling across the platform. The frozen creatures crashed to the stones and shattered into piles of quicksilver shards.

"You know," said Jack, breathing hard, "once you've figured out the white-ball-brain thing, those two are more of an annoyance than anything else."

Liu Fai grabbed his elbow and yanked him to his feet. "That did not play out *at all* as you said it would."

"You're too funny." Jack pushed the emissary away as fire torched the air between them. The two boys split, running for the cover of the columns. The clockwork dragon crashed into the roof above. Gold tiles rained down.

Sadie ducked behind the jasper table. "What happened to Gall?"

"Don't know." Jack pushed his senses through the racket and found a muted, angry shouting within the emperor's bronze sarcophagus. He bobbled his head. "Sounds like Ghost put him in a box with his hero. She must have figured out how to zap through solid metal."

"So where is she now?" asked Liu Fai, pressing himself against a column as more flames streamed past.

"Not a clue. I—" Jack's reply caught in his throat. The clockwork dragon, the thing that plagued his nightmares, had landed behind the throne. It spread its metal wings, steel jaws open, hanging over Gwen.

"Come and save her."

Jack tried his new telekinetic skill, but the wavering molecules at his fingertips fizzled. Before, he had used the molecular strings of Gall's telekinetic power as a guide. He didn't know enough to work without them. His eyes drifted from the creature's face to Gwen's, in peaceful repose on the throne.

He couldn't save her.

Fireballs wouldn't work. He'd tried that already, with an army of long wushi and three real dragons to back him up.

Real dragons.

"Wait," he said out loud, holding up a hand as if asking for a time-out.

Off through time and space I soar
Through forest green, through planet's core.
Am I the answer? Can I destroy
The monster that still haunts the boy?

"Sadie, call the dragons—the way you called them in the forest."

His sister, still hiding under the jasper table, scrunched up her nose. "The gate is closed. They can't get down here."

"Actually, one of them can."

Red eyes flared. Jack fired his last dart into the left one, and it sparked and sizzled. The creature roared, reeling back.

Jack had bought some time. He tried to buy a little more. "You wanted fire, right? That's what I took from you. Well, now you can have it back!" He shot fireball after fireball.

Liu Fai added ice, and steam billowed from the blue-green armor.

With a single beat of its wings, the creature jumped up onto the roof behind the throne. "Burn, Jack. Burn all!" Fire crackled in its jaws.

Friend. The thought was not Sadie's. It was deep, reverberating, threatening to split Jack's brain in two. A torrent of blue flame, the color of a starry midnight sky, flashed out from behind him and eradicated the clockwork beast.

The golden roof collapsed on three of its ten sides. Mercury bubbled up from an exposed pump beneath the broken travertine. Quicksilver would soon flood the jasper platform.

The long wushi's matriarch dragon settled into the decagon, her massive obsidian wings casting their protective shadow over Gwen. The dragon lowered her head, curling her great long neck, and allowed Sadie to place a hand on her nose.

Friend.

Jack winced at the pain. "One day we'll have to do something about that inner voice of hers. Right now we have to get out of here."

Liu Fai understood. He took Sadie's hand and the two of them climbed up onto the matriarch's back. At the same time, Spec emerged from Jack's pocket and carefully lifted the green sphere from the chalice on the throne.

Jack touched Gwen's arm. "Wake up. Please wake up."

Quicksilver brimmed over the edges of the platform, inches from the pixiu's white spheres.

"Try this." Liu Fai bent down and spread a thin layer of frost over Jack's palm, sending goose bumps up his arm. Jack laid the icy hand against Gwen's cheek.

It worked.

Gwen's eyes fluttered open. "Jack? How did you get here?" As the fog cleared, her gaze broadened to take in the massive creature behind him. "Scratch that. How did *she* get here?"

Jack helped her off the throne. "No time to explain. Just get on the dragon."

Chapter Fifty-Five

THE DRAGON ROSE FROM the broken circle, drops of quicksilver falling from her wings. As the mercury flooded the platform, the two snarling pixiu took form. One immediately jumped for the dragon's tail, claws flared, and got more than it bargained for.

The matriarch gave the little monster a dismissive glance, whipped her tail in a circle, and smashed the white sphere out of its head. The other pixiu watched the whole episode and reconsidered its own attack. It ran off to chase the ball instead.

"What about Ghost and Gall?" asked Liu Fai.

Jack's gaze tracked along the plateau to the bronze sarcophagus. He could swear he saw it quiver. "Gall made his bed, so to speak. And if Ghost has figured out a way to zap through walls, she'll find her own way out."

Pearl stars flashed by. Planets crackled with electricity. Jack bent close to the dragon's head and pushed a single thought. *Speed*.

The matriarch weaved left and right to through the mercury waterfalls, hugging the rim of the dome. Down below, the lakes spilled over their shores.

"What are we doing?" asked Liu Fai.

Jack held on tight as the dragon banked over the golden stairway to start another circuit, still picking up speed. "Remember that vial of blue liquid you used to create the dragon portal?"

"Yes, of course."

"The fire it made matches this dragon's fire. It has to be an extract from the matriarch." They reached the northernmost point of the chamber. The falls were coming up again, and still the dragon accelerated. Jack could feel her jubilation. Heat welled up within her. He glanced over his shoulder and shouted at his sister. "Sadie, think of home!"

The silver falls were coming up too fast for the dragon to avoid them. Her scales burned Jack's legs through his jeans. "Now?" he asked her, using speech and thought at the same time.

Now.

The dragon let out a burst of blue fire that exploded into a circle filled with twinkling stars. An instant later, they crashed through.

Galaxies passed overhead, so much deeper and more colorful than the jewel dust in the emperor's mausoleum. A flat plane of liquid rushed toward them.

"Tell me that's not Liu Fai's liquid iron," said Gwen. "Tell me we're not headed for the long wushi landing bay."

Jack could not imagine that going well. Thankfully, the rippling liquid did not look like the long wushi's iron deceleration pond. It looked like . . . a river.

The obsidian dragon burst through the water, going straight up into a full moon. A bridge with two towers passed by. Even soaked and disoriented, Jack knew its shape. He shook the water from his eyes and saw Parliament and the green glow of Big Ben.

Home.

The thought came to him. Jack winced at the force of it and laughed. "Yes. Home. Sadie, you should have specified *which* home, ours or the dragon's."

His sister leaned out from behind Liu Fai and shrugged. "I did."

In no time at all, the familiar awnings of Baker Street appeared beneath them. Jack was thankful for the late hour. A shiny purple-black dragon landing on top of the Lost Property Office might have drawn more than a few stares.

The matriarch did not linger. After a few hugs and a kiss on the nose from Sadie, she flew off into the night.

"Extract?" asked Sadie, watching her go. "So you're saying some long wushi has to milk the giant dragon?"

Jack hadn't thought about it in quite so much detail. "Um . . . Sure."

"Well, that's kind of a short-straw chore, isn't it?"

As the dragon disappeared in a halo of blue fire, it dawned on Jack that Liu Fai was still standing beside him. "You didn't want to go back to China with the matriarch?"

Liu Fai stepped out in front of him, shoes crunching on the gravel roof. "I did. But you and Gwen still have much to face." He took Jack's shoulders, squeezing them with a strong and slightly frosty grip. "You will want your friends beside you."

Jack found his mother asleep in the chair at his father's bedside, and he lit the gas lamp on the nightstand to brighten the room—using a match, if only to feel a little normal.

She sat up in the chair, yawning. "You're back."

The others filed in, with Spec hovering at Gwen's shoulder,

clutching the green-and-gold sphere. Sadie pressed her head against her mother's chest. "We all are. How's Dad?"

Jack got the answer from his mother's face. *Not good.*

"He hasn't woken up since you left. Doc Arnold is afraid he hasn't much time."

Jack took the sphere from Spec. "We'll see about that."

Gwen stayed beside him as he walked to the bed. "A green sphere. The red sphere siphoned off your consciousness. The white spheres of the pixiu were neutral, used as their brains. Green must transfer a consciousness out of the stone and into another mind."

"Gall did say that I had reversed the polarity." Jack gently lifted his dad's hands onto the covers and placed the sphere into his right palm. He covered it with the left, then pressed both his father's hands between his own. "Dad?"

No one breathed. There was no sound but the slow, steady beep of the heart monitor.

The beeping spiked. John Buckles convulsed, body arching over the mattress.

"Hold him down!" cried Jack's mom, coming out of her chair. "Get that thing away from him!"

Too late. Jack could not unclench his father's fingers. A tube came out of his arm, and the IV stand crashed to the floor.

Sadie, Gwen, Mary, and Liu Fai together could not control the fit. The beeping accelerated until the pulses merged into a single, unthinkable tone. The pattern of orange spikes on the monitor flattened into a line.

"No, Dad!" Jack shouted, still trying to pry the sphere away. "No, no, no!"

His father's hands finally parted, and his left arm dropped beside the bed. The sphere rolled across the floor.

"Move!" Gwen shoved Jack out of the way, holding a set of paddles with wires that ran to a white box on the nurse's cart. A red light flashed. "This isn't over!"

The whine of the building electric charge filled the room. Gwen held the paddles at the ready. The red light turned green. "Clear!"

"Don't, Gwen," said a still, quiet voice.

Sadie stood apart from the rest, tears staining her cheeks. She held up the sphere, now white, and made a slow nod toward her father. "I can see him."

The monitor beeped. And then, a long, agonizing second later, it beeped again.

As Gwen backed away, John Buckles opened his eyes and looked up at his son. A weak smile spread across his lips. "Jack. I knew you could do it."

• • •

Doctors and nurses crowded into the upper bedchamber of House Buckles. Jack's father was having a hard time breathing, mostly because his daughter and wife were squeezing him so hard, but he managed to ask, "Who's this?" shifting his gaze from Jack to Liu Fai.

"A friend," said Jack.

"The Earl of Ravenswick!" declared Sadie at the same time.

Jack did not want to waste time on introductions. He had too many questions. "Dad, our time together in the Mind of Paracelsus, and our battle with Tanner, do you remember any of it?"

His dad gave him a proud nod. "I remember all of it, even the ghost of Genghis Khan. The part of my consciousness trapped in the Mind returned to me through the combined stone."

"Big Ben, too?" asked Gwen.

"Yes, that too. Gall and the Clockmaker had me in that tower for days until they finally gave up on their alchemical experiments."

Gwen sat down on the bedside and placed a hand on his wrist. "What about the poem that guided us to China and the First Emperor? How did you manage it?"

"That part is fuzzy." John Buckles scrunched up his face. "I think the part of my mind Gall had trapped in his pyramid was . . . unlocked under the stars of the First Emperor's mausoleum. After all, the entire place was designed to facilitate mental transference."

Jack raised an eyebrow. In the thirteen years before the coma, he had never once heard his dad use the word *facilitate*.

"And that, in turn, unlocked a portion of your mind here," said Gwen, nodding, eyes clearly lost in some book she had read. "We're talking about a form of quantum entanglement at the level of neurons, far beyond John Stuart Bell's theorem or Einstein's spooky action."

Jack's dad squinted at her for a long moment, and Jack expected him to tell her she had lost him. But then, in a rapid cadence eerily similar to Gwen's, he answered, "True. But spooky action can't account for the predictive nature of the poem. That necessitates involvement of a higher plane, the soul or spirit, and their linkage to the mind, as in the work of Thomas Aquinas."

Gwen raised a finger. "But combined with the Platonic theory of Forms."

The two went on in a language all their own.

Liu Fai pulled Jack back a few paces. "I am not so sure you

interrupted the transfer of Gwen's mind early enough. Your unacknowledged girlfriend now appears to have a permanent mind-meld with your father."

"Yeah," said Jack, watching Gwen and his dad with a worried stare. "That's gonna be awkward."

Sadie leaned against her brother, wrapping an arm around his waist. "Cool."

Chapter Fifty-Six

FIVE DAYS AFTER JACK'S dad woke up, the trial reconvened at the Black Chamber. Jack, his parents, Sadie, and Gwen all arrived together, making for a crowded elevator—especially considering the quantum thruster wheelchair Jack's dad required.

A blond woman waited in the corridor below, wearing the gray overcoat and red scarf of the dragos. Spiked heels added to her already significant height.

"Lady Ravenswick." John Buckles gave her a respectful nod as he passed. "How nice to see you. You'll pardon me if I don't get up."

"Mr. Buckles." Lady Ravenswick shifted her gaze to Jack and

cracked a smile. "And Mr. Buckles. I see you both managed to survive." A lingering question hung in the statement.

Jack touched his mom's elbow. "I'll catch up."

Lady Ravenswick waited until the door to the accused's anteroom had shut. "Have you given any thought to my offer? And remember, we're talking a title, privilege"—she traced a long, red nail down the length of his arm and hooked his hand, turning it palm up—"and training. We can also shelter your parents from this Section Eight nonsense. Your father is awake, Jack. There *will* be another trial."

"I know." Jack pulled his hand away, hiding it behind his back. "And I'm grateful for your kindness. But my family and I are willing to take our chances with the Ministry of Trackers."

"I'm very sorry to hear that." Lady Ravenswick put a hand on Jack's shoulder, releasing an uncomfortable volume of heat before walking off down the hall. "Very sorry indeed."

Zzap.

Jack felt a concussive punch to his gut, and a girl in a hooded black cloak popped up beside him, casually leaning against the wall.

"Well, that one's a piece o' work, in'n she?"

"Ghost?" He checked over his shoulder to see if Lady Ravenswick had noticed, but she had turned the corner. "Um . . . Hi. And thank you . . . for what you did in the tomb, I mean."

"That's what I was there for, wan'n it?"

Jack looked down at his sneakers. "So how does it feel?" He hesitated, then raised his eyes. "You know, now that you've gotten revenge against the man who killed your brother?"

Ghost's smile faded. "Not like I'd hoped. Arthur's still gone, yeah?"

"Yeah." Jack didn't know what else to say. He tried changing the subject. "How did you escape the tomb?"

"You have your secrets. I have mine, yeah?" Ghost tried to laugh, but it quickly dissolved into a coughing fit. Her shoulder slid a few inches down the wall. Her use of the Bridge had weakened her.

Jack took her arm to hold her up. "You need a doctor. We have to get you to a hospital."

"An' miss the trial of the great Jack Buckles? Not a chance."

"Afterward, then." He narrowed his eyes. "Promise me."

She gave him a little shrug. "Whatevs." That was the best he was going to get.

Jack frowned. "Until then, keep out of sight. Okay?"

She gave him a weak half smile. "It's what I do, yeah? I'm a ghost."

Zzap.

Jack fell against the wall as the thief vanished.

— · Chapter Fifty-Seven · —

NOT LONG AFTER JACK joined the others in the anteroom, that dreadful black slate door cracked open, marking the beginning of the night's proceedings. The air seemed to leave the room.

And then a familiar face peeked in.

"Will!" Gwen rushed into the clerk's open arms, and Jack could not blame her. The clerk looked sharp as always, in a gray suit and red striped tie. But Gwen returned to Jack as quickly as she'd left, slipping both hands into the crux of his arm. "You should have seen him, Will. Riding dragons. Facing down Gall."

The strawberry-scented, pinkish-purply haze filled Jack's senses. He flushed and whispered. "You didn't actually *see* me face him down. You were unconscious."

"Yes," Gwen whispered back, "but I know you were amazing, because you're you. And it's about time the world knew it." She raised her voice. "*A-maz-ing*. That's my Jack."

Her Jack. He flushed a little more.

Will gave him a rueful smile, clearly hating to spoil the moment. "It's time, Jackie Boy."

As the two reached the accused's podium, the Master Recorder gave them a chin raise that said *Don't bother sitting down*. "All rise for the Right Honorable Sir Alistair Drake."

The Royal Arbiter entered from the side door, wig slightly askew, and cringed at the stack of papers in front of the Master Recorder. "In the interest of time," he said, motioning for the crowd to be seated, "would the Ministry of Secrets waive a second reading of the complaint?"

A gray-bearded man stood at the spook podium. "Has my lord made another reservation at the Wig and Pen?"

"That'd be Lord Wyllt," whispered Will, nudging Jack with a sharp elbow, "the Undersecretary for Things to Come. He'll be proxy-in' in for Gall."

"I have," said the Royal Arbiter.

Lord Wyllt offered a solemn nod. "Then yes, we will waive a second reading."

"That is excellent news." Sir Drake signaled the Master

Recorder, who was frantically tossing aside all the parchments he had bypassed.

She found the right one and raised it to her eyes. "In the light of new evidence provided by one Gwen Kincaid and corroborated by Stephen Corvus, Earl of Ravenswick, and his esteemed father"—she glanced at Liu Fai and his dad, who sat side by side in the drago section—"it is clear that the late Lord Gall precipitated *all* the calamitous events noted in the complaint against young Mr. Buckles. As such, the complaint is made void. This tribunal is adjourned."

Gwen let out an exuberant "Yes!"

The spooks and toppers shouted out protests that were summarily ignored.

But before Sir Drake could escape the platform, Lady Ravenswick raised her voice above the clamor. "Point of order, my lord!"

The brow beneath the canted wig furrowed. "We will *not* reconsider, Lady Ravenswick."

"Yes, my lord, but I fear we have forgotten the violation of this so-called Section Eight."

Mrs. Hudson rocketed up from her chair. "*That* is an internal matter for the Ministry of Trackers. You have no right!"

"Don't I?" Lady Ravenswick cocked her head. "We've all heard rumors of the events surrounding this boy. If this is the sort of confluence of power that Section Eight was designed to prevent, then I suggest all four ministries give it the attention it deserves."

So that was what she had meant by *very sorry, indeed*. Jack had rejected Lady Ravenswick's offer. In retribution, she would bury his whole family. He dropped his head into his hands.

"Something I should know?" asked Will.

"Only that I made a bad choice. A *really* bad choice."

Lord Wyllt's previous indignation vanished. "Oh yes, my lord. I quite agree with my esteemed counterpart. I second her motion to consider this important issue."

The motion carried. Sir Drake sighed and turned to address Jack's parents. "Mr. and Mrs. Buckles, do you deny violating the rules of Section Eight?"

"No, my lord." Mary Buckles took her husband's hand and stood, speaking for them both. "How could we?"

"The question before us, then, is one of consequences. Each ministry will vote, and the Ministry of Trackers must abide by the decision." Without taking his eyes off the pair, he motioned to the Master Recorder. "Go ahead, Asha."

"Oh. Yes. All right." The Master Recorder took up her quill and parchment. "Um . . . What does the Ministry of Secrets say in the matter of consequences for the Section Eight violation?"

Lord Wyllt kept his bearded face deadpan, eyes straight ahead. "Prison. Send them to the bottom of the Mobius Tower, and let them rot there until the end of their days."

A murmur swept through the crowd. Will leaned close to Jack's ear. "Well, that's a bit *disproportionatious*, innit?"

Through it all, Jack had not lifted his head from his hands. He rocked to one side, glancing up at Will. "My parents are being condemned and you're still making up legal terms?"

The color drained from the Master Recorder's face as she scribbled down the spook's exact response. "Er . . . That was . . . quite specific. Yes. And now the Ministry of Guilds?"

Sir Barrington Rothschild leaned across his podium and grinned. "The Ministry of Guilds concurs with our learned colleague. Prison. Mobius Tower. *Life sentence.*"

Jack's mother let out a shocked whimper. His father patted her hand.

"That's all but done, then," said Will with a light sigh. "We know 'ow the Lady Ravenswick'll vote." He slapped Jack on the back. "Cheer up, though. It's not as black as it seems.

There's never any rain down there in the Mobius Tower, is there?" After a long pause, he added, "'Course, there's never any sunshine, neither."

Jack's throat was too dry to answer. What had he done?

When her turn came, Mrs. Hudson defied the upper echelon of the trackers and requested a complete pardon. "This family has suffered enough," she said, spectacles held regally at the bridge of her nose. "The Ministry of Trackers recommends no punishment." Not that it mattered.

"Yes. Good." The Master Recorder's feather pen quivered in anticipation of what they all knew was coming next. "And now the Ministry of Dragons."

Lady Ravenswick regarded Jack's parents for a long time. "Mrs. Hudson is . . . entirely correct." Her ruby lips spread into a smile. "The Ministry of Dragons recommends a full pardon."

Jack raised his head in surprise. "What?"

Will slapped his leg. "Whaddaya know?"

"She can't!" cried Sir Rothschild.

"She *can*." Sir Drake pressed his bushy eyebrows into a scowl that knocked the topper back a step. "The countess may vote however she wishes. And since the vote is now split two to two, the decision goes to the arbiters. Give us a moment. It *won't* take long."

As the council rolled their chairs together, Will whispered in Jack's ear. "Now it's anyone's game, innit? They could go for something a little less *perma-nentary* than prison—house arrest for a decade, or per'aps ship 'em off to Australia for a spell like the old days."

The chamber grew quiet as the council members rolled back to their stations.

The Royal Arbiter turned to face the room, and Jack's mom squeezed her husband's hand so tight that her knuckles whitened.

"Mr. and Mrs. Buckles," said Sir Drake. "We grant you a full pardon. You are free to go."

A cheer went up. Ash, Sadie, Gwen, Jack, and his parents shouted and hugged one another. Shaw pouted beside them. Liu Fai jumped up with a brash "Yeah!" but his dad quickly pulled him down into his seat.

Sir Drake took off his wig. "*Now* may we adjourn?"

"You may not!" A man in a hooded cloak marched to the center of the chamber.

Sir Drake was not amused. "Oh, rea—" He fell silent as the man lowered his hood with a clockwork hand, revealing a bald head streaked with lines of mercury.

The elevators opened, and spooks filed out, some rising

over the bleachers on ankle thrusters. Ignatius Gall let out a sickening laugh. "What's wrong, Alistair? Surprised to see me? Did you really think you could send children to do your dirty work?"

The wardens were having none of it. Three tweed giants pushed out through a wooden gate from the crumb bleachers, but they did not get far.

Gall flicked his hand and they flew back, shattering the rail. "I tried to do this gently," he growled, pacing up the floor with floating supporters on either side. "A little subterfuge. A quiet coup. But by sending the boy, you forced my hand." Gall stopped a few meters from the platform, fingers twitching at his sides. "I no longer recognize the authority of this council. Sir Alistair Drake, you're fired." He threw his hands together and shot out a blue-green ball of flame.

———·Chapter Fifty-Eight·———

THE SLATE MURAL BEHIND the platform exploded, sending Sir Drake and the council members flying. When the dust cleared, there was a three-story hole in the chamber wall, framed by twisted pneumatic tubes.

Spooks, dragos, and crumbs all jumped the barriers and clashed in the middle. The toppers, for their part, fell over one another in a bid for the exits.

Jack had never experienced a fan fight at a British football match, but from Gwen's descriptions, he imagined this was what it looked like—so much noise, so much movement, with streams and flashes of color that merged into a gray storm, clouding his senses.

Lady Ravenswick drew the sword from beneath her coat

and shouted commands. With Liu Fai, his father, and a platoon of dragos, she charged down the bleacher steps to protect the fallen council members. At the same time, Lord Wyllt and a cluster of spooks mounted their own rescue effort. Clearly, a portion of the Ministry of Secrets remained loyal to Crown and Country.

Tracker wardens roared. Drago fireballs soared up to singe black robes. Floating spooks answered with blue-white bolts from chrome weapons, setting wood railings aflame. A line of spooks remained stock-still in their bleachers and glared across the chamber. Several dragos grabbed their temples and dropped to their knees.

Jack's dad was not idle, despite his weakened state. He kissed his wife's hand and rose skyward in his quantum thruster wheelchair, falcon-head cane at the ready. Mary Buckles watched him go for a moment, but then one of Gall's black-robed goons ran up the steps to attack her. She balled up a fist and punched him in the nose, knocking him unconscious into the benches. Beside her, Sadie stared hard at the line of concentrating spooks. Two of them crumpled.

"No point standing 'ere gawking, eh?" Will vaulted down from the accused's podium.

Jack shrugged and followed.

"Jack!" His dad unsheathed the sword from his cane, catching a floating spook across the chin with the falcon-head pommel before tossing it down to his son. "Fight your way out. We'll face him another day!"

"No way!" countered Jack. He caught the sword by its hilt and started toward the battle. "This ends tonight!"

He did not make it far. Two steps in, his foot bumped against a chunk of rock—a piece of the shattered mural. The black slate facade was only two inches deep. The rest was gray and glossy, furrowed with rivers of blue and red. Jack picked it up, feeling the heat course into his arm. "Drago-nite?" he asked under his breath.

Will was several paces ahead. He scowled over his shoulder. "Come on, Jack! Sir Drake is in trouble!"

But Jack was still processing the implications of the dragonite. He glanced around the room. Books and scrolls were scattered across the floor, burning and smoldering. Suddenly he under-stood. The Black Chamber sat adjacent to another of London's secret underground strongholds—one that he knew well.

"Too late," said Will, backpedaling to Jack's side. "Looks like the fight's coming to us."

The men and women fighting at the center of the chamber fell back like parting curtains. Gall strolled between them.

Gwen appeared to Jack's left. "Um. Yeah . . . I think that was a given." She held what looked like a wooden baluster at the ready. When Jack gave it a questioning glance, she shrugged. "What? I improvised."

He offered a quick smile, his own version of Gwen's freckle bounce—without the freckles. "I'm glad you're here. I can't do this alone."

The moment he spoke those words, they echoed in his head. *I can't do this alone.* He'd said it before, hadn't he—climbing out of the long wushi well? How had Gwen answered him?

You don't have to.

You've never had to do any of this alone.

The thought hit his brain with far more force than a memory. Jack shifted his gaze to the crumb bleachers and saw his sister looking straight at him, serenely calm as their mother kicked an approaching spook in the chin and sent him tumbling down the bleachers.

Sadie smiled.

We've always been here, Jack. Right beside you.

She was right.

In the bell tower of Big Ben, Gwen had been there to help him defeat the Clockmaker.

In the subconscious battle within Genghis Khan's ruby, Jack's father had fought beside him.

In the tomb of the First Emperor, Ghost had saved Jack from Gall, and Sadie had called in the matriarch to obliterate the clockwork dragon.

Despite the isolation Jack had felt since the Clockmaker first dragged him into the secret world of the four Elder Ministries, he had never been alone.

He knew what to do.

Jack needed his sister's help, but he didn't dare risk pushing a thought her way, not with Gall so close. "Gwen, look." He showed her the lump of dragonite.

It took less than a second for the usual *I-have-it-all-figured-out* expression to wash over Gwen's face.

"Gather the troops," whispered Jack.

She gave him a single nod and rushed away, heading for Sadie and his mother. On the way she swept the legs out from under a spook with her baluster, freeing Ash from a chokehold. She beckoned for him to follow.

Gall strode through the chamber, shoving dragos and wardens out of the way without even touching them. Shaw rushed him like a bull and Gall knocked him aside with a telekinetic backhand. The warden slid across the floor, unconscious.

"I guess it's up to us, then," said Will.

"Not entirely." Jack siphoned heat from the dragonite. His sword burst into flame. "I think I have a plan."

"You think?"

"Get ready. Here he comes."

The spook slowed to a halt a few feet away, regarding their combative postures with derision. "We've already been over this, boy. You don't have the skills to fight me." He stretched out a hand wreathed in blue flame. "And neither does your little friend."

Jack felt Gall's telekinetic power licking at his skin, and he felt Will's barrier go up to absorb it. The strain of the effort tightened Will's features. Sweat beaded at his brow.

"See? Young master Will already begins to crumble. He will fail, and once again, you will be all alone."

A green fireball came next. Jack dropped the dragonite chunk and answered with a fireball of his own. As the flames exploded between them, dark thoughts entered his mind.

Did you think you had won? Did you think a bronze box could possibly hold me?

The fire covering Jack's blade dwindled.

Will dropped to a knee, pushing out with both hands, his telekinetic shield failing.

Your friends cannot save you, Jack Buckles. Your mind. Your abilities. They all belong to me.

Gall's words wrapped around his brain like barbed wire. Jack let out a cry.

You are suffering needlessly. Give in and it will end all the sooner.

The pink ribbons of a second, melodic voice broke through.

Leave my brother alone!

Several strands of the barbed wire snapped. The pain lessened. At the edge of Jack's peripheral vision, he saw Sadie stepping down from the bleachers. Three quartermasters—Gwen, Ash, and Jack's mother—surrounded her, fists, cane, and wooden baluster flying to defend her from all attackers. Sadie's paced forward, eyes burning.

You're finished, Gall.

Another wire snapped. Jack drew a breath. Then, for just a moment, Sadie glanced away.

Wake. Wake now!

That last telepathic call seemed to catch Gall's interest. He furrowed his silver-streaked brow, as if wondering what the little girl was up to.

Jack knew. But before he could act, he heard a familiar *zzap* and a dreadful cry.

"Ghost, no!" Jack reached for her.

The thief had tried the same tactic as before, but this time Gall saw her coming. With a flaming blue hand, he stopped her in mid-flight. Her features twisted in agony. Her body flickered like the ghost she claimed to be. Gall released her and she dropped to the floor.

Jack grit his teeth. "You'll pay for that." He looked to the others around him. "Now!"

Hovering above, Jack's dad fired a bolt of electricity from the sheath of the falcon-head cane.

Sadie pressed closer, thoughts pounding the spook.

The bronze wolf's head shot out from Ash's cane, trailing a wire.

Will thrust out both palms, unleashing a rippling blast wave.

The onslaught overwhelmed the senior spook. Gall swatted the air with flaming hands as if fighting off a swarm of mosquitos, and Jack did not waste the opening.

"Aaagghhh!" With a shout, Jack slung a white ball of flame, the biggest he could muster. The fireball sailed past the spook, skipped off the arbiters' desk, and disappeared through the black hole in the wall.

Gall watched it go, panting. He sneered. "You missed, boy."

"Nope." Jack kicked off his sneakers and stepped up onto a big slab of dragonite. "I didn't."

Ffffooomp. A deep burgundy light flashed in the darkness beyond the gap, illuminating curving shelves of books. The Archive. The Black Chamber, it seemed, backed up to the giant well, and Jack had tossed his fireball down into its depths, betting on what lay waiting there—a creature Sadie had just awakened.

The flame!

A roar shook the chamber, like the blaring of a thousand ships' horns.

The defiance dropped from Gall's expression, replaced by a look of sheer terror.

The heat of the dragonite filled Jack's body. He wrapped both hands around the hilt of his cane sword, and with a swing worthy of a home run, he slung the fire from his blade.

Whirling, burning gasses trailed the fireball. It slammed into Gall's chest with an ugly *thump*, sending him flying backward through the gap in the wall. A blast of dark red fire filled the Archive well. When the flames fell away, Gall had vanished.

Jack ran to Ghost. "Imogene," he said, using her real name. "Are you okay?"

Ghost raised herself up on an elbow. "I . . . I think so." But the moment her eyes found focus, they went wide, staring past him. Jack turned to see a massive ruby dragon head filling the gap in the wall. The creature gripped the edges with garnet claws the size of sports cars. It opened its jaws. A vortex of starry red fire swirled within.

"Liu Fai!" shouted Jack, pointing frantically. "Douse it! Douse it now!"

Liu Fai poured frost and snow into the dragon's mouth, advancing, straining, leaving a trail of frozen footprints across the wooden floor. Lady Ravenswick aided her son, drawing moisture from the air to feed his efforts.

The fire dimmed, and then the frost snuffed it out altogether.

The giant patriarch dragon snapped its mouth closed, gave Jack a sorely disappointed glower, and dropped back down into the well.

———·Chapter Fifty-Nine·———

THE MORNING AFTER THE battle, QEDs and workers on glowing ankle thrusters worked to repair the hole in the Black Chamber wall.

"No time wasted," said Gwen, handing a block of dragonite to a waiting drone. But she and Jack had not come to help with the repairs. They had come to say goodbye to their friend.

Jack sat down on the judges' table, right next to Liu Fai. "So it's back to China, then?"

"My father has given me no choice." Liu Fai cracked a smile. "He is simply too proud. Father has been on the phone all night, telling anyone who will listen how his son battled rogue British agents and subdued a patriarch dragon." He inclined his head toward the gap in the wall. "Speaking of which, how did you know?"

"Elementary, my dear friend," said Jack, giving Gwen a wink. He slapped Liu Fai on the arm. "You were the one who told us about the matriarch. And the portals in the Citadel were so like the Chinese portal device that I realized the dragos must have access to a similar creature. Suddenly, all the rumblings I've heard from the bottom of the Archive made sense."

Gwen folded her arms, jumping in. "I told Sadie to wake the dragon with telepathy, and Jack tossed a fireball down the well to light its flame." She gave Liu Fai one of her trade-mark freckle-bounce smiles. "I think I speak for all of England when I say we're grateful you were able to douse it again."

"And the thief who saw the dragon first? What of her?"

"Recovering," said Gwen. "The Einstein-Rosen Bridge is safely locked away in the Keep vaults, and Ghost's rather unique inju-ries are being *well* tended." She and Jack exchanged a sly look.

Liu Fai pressed his lips together, trying to decode the odd exchange, and then smiled. "You are referring to Will."

"Excellent deduction," said Jack, touching his nose. "Will helped carry her down to the Keep's medical wing and now Mrs. Hudson can't get him to leave."

Gwen giggled. "The thief and the legal clerk. They have so much in common."

All three laughed and Liu Fai pushed himself off the table. He clasped Jack's hand with both of his. "Thank you, Jack. My father and I . . . Well. Things will be different now."

"Yes." A melodic voice interrupted from the darkness of the well. "Very different."

The Archive's purple balloon, with its gilded ropes and spherical lanterns, descended into view. A Chinese woman in a silk robe worked the controls.

"Dailan?" asked Gwen.

The mountain hermit pushed open the gondola gate, and four QEDs scurried down to make a bridge, sliding into position in time for each graceful step. "I was told my help was needed. And"—she shrugged—"I am quite good with ancient documents."

Jack offered a hand to help her over the rubble. "You're the new Archivist."

"It is a difficult thing. I cannot replace one whom you loved so much." She glanced over her shoulder at the gondola. "And . . . I certainly don't get along with her cat."

The calico strolled out through the gondola gate to cross

the makeshift bridge, giving one of the drones the evil eye when it tried to move too soon.

"That's okay," offered Gwen. "The Archivist never got along with him either."

"And it looks like you've got some extra help." Jack thrust his chin at the gap.

A blue snout poked out from behind the balloon. Xiaoquan gave Jack a bright water-dragon grin and flew into the chamber. He circled low over the cat, dodged a swipe from its claws, and retaliated with a stream of water. The calico retreated into the cover of the rubble.

An alarm sounded, the *wee-oo, wee-oo* of a police siren. Gwen's pocket lit up with spinning lights and Spec flew out.

"Time to go?" she asked as the drone settled in front of her.

Spec did a flip and a twirl.

"Excellent. Now get back in the box."

Spec dimmed his thrusters and drooped a bit, but when Gwen opened the pillbox, he obeyed.

"Forgive us," said Gwen as she and Jack took Dailan and Liu Fai's hands. "But we have an appointment across town."

They found Mrs. Hudson in the Keep's Botanical Artifact Conservatory, snipping at an unruly stranglervine.

As the open lift brought them up to the third level, Gwen whispered, "Tell me again why we're meeting in the Dodgy Plant Vault?"

Mrs. Hudson heard her. "Because I like the trees here," she said, still sparring with the vine. Out into the open center of the greenhouse, the Kite-eater tree made a grab for a QED and missed. "Most of them. And this vault doesn't have any extra ears. Except for those." She pointed her shears at a potted tree with big floppy leaves growing from its trunk. The card at its base read HOUNDDOGWOOD (*CORNUS BASSETUS*).

As Jack and Gwen stepped off the lift, Mrs. Hudson caught the wiggling vine with her shears. She ground the blades through, cutting off a foot or so. The severed end shriveled up, and the remainder retracted into the bushes. "That'll do for the day, Nigel," she called after it. "Same time tomorrow?" She dropped the tool into a belt holster like a western gunslinger and started down the path.

Jack and Gwen fell into step behind her.

"It was no small thing that you two did," she said, spritzing flowers and shrubs as she went, "stopping Gall. The realm is safe. Sir Drake and his council will recover from their injuries. All is not right with the world by any stretch, but it certainly could be a lot worse."

They passed a line of tall look-at-me flowers, all vying for Jack's attention. He let several brush against his fingers. They were soft and sweet. "We had help."

"I know." Mrs. Hudson lowered her spectacles, and from over her shoulder—whether by accident or design—Jack glimpsed a marking on the base of their stem that he had never noticed before. It was a seal, a falcon and a dragon. "Nevertheless, you proved yourselves. Normally we withhold the rank of journeyman until sixteen years of age. But the regulations permit the occasional waiver."

They came to a small courtyard with a fountain, where Ash waited, newsboy cap on his head and wolf's-head cane laid back against his shoulder. Mrs. Hudson nodded to the quartermaster, who reached into the pocket of his waistcoat and pressed something into her waiting hand. As she turned to face Jack and Gwen, he gave them a wink.

"All journeymen carry challenge coins," said Mrs. Hudson, presenting them each with a bronze marker stamped with the ministry's falcon-head seal. "With these you can identify friend from foe in dark and dangerous places. Keep them on you at all times."

"You mean—" said Gwen.

"Congratulations. You are both hereby promoted."

"Welcome to the club," said Ash, touching each of their shoulders in turn with his club like a king knighting a squire.

Jack and Gwen pocketed their coins and exchanged a knuckle bump.

Mrs. Hudson interrupted with a cough. "I will expect those waiver applications by this evening. In triplicate." She returned to her spritzing, working her way around the courtyard, as if nothing whatsoever unusual or knuckle-bump-worthy had happened.

"Mrs. Hudson?" Jack pushed at the pavers with the toe of his sneaker.

"Are you three still here?"

"Well, I . . ." He frowned. "Was there anything else you wanted to tell us?" She had hinted that she did not want their meeting to be overheard, but a promotion to journeyman was not something either of them needed to keep secret.

"Oh yes." Mrs. Hudson snapped her fingers. "The titles of journeyman tracker and journeyman quartermaster imply that you two are ready to train new trackers, the same as Mr. Pendleton here."

Jack didn't understand. "There *are* no new trackers. There won't be for a full generation."

She raised her spectacles and stared at him as if she expected better deductions than that.

"The exiles," said Gwen.

Mrs. Hudson's thin lips stretched into something close to a smile. "High marks, Miss Kincaid."

"But the tracker regulations—" protested Jack, stepping to the side as a strange flower leaned out and tried to kiss him.

"Are indisputable," Mrs. Hudson finished for him. "Rules, I am afraid, are *not* meant to be broken, no matter what Miss Kincaid says. So I must know nothing about it. However, if *I* were Mr. Pendleton, *I* might choose to help you gather said exiles and find a secure location to train them."

Ash stepped up between the other two. "Sounds good to me."

"I'm sure it does." Mrs. Hudson turned to leave again, then stopped, glancing back. "Out of curiosity, if you three *were* to create a new, secret organization under the auspices of the Ministry of Trackers, what might you call it?"

Jack and Gwen exchanged a smile, then both answered together.

"Section Thirteen."

ACKNOWLEDGMENTS

As always, my wife, Cindy, deserves top billing. She is my first line editor, my cheerleader, and my shoulder to cry on. Without her, my books would not be possible. Also, without her, I would probably starve, so there's that.

David Gale, Amanda Ramirez, and Jen Strada at Simon & Schuster Books for Young Readers are a fantastic team, and I will be eternally grateful for their commitment to this series. I am also grateful to my agents, Harvey Klinger and Sara Crowe. It is wonderful to have such an incredible group fighting in my corner.

No author worth his or her salt can make it without the support of friends and volunteers. The list of the usual suspects continues to shape my writing with critiques, encouragement, instruction, and advice. Author Steven James, Susie, John and Nancy, Chris and Melinda, Seth and Gavin, Danika and Dennis, Rachel and Katie, James and Ashton, Nancy and Dan, Steve and Tawnya, Randy and Hulda, and the Barons. God has blessed me through all of you, and I am grateful both to you and to Him.